The Zook Family Revisited

Book One

Waiting for Belinda

Other Books by Author

All About Grace - A Chrisitan Romance Novel

Inn Sane - My memoirs as an Innkeeper

The Zook Sisters of Lancaster County Series:

Book One - Ruth's Dilemma

Book Two - Emma's Choice

Book Three - Katie's Discovery

Available in e-books:

A Long Way to Go - Historical Fiction

(Paper Edition - Oct. 2013)

Moving On - A novel about Christian Divorce

(Paper Edition—Feb. 2014)

A Special Blessing for Sarah

(Paper Edition—Feb. 2014)

The Inn Game—Christian Romance

The Landlord—Christian Romance

Waiting for Belinda

A Novel

June Bryan Belfie

Dedication

To all the faithful readers of Amish fiction:
I hope you enjoy this series about a remarkable society
of deeply moral and hard-working people.
Whether Amish or English,
we can all appreciate the life-style
of our Amish friends and neighbors.
It is a peek into a life where family is paramount,
where hard work and independence are valued,
and where God is placed first.
Our society could learn much from the Amish.

JUNE BRYAN BELFIE

Chapter One
Holmes County, Ohio

Belinda Glick waved to her friend, Jeff, when he pulled quietly away from the entrance to the driveway. She trudged through the snow toward the back door as two deer broke the silence. They darted across the lawn, startling the seventeen-year-old Amish girl while she reached for the doorknob.

Why was the door locked? She was certain she had left it unlocked when she tiptoed out the back kitchen door two hours before.

The moon was nearly full, allowing Belinda to find the hidden key under the brick by the outside basement door. Shivering from the single digit temperature, she brushed off some newly fallen snow, lifted the brick and removed the key. She turned it in the lock carefully and then replaced it, even taking the time to scatter some snow back onto the brick.

Belinda noted with relief that there was no light downstairs. Sometimes her mother read if she had trouble sleeping, but tonight all was well.

After leaving her boots on the back porch, she hung her woolen shawl on a peg and headed toward the staircase. The only light was shed by moonbeams entering through the window. Belinda thought she heard faint voices coming from her parents' room. She hoped the stairs and old wooden pine floors wouldn't creak as she made her way past their bedroom to her own room in the silence of the night. Perhaps she had imagined their voices. Goodness sake, was she losing her mind? Or maybe the beer did it. Jah, probably, since she wasn't used to drinking.

Belinda removed her jeans and her pink and red tie-dyed shirt, purchased earlier from a local thrift shop, and rolled them into a ball. Then she unwrapped her Amish frock, which she'd worn over to her friend's house and laid it over the maple side chair her grandfather had made for her when she had turned sixteen. She remembered how pleased he seemed at her reaction. She'd even given him a hug—something rare for her grandfather to receive, since his proper mannerisms and scraggly beard made him appear unapproachable to most.

Her *kapp* lay crushed in the apron pocket, which was folded inside her dress. She removed it and set it on her dresser, plumping it up to remove the wrinkles. Then she laid her apron across her dress for the morning.

She slipped on her nightgown and headed for bed. Tonight had been so exciting—so different from her Amish events.

She had met Carrie Richardson, her English friend, at the market where her parents had a stand on Wednesdays, and they had become good friends. Carrie's mother sold health products and gift items a few stands from theirs, and the girls often took breaks together to chat about their lives. Carrie was planning to attend college in the fall and even had a small rose tattoo on her shoulder. Belinda could not quite understand why girls did such things to their bodies, but it was nicely done and looked almost real under certain lights. Still, it wasn't something she would ever do.

Carrie loved to dance and the first time Belinda went to a party at one of their friend's, Carrie talked her into wearing English clothing. Since they wore the same size, Carrie loaned Belinda one of her own outfits.

What a shock to look in a mirror and have this stranger stare back at her—this girl with wavy blond hair nearly to her waist wearing a revealing stretch shirt over tight jeans, adorned with lipstick and eye make-up presented in such a way as to add five years to her natural age. Jah, she looked beautiful—no denying it. When Carrie's older brother Jeff saw her, his eyes nearly popped out of his head. He whistled and scanned her from head to toe, causing a very uncomfortable feeling. No man had ever looked at her like that before. She wasn't sure whether she liked it or not, and it made her ever so self-conscious.

Belinda let out a sigh as she checked the clock. It was already midnight. She was expected to be up early to help prepare breakfast for her *daed* and brother, Gideon, who would be headed for school after helping his father with the animals. He couldn't wait to turn thirteen, though it was only February and his birthday wasn't until the end of August. He hated school with a passion and barely passed his subjects. Daed had been firm about the importance of gaining his education, even though it was only to eighth grade. "You need to read real *gut, sohn,* because one day you may be called upon to preach. Learn English first and study your German. Take it serious and you'll never regret it."

The words were repeated frequently enough, that half way through the lecture, Gideon would add his voice and they would end together repeating the same words, grinning like silly boys. Belinda thought it rather ridiculous, though she agreed that reading was important. Her English friends sneaked paperback books to her sometimes, which she devoured, though some of the terminology went over her head. It was probably just as well, she figured, since some of the covers looked rather risqué.

After she pushed the ball of clothing into the back of her closet, she tiptoed to her bed. When she pulled up her quilt, she heard her fourteen-year-old sister, Nellie, whisper, "What time is it? Where were you?"

"Shhh. Go to sleep."

"You were out again, weren't you?" Nellie's voice caught and Belinda reached across to her sister's bed and touched her on the arm.

"It's okay. Jah, I was out with my friends. Don't tell anyone, all right? Nothing happened, honest. I just want to have fun."

"Daed would have a cow if he knew you sneaked out."

"Well, he won't find out unless you tell."

"I won't, I guess."

"Go back to sleep."

Belinda had trouble dozing off from all the excitement of the evening. She was glad she'd only drunk half the beer from the bottle. She didn't like the feeling and hated the taste. Maybe next time she'd just have a soda. After she finally settled down, she fell off to sleep, but it seemed no sooner had she lost consciousness than she heard her mother knock on the bedroom door. "Time to get up, Belinda. Hurry now."

She rolled over and stared at the ceiling. Some of her mascara had smeared on her pillowcase. She'd have to get a fresh one and stick this one in the laundry basket before her mother caught sight of it. Checking the mirror, she noted circles under her eyes. If any of the boys from the night before saw her now, they'd surely think she was most unattractive. Probably not even cute enough to dance with. The music went through her mind while she took her washcloth and wiped off the make-up, rinsing it carefully to remove signs from the cloth. She brushed her long silky hair and tied it into a bun before reaching for her kapp. Why did the Amish have to be so old-fashioned? Wasn't it enough to give up electricity? *Nee*, women had to hide their most beautiful asset— their locks of hair. Surely if God didn't want it to be seen, he would have made them bald.

Belinda noticed her sister staring at her image through the small mirror before her. She was pouting.

"You don't have to get up yet, Nellie. Why don't you sleep some more."

"You look awful."

"Danki. Just what I need to hear."

"Your eyes look like someone punched you."

"It was eye make-up. It's hard to get it all off."

"Not gut."

"Well, it didn't look bad when I first put it on, silly."

"I never want to use stuff like that." Nellie turned onto her back and stretched her arms above her head, bumping the white metal headboard. "I'm gonna get up anyway. I have to feed the barn cats."

"They have mice galore, Nellie. You don't have to worry about them."

"I know, but I love cats. They're so sweet."

Belinda laughed and slipped on her leather shoes. "I'll see you at breakfast."

"Belinda?"

"Jah?"

"I don't want anything to happen to you."

Belinda went over to her sister and sat on the bed. "Don't worry, little *schwester,* I'll be fine, that's for sure." Then she kissed her cheek and headed downstairs.

Her *daed*, Jedidiah, came in from the barn to have breakfast and mentioned the scrapple wasn't crusty the way he liked it.

"Sorry, Daed, I was late coming down."

"Jah? You still look tired. Not getting enough sleep?"

"Uh, I had trouble sleeping, is all."

"Sorry to hear that. Get to bed earlier tonight."

"I'll try." Belinda took the fry pan over to the sink and added water and detergent. She looked out at the bleak Ohio landscape. A white covering of snow lay over the rolling acreage. The painted red barn added a touch of color to the dull gray image before her. She hated winter and it wasn't even mid February yet. Spring seemed like years away.

"*Dochder*, I asked you for another piece of toast."

"Sorry, I'll make some and get you more *kaffi*."

"Never mind, I have a full cup yet."

"Did Gideon eat already?"

"Jah, he ate early. He's feeding the animals. So what are you going to do today with your *mamm?* Bake your famous cinnamon bread?"

"I guess."

"You seem sad, Belinda. Anything upsetting you?"

"Nee. Just bored with winter is all."

He laughed as she took the bread from the toaster and laid it on his plate. "You have a long way to go before winter's over with."

"I know—only too well."

The day dragged on. She and her mother, Grace, baked five loaves of bread while Nellie worked on laundry. Since it was too cold to hang out today, Belinda joined her sister to help pin the clothing on lines in the basement. The coal stove pumped away, heating the sterile white kitchen. The aroma of cinnamon and yeast infiltrated the large eat-in room and wafted into the other three rooms on the first floor. The rest of the house remained chilly no matter how hard they tried to keep the fireplaces running, so the family members spent most of their time in the large kitchen and the adjoining room with the upholstered furniture. In the winter months her family went to bed before eight most nights, saving on the kerosene as well as their eyesight. No wonder Belinda had to get out with her friends. After all, she was old enough for her *Rumspringa* and unlike a couple of her friends, she stayed at home—only going out on occasional evenings. One acquaintance, Rebecca Yoder, had decided to leave her Amish community and run off with an English boy she'd met at market. It was the talk of all her friends. Belinda would never want to leave her family. Never. And as far as going out, well—it really wasn't a big deal.

"I got a letter from my brother, Gabe," her mother mentioned that evening while the family sat in the sitting room, each actively doing their own project. Grace knitted on a scarf, while her husband read the farm paper. The three children sat hunched over a card table to play a game of Monopoly, which remained in a state of progress for days at a time.

Jed looked over at his wife. "Jah? How is he?"

"Excited. Seems his new wife, Emma, is in a family way."

"That's nice. I hope the two children from his first marriage are excited as well."

"I'm sure they are. 'Specially little Lizzy. She'll be seven next month."

"How old is her brother again? Twelve?" Jed rested his paper on his lap and gave his wife his full attention.

"It's hard to keep track. I think he turned thirteen already this month."

"He's lookin' forward to getting out of school, I bet ya," twelve-year-old Gideon said with a grin.

"I believe so. He loves working on the farm, I know that."

"I guess we should go see them one of these days," Jed said, returning to his newspaper.

"It seems Emma's younger sister, Katie, is already talking about marrying next year." Grace redid a row on her scarf, after she accidentally dropped two stitches.

"That's odd. Girls don't usually talk about wedding plans until near time. Does she have a fellow picked out?"

Belinda looked up and grinned, "Daed, she must have a fellow, if she's planning a wedding."

Jed laughed. "Makes sense to me, it does. Still, odd they've told anyone already. What if the boy changes his mind?"

Nellie giggled and Belinda rolled her eyes. "He wouldn't dare. Uncle Gabe would defend his new sister-in-law, I bet," Belinda stated. "Why don't we go see them? Reuben could watch the farm for a few days, couldn't he?"

"Oh, your brother-in-law has a lot to do. His equipment was breaking down something fierce in the fall," Grace said while she turned her needles to start the next row.

"Our house is warmer. I bet Rachel would rather be here when it's cold like this."

"Your older sister complains unless it's eighty degrees out," her father said with a grin. "She'd better get some meat on those bones."

"Reuben likes her skinny. Says after she has seven or eight *boppli*, she'll fill out her dresses real nice," Belinda said.

"I wish she'd get in a family way soon. She's nineteen, you know." Nellie added. "I want to be an *aenti* so bad."

"Won't be long before you have your own," Gideon teased.

"I can't wait. I'm going to get married when I reach sixteen."

"Takes two, little one," her daed reminded her.

"I'm already looking around," she announced with a degree of pride.

"Oh, now, listen to this one," Grace said, her mouth spread across her round face, dimpling her cheeks.

"I bet she is and I bet the boys are noticing her as well," Jed said with a nod. "Though fourteen is a little young to worry about boys. On that note, I'm going up to bed early. This cold makes my bones creak. I'll need an extra quilt tonight, Grace. Is there one in our closet?"

"Nee. I'll be up in a minute and get one out of the cedar chest in the spare room. I want to finish this row before I go to bed."

"*Gut nacht*, everyone. See you in the morning, God willing."

Belinda watched her father climb the stairs with a separate lamp. He still looked young, she thought, but then he was only forty-three. She glanced at her mother, who was finishing up the row. Her gentle features took on a rosy hue from the light of the lamp. She was quite beautiful and only forty. Even though she was plumper than she was when she was a bride, she walked with an erect posture and an aura of confidence. Hard work seemed to agree with her. Belinda wondered if she could handle all the chores her mother did so gracefully—without a word of complaint and so efficiently that her daed broke the Amish rule of never displaying *hochmut*, or pride, and bragged on occasion to his family and friends about his wonderful-*gut* wife.

After her mother retired, Belinda took the last remaining lamp, and she and her sister headed up to bed with Gideon following close behind to take advantage of the faint lighting on the stairs.

Chapter Two
Holmes County, Ohio

Two weeks passed without Belinda leaving the house. Her mood darkened and her mother asked her if she was feeling ill.

"I'm just so bored," she said while she stirred the potato soup for supper.

"I don't know how you can say that. We keep so busy. Maybe you should go see Rebecca. The Smuckers' place ain't that far and your daed said the roads are pretty clear."

"Maybe, but Rebecca is dull. She has no interest in anything besides quilting."

"She could teach you a lot, young lady. Her stitches are near perfect, that's for sure."

"But I don't *care* if I can quilt or not. No one seems to understand." She placed the wooden spoon on a plate and checked the pumpernickel bread baking in the oven. It still needed a few minutes. She hadn't meant to slam the oven door, but it clunked loudly, drawing her mother's scowl.

"You think too much about yourself, Belinda. One doesn't have to be happy all the time. Why don't you read the scriptures?"

"Oh, Mamm, you'll never understand. I guess I may as well go over to Rebecca's for a while. You don't really need me right now anyway. The clothes are still damp and Nellie can fold them when they're dry. The bread only needs about ten more minutes."

"Jah, go. I'll watch it. Just be home by four. Get Daed to hook up the buggy for you and add a heater."

"I can do it. Daed's sharpening his tools. I don't know how he stands it out in the barn all day in this cold, with only that small wood stove."

"Your daed likes to do his man chores and he stays warm between the stove and the heat from the animals, but you can tell him I'm putting tea water on and he should come in for a break."

After Belinda freshened up and re-did her hair, she placed her black bonnet over her prayer kapp and donned her warm woolen coat for warmth. Fortunately, the ride over took only fifteen minutes. In good weather she walked, but it was still in the low twenties and the wind gusted, dragging the temperature even lower.

Rebecca greeted her at the door and invited her to join the family for coffee and fresh baked molasses cookies.

Rebecca's youngest brother was in school, but two of her older brothers were in the barn with her daed, leaving nineteen-year-old Zeke busy painting the pantry cupboards for his mother. At his mother's instructions, he went out to get the others.

Rebecca was the middle child of five and the only girl. The family was ruled over by a strict father, who rarely smiled—a sharp contrast to Belinda's daed, who had such a cheerful demeanor and frequently teased his children in his good-hearted way. Rebecca told Belinda once that she loved being at Belinda's home because of the pleasant atmosphere.

When everyone was seated, Rebecca's mother poured coffee and laid platters of the fresh, soft-baked molasses cookies at each end of the long trestle table. No one spoke for a few moments. Zeke sat across from Belinda and gave the appearance of being unaware of her presence, though Belinda caught him looking at her more than once. He'd quickly turn his gaze away, but the scarlet flush on his neck gave away his interest. He pushed his blond curls back off his forehead with one hand, while he reached for two cookies with his other. Dabs of white paint decorated his nose and chin and Belinda stifled a laugh, not wanting to embarrass him.

"So, Belinda," Mrs. Smucker began, "how's the family?"

"Gut. We're all fine."

"I'm glad."

Rebecca passed the cookies to Belinda, who took one and bit off a small piece. "These are delicious, Mrs. Smucker."

"Rebecca made them."

"Oh, jah."

It was so quiet in the room, Belinda could hear herself chew. She almost wished she'd stayed home. This was even more boring than being alone, for heaven's sake.

Becky's daed motioned toward the coffee pot and his wife rose immediately to retrieve it from the coal stove. She moved swiftly to fill his mug again. He nodded with his mouth in a straight line and his long reddish beard popped up and down as he chewed a cookie and stared straight ahead. At long last, the ordeal was over. Zeke went back to his painting and the other males returned to the barn. Mrs. Smucker went upstairs to change the beds leaving Belinda alone with Rebecca. They sat together on a long worn sofa.

"Do you want to do anything special?" Rebecca asked her visitor.

"Like what?"

"I don't know. We could sew."

"Nee. I don't think so."

"Want to go for a walk?" Rebecca asked with her brows raised.

"It's too cold. I wish we could dance."

"Belinda, I have absolutely no idea how to do that."

"I can show you."

Rebecca giggled. "With no music?"

"I can hum a tune I know."

"You went out again with the English, didn't you?" she asked with a sly smile crinkling her lips.

"I got out a couple weeks ago. We had a ball. I danced with three different guys."

"Wow! Did they kiss you?"

Belinda clucked her tongue. "Of course not. I know they wanted to, though."

"How did you know?" Rebecca leaned toward her friend

"A woman can tell, is all." Belinda laid her head back against the sofa and folded her arms.

Rebecca pulled back and stared at her friend. "I think you're taking your chances with guys like that, Belinda. You'd better be careful."

"They seem to respect me. They don't even curse around me much."

"Much?"

"Well, not at all. Most of the time."

"What would you do if someone tried to get fresh?"

"I'd lay down the law. I'm not gonna do anything stupid."

"You never drank or smoked?" Rebecca cocked her head to the side.

"One little bit of beer only once and I'll never do it again."

"So, what do you do when you're with them?"

"We dance. Sometimes we play computer games. They have a neat game where you pretend you're playing baseball. You swing an invisible bat and—"

"No way! You know how to use one of those computers?"

After removing her shoes, Belinda tucked her legs under her and relaxed. "Not real gut, but I can do other games, too. It isn't that hard."

"Do your parents know all this?"

"I don't tell them everything, but it's okay since I'm seventeen you know. You could do it, too."

"No way. My daed would never let me do stuff like that. He doesn't even like me going to the sings, but Mamm says that's okay. How else will I find a husband? You don't come anymore. If you're not careful, you could end up with no proposals, Miss Belinda."

"So? I don't care. Maybe I don't want to get married anyway."

"Oh, right. You don't fool me. You told me yourself you wouldn't leave the community. You haven't changed your mind, have you?"

Belinda let out a long breath and looked up at the ceiling. "Nee. I want to stay Amish, but I get really bored sometimes. I get tired of working and I'm not sure I want a hundred kids."

"I thought you liked boppli," Rebecca said as she held her knees up and circled her arms around them, careful to keep her skirt in place.

"It's not like I don't want any, but look at the Millers up the road. She's gonna have her eleventh and she's only in her early thirties!"

"Jah, that's true. She sure doesn't have much time to relax."

"That's for sure and for certain."

"Belinda, I think Zeke likes you."

Belinda's brows rose. "Really? Actually, when I think hard about it, I bet you're right."

"Jah, he always listens careful-like when I talk about you."

18

"Does he know I go out with English?"

"He knows, but I didn't tell him. Word gets around. Someone saw you in English clothes once, you know."

"Who?"

"I daresn't say."

"You're my friend. You have to tell me."

"I don't know. I don't want hard feelings…"

"Never mind. I don't care anyway. It's my business and it's not like I'm taking drugs or doing immoral stuff like some girls. I just like to have fun."

"Be careful though, because the Amish guys don't like it when we fool around with English guys. They sometimes make remarks about girls that do."

"But it's okay when they go out with English girls! Somehow that's different!" Belinda's eyes shot fire when she contemplated the difference in attitude.

Rebecca shook her head. "It will always be different. Fair or not."

"It's not right. So, anyway, do you want me to show you how to dance or not?"

"My mamm is right upstairs and Zeke's in the other room. Maybe some other time. He'd make fun of me. Why don't we make fudge. I could go for some."

"Booorrrring."

"Honestly, Belinda, sometimes you make me mad. If everything is so boring, why don't you leave the Amish and you can be as fancy as you want!" Rebecca's blond hair loosened while she shook her head vehemently at her friend.

"Rebecca! I thought you understood."

"It's just you act so superior now to the rest of us. Like you're so smart and sophisticated. It hurts us, you know. We've always been so close, but now it's like you treat me different. Like I'm stupid or something."

Belinda's mouth dropped open and she moved closer to her friend who was sitting on the other end of the long sofa. "Rebecca, that's not true. I don't think that at all and you'll always be my very best friend."

Rebecca wiped her eyes with her apron hem and sniffed. "It doesn't seem like it. I even hoped you'd end up someday with my brother so we could be even closer—like sisters."

"Oh, Rebecca. I'm so sorry. I like Zeke. I really do, but I don't know if I could love him."

"You could give it a try."

"He's never even asked me to a sing."

"He would, if you encouraged him even a tiny little bit."

Belinda looked away and leaned back. "I need to get this restlessness out of my system or I won't be a gut wife to anyone, Beck. Give me a little more time and I think I'll be okay again."

"Jah. Take as much time as you need, Belinda. I will always love you and you'll always be my best friend."

The girls reached over and embraced. Belinda sniffed deeply and blinked rapidly to hide her own tears. "Let's go make fudge."

"Jah, okay. You can take some home with you."

"That's sweet of you. My daed will be super happy." The girls went hand-in-hand to the kitchen to begin mixing the chocolate delight.

Chapter Three
Lancaster County, Pennsylvania

Gabe closed the barn doors after milking the cows and pulled his woolen jacket closer to his body. The winds whipped through the open drive area. He headed back to the house where he could nearly smell the coffee brewing on the back of the coal stove. February was brutal enough when the temperatures dropped to single digits, but now with the gusts added, he felt the bitterness of the wind in his bones.

His dreams were reality when he entered the cozy, bright kitchen where his wife, Emma, not only had coffee prepared, but had just pulled sticky buns from the oven. She set them on the side of the burners to cool slightly before presenting them to her husband. Gabe's two children by his first wife were in school. Lizzy and Mervin would not be expected home until mid-afternoon when Gabe planned to take the closed buggy to pick them up. Though the school was walking distance under normal circumstances, the harsh winter was excuse enough to bring them home in a protected carriage. Lizzy's low resistance to viral infections was an additional reason for Gabe's extra precaution.

For now, Gabe and Emma enjoyed their moments uninterrupted. With a baby on the way, they knew this 'honeymoon' stage of their recent marriage, would be short-lived. Emma enjoyed this time of her pregnancy. At five months she was not uncomfortable yet and popping enough so she wasn't asked anymore if she was just gaining weight. It was obvious she was in a family way and she and Gabe were thrilled at the prospect of having a child born of their union and the love they shared. After Gabe's wife passed away, he had thought his life was always going to be one of loneliness and heartache, but the delightful elder Zook daughter, though considerably younger than he, had not only fallen in love with his two needy children, but miracles above miracles— with him as well.

"I wrote to my sister, Grace, in Ohio a couple days ago, Emma," he remarked while he stood and poured a mug of the strong brew and eyed the steaming sticky buns, coated with melted butter and brown sugar.

"Oh, jah? That was nice. I hope someday to meet her and her family. You can wait five more minutes for the bun," she said teasingly, as she reached for small bread and butter plates.

Gabe smiled and kissed the side of her cheek when he passed by her to go to the sink to wash up. He set his mug on the counter. "I asked them to come out whenever they have a chance. It was too bad they couldn't make our wedding. Maybe after the baby…"

"Jah, that would be ever so nice. I heard about her husband from Mervin. He's apparently a friendly sort of man."

"He is. Lots of fun to be around."

"They only had four children, ain't that so?"

"Jah. Four who lived. She miscarried a couple times, sad to say. Their oldest girl, Rachel, was the one who got married last year. Remember, I was going to go out for the wedding, but then we had problems with Mervin?"

"Oh, jah, I remember now. They have three girls and one boy, right?"

"Gut memory, Emma. Jah. So, can I have my sticky bun yet?"

Emma smiled as she scooped it onto a plate with a butter knife. "More butter?"

"Nee. Bad enough I eat it at all. Have to watch my figure," he teased. Emma came over to the sink where he was drying his hands. She set the bun down next to his mug and wrapped her arms around his lean waist and kissed him tenderly on his lips. He moved back and patted her tummy. "Our little one is stirring?"

She smiled and nodded as they went over to the kitchen table to sit. "All the time. Getting stronger, too. I bet it's a boy."

"I don't really care what it is so long as our boppli's healthy and doesn't give you a rough time."

"I'm not frightened. I know everything will go just fine. I'm strong, you know."

"You are, honey. I can't believe all you can do. You're so petite in ways and yet strong in others. I love you, Emma, with all my heart."

"Oh Gabe, I'm so happy—not only because you're my husband, but I've been blessed with your children as well. I feel God has brought us together as one family. I just hope Lizzy won't be jealous of the baby when it comes."

"I don't think that will be a problem. She talks about it a lot and I think she's excited to be old enough to help."

"I'm counting on that. So, let's enjoy our sticky buns and relax for a while. It's too cold to be outside, ain't it?"

"It's bitter out there today. Jah, I'll just do what's necessary and then spend my time with you."

While they enjoyed their coffee break, it began to snow for the second day in a row. While they looked out the window above the sink, the wind swelled and the snow began to brush against the panes, never accumulating, but instead swirled, forming intricate patterns.

"It's so beautiful, Gabe."

"Jah, beautiful, but dangerous on the roads."

Emma watched later when Gabe attached the buggy to his faithful horse. He was nearly invisible through the increasing volume of snow plastering the area as he headed over to the schoolhouse to collect the children. After he rode out of sight, she said a prayer for his safe return and then added a shovel full of coal to the stove, thanking the Lord for the safety and warmth of their home.

Emma's younger sister, Ruth, held her six-month-old son, Nathanael, over her shoulder covering him with one of the hand-crocheted blankets her mother, Mary, had made last winter when she knew her daughter was expecting her first child. She tucked it around his shoulders, restraining his arms to keep him warmer. He had finally cut his lower front teeth and was more content now. His constant fussing and crying had been difficult on her nerves and she welcomed the respite before the next teeth worked their way through his tender gums.

He was indeed a handsome young boy, so like his father, Jeremiah. She could see the resemblance to her husband through the eyes and some of his facial expressions—especially when he was fussy. She loved teasing Jeremiah about his son's frown resembling his own.

After living several months with her Aunt Esther, a professor at the university in Philadelphia, Ruth was afraid the Amish way of life would seem dull and difficult in comparison, but she never once regretted her decision to return and marry the only man she ever loved—Jeremiah Fisher.

He worked in a buggy shop with her brother, Mark, and was skilled at what he did. Sometimes she wished he worked the land for a living so they'd be together more, but as of now, he enjoyed his work and he was usually home by five. The money came in regularly, which helped with the few bills they accumulated.

Bored? Never. Dear little Nathanael saw to that.

Her heart beat rapidly as she watched the blizzard developing outside her snug clapboard home. Visibility had gone from fair to impossible in only a few short hours. Surely they'd close the shop and head for home before it got any worse. It wasn't fair to the horses to put them through weather so dreadful and it wasn't safe on the roads without brake lights. While the large red triangle the law insisted they use on the back of their buggies and the small red reflectors helped under normal conditions, they'd be nearly impossible to see through the snowstorm emerging. Ruth said a prayer for safety for all on the road and went over to the rocker to rest. Her baby was asleep, but instead of laying him in his crib, she wanted to feel his warmth and his soft breathing on her neck, reassuring her of his safety. Now if only Jeremiah would come through that door.

Right after her last pupil left the schoolhouse, Katie started for home. It took twice as long to make it through the treacherous weather as it would in normal conditions. She released a deep breath when she turned down the drive to the farmhouse.

After her younger brother, Wayne, met her and offered to take care of the horse and buggy, she made her way to the back porch and left her boots on the steps. After a hot cup of cocoa and one cookie, she took over the job of kneading bread from her mother, who wanted to start preparing rutabaga for supper.

Katie shifted the mound of dough a quarter turn and punched with her fist at the elastic blob of future bread. She continued kneading the yeasty mass, glancing across the room at her mother, Mary. Her mother's pallor and persistent cough troubled the entire family, yet she refused to see the doctor. Even though Katie's daed was now a strong advocate of the medical profession, and tried to convince her to make an appointment.

Perhaps his experience of the past year with his own issues of high blood pressure and dizziness, had made him more aware of the advantages of catching problems before they became serious. So far the beta-blocker had done its job and he had returned to his farming with new vigor. Yah, Katie would try to convince her mamm to see the doctor if she didn't improve soon.

Katie covered the dough with a clean dishtowel and walked over to the window to check the weather. It seemed to worsen by the minute. At least she knew her fiancé, Josiah, was safe from the blizzard. He had decided to spend the week working on their new home. He'd be warm and safe judging from the amount of wood he'd cut and stacked on the repaired porch and she had seen to it that he had enough food for at least a week. They were excited to know they'd be married within a year and living in their own little place.

Her seventeen-year-old brother, Wayne, sat quietly next to a kerosene lamp and worked on a horse he was carving for one of his young nephews. He had even sold one at auction for twenty dollars. Katie was quite proud of him, though she couldn't boast to her friends. It wouldn't be humble to brag.

Katie pictured her family scattered across the valley and prayed everyone was safe at home already. It was at times like this, she wished she could talk by phone to her loved ones. How reassuring that would be. But her Amish roots forbade such modern conveniences. Way too worldly. And she was an Amish woman, through and through.

A rapid pounding caused her to leave her reverie abruptly and she nearly ran to answer the door. There stood her older married brothers, Mark and Abram. Their stone-like expressions placed fear in her heart. What on earth had happened?

Chapter Four
Holmes County, Ohio

The blizzard had not amounted to too much after all. The predictions of failing power lines and days of snow removal were exaggerated, though they heard from travelers that Pennsylvania had been hit harder than Ohio by the same storm front. The day after the snow stopped, plows came through opening the roads enough for the family to go to market. Most of the stands were open and Belinda noticed Carrie's mother was already set up with her health food and supplement display when they arrived. They waved to each other and then Belinda helped arrange the root vegetables and apples in the proper bins when her brother brought them in from their buggy. Her mother chatted with another Amish woman who sold breads and other bakery goods in the next booth. Her own family stuck with produce, since they didn't want to compete with their long-time friend, Hettie.

Usually Carrie came by after school to work with her mother, though Belinda had missed seeing her these past two weeks. Belinda hoped she'd show up this afternoon. She needed desperately to get out of the house and do something different! Anything! Hopefully, they'd make plans.

Around four, sales slowed down and Belinda's mother suggested she take a break. Belinda noticed Carrie coming through the front double doors with her brother, Jeff, in tow. He caught sight of Belinda before his sister did and gave her a welcoming grin. The three met in the center of the aisle and chatted about the snowstorm and then Jeff went to their stand while Carrie and Belinda sat on a nearby bench to catch up on their lives.

"We missed you last week-end. I thought you'd show up at my place Saturday."

"Did you have another party?"

"No, but a couple girls came over in the afternoon. We went shopping together. It would have been fun to have you there."

"I wanted to come, but I couldn't find anyone headed in your direction. But this Saturday, my brother-in-law offered to drop me off in town if I needed to go. I haven't checked with my mamm yet, either. But if I'm home before dark, she's usually okay with it. I'd have to count on someone to drive me home though. I hate to walk in this cold."

"No prob. Jeff has his own car now and loves to have an excuse to drive. It's a Honda and practically new."

"Do you have others coming over?"

"I'm gonna ask a lot of my friends. My parents have to go to my aunt's house an hour away. It's their anniversary and they plan to stay over." Carrie's eyes brightened when she spoke. Belinda felt a wave of apprehension go through her, not even understanding why, though she suspected it was because of the possibilities that loomed in her mind. A party without chaperones? Was she prepared for something like that?

"Is it okay if I get there mid-afternoon? That's when Reuben, plans to head for town."

"Great! We can spend the afternoon together. Ginny plans to come early, too. I have a new dance step to show you. Don't bring your old jeans, since I have a darling new outfit you'd look great in. It's a mini-skirt and sweater combo. You'll love it."

Belinda gulped at the thought of exposing her legs that much, but she certainly didn't want to be a prude. After all, it was just clothing. "Okay. Sounds like fun. What about shoes?"

"Oh, you can go barefoot or be super cool and wear the heels I showed you last time. They'd make you look taller and older. My mother just waved. I'd better go help out. Looks like they have five customers all at once. I'll see you Saturday. Why don't you spend the night? Ask your mom."

Belinda nodded and watched Carrie remove her knit beret and toss her long sleek hair over her shoulders as she made her way over to the stand. Jeff winked over while he made change for a customer. She had a quickening of her heart rate when she noted his wavy blonde hair and dimpled chin. The whole family was attractive and according to Carrie, her mother had actually been a model before she married. She even ran for Miss Ohio when she was younger. Carrie attracted guys wherever she went. Sometimes Belinda felt invisible when she was with the group, but lately, she noticed she too was gaining attention from the guys. She was determined not to let it go to her head, but it was more difficult all the time to remain humble. In fact, that's about all she thought about when she lay awake at night. The 'other world' was looking more attractive all the time. Oh, mercy, what would her parents say if she decided to leave her close-knit community.

Belinda returned to the stand and straightened out the rows of winter squash. Her heart was heavy, though thoughts of Saturday night put a smile on her face. A new dance step. Maybe Rebecca would decide to join her some night. She'd teach her the steps and then convince her to loosen up and have some fun in her life. After all, you're only young once.

Miracle above miracles, Belinda's mother agreed to let her remain at Carrie's house overnight. It helped that she knew Carrie's mother and trusted her. Carrie forgot to mention the parents would be away and boys would be attending. She pushed her guilt into the dark recesses of her brain and rationalized those were unimportant details.

Lancaster County, Pennsylvania

Katie held the door open while her brothers removed their hats and stepped inside. "Where's Mamm?" Mark asked, turning his head toward the kitchen. Their somber expressions told her something was wrong—terribly wrong.

"Upstairs. What's happened?" Katie could barely swallow. Fear enveloped her whole being.

Abram didn't even remove his boots, but went to the base of the stairway and called up to his mother. Mary appeared at the top of the steps, her eyebrows gathered and mouth drawn. "What's wrong? Why are you here now?"

"Mamm, come down. Please." Instead of waiting for her to come unassisted, Abram met her half way and took her elbow, guiding her down the remaining steps. When they got to the bottom, he dropped his arm and looked over at his brother. Katie felt she'd pass out from the stress that permeated the room.

"It's about *Dawdi* and *Mammi Oma*. Their buggy was hit by a car."

"Oh, dear heaven," Mary grabbed hold of the railing and bent over, breathing heavily. "How bad was it?"

"Bad, Mamm. I'm afraid...I..." Abram looked over at Mark, his eyes pleading for help.

Mark moved quickly to his mother's side and took her in his arms. "Mamm, Oma is real bad, but she's alive. We heard they have her in intensive care already."

"Oh, thank you, Jesus. At least she's alive." Mary looked at her sons. "And Daed? What about my father?"

The men exchanged glances and looked down. Tears ran down Mark's cheeks as he shook his head.

"No, no. Don't even tell me! He can't be. Oh, dear God in Heaven—no!"

Katie stood motionless. It was a nightmare. Soon she'd awaken and it would be over. Yet she knew better. It was true. This was a nightmare she would be unable to shake off. This was life, or really—the awful opposite. This was what one prepared for and yet? One was never prepared for a loved one suddenly having life snatched away. No time for good-byes. No last moments to express the love felt. Katie went to her mother and brothers and they formed a ring. A ring of grief. The deep love they shared as well as the mutual pain of losing a family member so dear to them—the ring was support. It rang of the family blood ties that ran through their veins. It spoke of eternity. Surely, Katie's *dawdi* was dwelling in the house of the Lord. His constant devotion and desire to be a man of God would count. He once stated that he had accepted Jesus into his very heart and he wanted to live the way his Jesus wanted him to. God's grace would cover his sins, his misjudgments, his moments of frailty and humanity. *Thank you, Jesus*.

Mary lifted her head. Her tears continued to stream down her face, dampening her Amish apron. "Go tell your father and Wayne. They're in the barn. We must go to Oma right away. There will be plenty of time to grieve later. Right now she needs us."

Mark nodded and headed for the door while Abram and Katie led their mother to the sofa. Katie wiped her own tears and handed her mother a tissue box from the table. Mary gathered several and held them to her face. Her body shook and her tears continued, though she sat erectly, obviously trying to compose herself. "Where do they have my mamm, *sohn*?"

"Lancaster. I stopped at Ernie's on the way here. He's on his way over to take us by car. I knew we'd need a driver. He's offered to loan us his son's cell phone for a few days." Abram wiped his face with the arm of his jacket and took a deep breath.

Leroy arrived beside them with Wayne and Mark. Their faces were ashen. Wayne sniffed loudly and knelt beside his mother, who placed her hand on his head and patted it lightly. "It's okay, sohn. We know where your dawdi is. It was God's will."

"Why? Why would God want to do this?" Wayne's voice cracked and his father, Leroy, knelt beside him, surrounding him with his arms. "Hush, boy. We all ask questions, but the answer is always the same. We don't have the mind of God. He knows best even when we can't understand. We must trust."

"It's so hard, Daed," Wayne turned his head and laid it against his father's broad chest.

"I hear a car," Mark said as he headed toward the door. "Jah, it's Ernie. Katie, get mamm's shawl. We have to go."

The group gathered what they needed and wordlessly trudged through the growing piles of snow to the waiting van. The sting of the snow turning to sleet added to their pain. The roads were still treacherous, but there was no fear—just grief. Their world was missing a Godly man and the void was already felt.

Chapter Five
Holmes County, Ohio

Finally Saturday arrived. Belinda was surprised her father didn't seem alarmed that she wanted to spend the night at her friend's house. She knew it helped that her mother knew Carrie Richardson's mamm and they had frequently taken breaks together. What her parents didn't know was Mr. and Mrs. Richardson were going to be away overnight. Somehow, Belinda failed to mention that fact.

Her brother-in-law pulled up to Carrie's home, which was along the main road. It was set back over a hundred yards and almost hidden by large hedges, which surrounded the brick two-story Federal structure. "Nice place," he said when he pulled the buggy off the side of the road. "You like coming here, Belinda? Ain't it a bit rich for your taste?"

"They're real nice people and don't act all rich and everything."

"Can't be too rich if she has to live off sales from her stand."

"Well her husband has his own business, too. He's a contractor or something."

"Want me to pick you up later on my way home?"

Belinda shrugged. "No, I'll get a ride home tomorrow, *danki*." She climbed down and waved while he pulled away from the curb. Her heart was pounding. All night? No parents? Was she really okay with this? Well, certainly she'd be safe with Carrie and her brother there. Her brother. Oh, my, he certainly was handsome. But he wouldn't be attracted to an Amish girl. His expression when he saw her in English clothes the first time came to her mind. He seemed to appreciate her looks that day.

When she got to the door, Carrie opened it and pulled her in. "It's freezing out there. Quick, I don't want the heat to get out." Warmth reached Belinda's cheeks immediately and she wondered if the whole house was this toasty. But then of course, why wouldn't it be with central heat? "Ginny didn't get here yet. Let's go to my room and I'll help you change. How do you stand such dreary clothes? I could never be Amish."

The girls climbed the carpeted stairs and went into Carrie's large comfy bedroom. Her walls were painted maroon and she had white furniture and carpeting. The spread was a brilliant combination of primary colors in abstract design—hardly something Belinda would want, but interesting nonetheless. Two black and white polka-dotted beanbag chairs rested at one end near a flat screen television and sound system. A desk with a computer sat along one wall with two shelves of books above it. Carrie kept her room neat and every time Belinda went there it seemed she had added something new. This time she noticed a contemporary floor lamp between the chairs.

"Wait till you try on this outfit. You'll love it," Carrie said as she opened her walk-in closet and took out a brief aqua skirt. "Here, try it on and I'll get the sweater."

Belinda's hands shook slightly when she removed her Amish frock and laid it across the end of the bed. Carrie turned and watched her friend put on the scanty mini-skirt. Belinda's face reddened when she looked down at her long slender legs, exposed. "It's kind of short."

"Yeah, that's the idea," Carrie said with a grin.

"But the guys—"

"Oh, don't worry about them. They're used to seeing legs. It's not a big deal. Here's the sweater. Isn't it cool?" She handed over a white long-sleeved pullover, which thankfully covered Belinda's upper body without accenting her full breasts.

"Do you have anything longer?" Belinda asked as she checked her reflection in the full-length mirror imbedded in the closet door.

"But look how cute you are! Wait till Ginny gets here. We'll ask her opinion. And if my brother ever wakes up, we can get his thoughts."

Belinda's cheeks went from pink to scarlet.

"Let your hair down, Belinda, and I'll style it. Can I cut it a little first?"

"Mercy no. We never cut our hair."

Carrie's brows arched. "Never?"

"That's the Amish way."

Carrie shook her head. "There's no way I could be Amish. I love the new styles too much. You should be English. What's the big deal, anyway?"

"It's too hard to explain, I guess. We don't want to be a real part of your world. Too many bad things happen."

"Like what?"

"Well, like divorce for one thing."

"Yeah, a lot of my friends have split homes, but they manage. You get used to it I guess."

"We don't want to be proud so we don't wear make-up or show off our hair. Only my husband will see me with my hair down."

Carrie laughed, "and my brother and my friends and—"

Guilt flooded Belinda's mind at the very words. "Oh, I'd be in trouble, big time."

"But it's your Rums— something, isn't it? You're *allowed* to fool around, aren't you?"

"Depends on the district. Our bishop allows it, though I know my parents would be upset if they saw how much I did."

"So they won't find out. Come on, sit on the bed and I'll brush your hair. It's so shiny. Our blond hair and complexions are so similar, we could pass as sisters."

Belinda did what she was told and Carrie brushed out her long tresses until her hair glowed. Then she pulled it back and put a satin elastic holder to keep it in a long ponytail. "Let me get eye make-up on you and lipstick. I have a bright red I just bought. I'll try that."

The front door bell rang and Belinda heard voices. Carrie's brother, Jeff, was talking with Ginny. Carrie leaned over the balcony and called over to her friend. "Come up. I'm fixing Belinda. Wait till you see her." Jeff followed Ginny up the stairs. He had a wide grin on his face. Belinda stood behind Carrie, unwilling to show her naked legs to him or anyone else at this point. Jeff went down the hall to his bedroom.

Ginny hugged her friends and then dropped her woolen jacket on the floor. "You look marv!" she said, looking over at Belinda, who sat down on the edge of the bed, gripping her legs together. "Except for your hair." She reached into her enormous red leather purse and pulled out a magazine. "Look what I found." She opened it to an article on hairdos for proms and weddings. The other girls leaned over and 'oohed' and 'aahed' over the glamorous models.

"Look at that one," Carrie said, pointing to a blonde with hair twisted in various positions, some locks floating down her shoulders. "We could do that on Belinda!"

"Yeah! Let's try." Ginny grabbed one of Belinda's hands. "Are you game?"

Belinda laughed a bit nervously. "Why not?"

"Oh, my gosh, this is gonna be so much fun. We'll tell Dan you're from Hollywood!" Ginny said. She and Carrie giggled.

"He'll believe it, too. He believes anything," Carrie said as she removed the ponytail holder and brushed Belinda's hair again.

"Have I met him?" Belinda asked Carrie, trying to recall a guy with that name.

"No, he goes to college, but he's home for the week-end and said he'll be here tonight. He never misses a party, but watch out. He loves the girls."

"And the girls love him!" Ginny added.

"I know one girl who does," Carrie said, winking at her friend.

"He's okay."

"Right! Just okay? He'd love to make out with you, Ginny, and you know it."

Ginny grinned. "Don't make Belinda too gorgeous. We won't stand a chance with any of the guys.

Belinda realized her heart was beating rapidly. Things were moving too fast. It was one thing to dress like them, even dance a little, but guys? Like allowing them to get personal? That, she hadn't thought through. It might be okay unless they really got fresh. She wasn't prepared to give up her purity to anyone but her future husband. Was this getting out of hand?

"Don't move, I'm trying to copy this do," Ginny said while she twisted several locks and pinned them in place. After a few changes, the girls stood back to admire their accomplishment. "Now make-up," Ginny added.

After several minutes of discussion on color, mascara, lash curling and liner, the new beauticians stood back to admire their work. Nodding, they took Belinda by the hand and drew her in front of the mirror. Whoa. This was overboard. She honestly didn't look like herself. There was no one in the entire world who would take her for Amish. It was scary. "Uh...I don't know," she started.

"You don't know? You're positively gorgeous! Wait, let me get my brother. He won't lie." Carrie ran out the door before Belinda could say a word.

Ginny adjusted a couple loose strands as Carrie and Jeff came through the door. Jeff let out a whistle and his eyes lit up like a Christmas tree. "Man! I can't believe you're the same girl!"

Belinda felt like she might *kutz!* Mercy, she couldn't throw up all over the beautiful carpet. She was so conscious of her bare legs and painted face that for a moment she wished she were at home, donned in her Amish frock and prayer kapp. But only for a moment. The admiration, especially from Jeff, went to her head and all the warnings about pride and self-centeredness flew through the brick walls and landed on another continent. This was fun!

Chapter Six
Lancaster County

Mary sat by her mother's bedside, caressing the frail motionless hand that had once held her when she was a newborn, tended to her every need while she grew up, and provided touches of love to all who knew her. Would it ever be so again? Would her dear mother be able to heal enough to one day return to her home? But then she couldn't return there, even if she was physically able. Not now. Not with the loss of her dear husband. Mary's throat narrowed as her inability to process the last two days of her life came crushing down.

Was it possible only days ago her life was so predictable? And she was so happy? Her two older daughters and her sons were married and living nearby with their young families. Katie was engaged to a wonderful young Amish man and Leroy, her dear husband, was healthy again with the aid of medication. He would surely live to an old age.

Then this happened. Her dear father was now in heaven and her mother, sweet soul, was on the cusp of death. "Dear God, please spare my mother's life, if it be thy will," she murmured while the ever-present tears continued their descent. Katie, who sat next to her reading the Psalms to herself, looked up and handed her mother another tissue.

"She's not in pain, Mamm. That's a gut thing."

"Jah. The only gut thing I can think of right now, Katie," Mary said, dabbing at her eyes with her free hand.

"Has she moved her hand at all?"

Mary shook her head.

A nurse by the name of Loretta, who had been with her from the beginning, walked silently to the other side of the bed and made adjustments to the IV hanging on a pole. "Her vital signs are improving," she whispered and gave Mary and Katie a weak smile. "Keep praying."

"Jah, that we do, but in the end, it's God's will and we must accept his decision."

Loretta nodded. "I understand. I'm going to sit over by the window for a few moments to fill out her chart. Let me know if there is any change."

Mary said she would and then she put her head back against the headpiece on the large leather chair. "I might sleep for a few moments, Katie. Will you take over?"

"Sure." After placing her Bible on the windowsill, she shoved her chair closer to the bed and took her grandmother's hand. She stroked it gently with her other hand. Within minutes, Mary was asleep.

Ruth came through the door and motioned to Katie to join her. Reluctantly, Katie placed her grandmother's hand on the blanket and tiptoed past her mother to the doorway. Ruth whispered to her. "I just talked to Aunt Esther. She and Martin are driving here to see Oma. They should be here within a couple hours."

"She must have been real upset."

"To say the least. They've been so distanced by her leaving the community and now this. She had so little time with Dawdi."

"Jah, that's got to be painful—all those years of not even talking."

Ruth moved back when a physician's assistant headed toward the bedside. "I feel in the way here. What can I do to help?"

"There's little any of us can do, Ruthie. I'm mainly staying for Mamm's sake."

"She looks so shattered."

"Jah, but she's holding up. She's strong."

"Like we're all supposed to be. I'm not that strong, Katie. I'll tell you that much."

"I guess when we need strength, the Lord supplies it. Is Emma coming by today?"

"She said she and Gabe would wait until this afternoon. Lizzy has a cold."

"I wonder how Becky's making out teaching by herself."

"She'll be fine. You said several kids were out sick, so she probably doesn't have that many to worry about."

"Who's watching Nathanael?"

"I left him with Hannah. She's such a dear. Even with her own four little ones, she always opens her arms to more when there's a need."

"Jah, you couldn't ask for a better sister-in-law. Of course, Fannie's always ready to help too." The sisters moved down the hallway and stood against the wall. "I'm glad Aunt Esther is coming. Hopefully, Oma will continue to be…"

Ruth nodded. "I hope so. Are they still saying it's unlikely she'll make it?"

"Last report was that she was slightly more stable. The nurse said her vital signs were somewhat better."

"She's a tough German lady, Katie. If anyone can make it, she will, of that I'm sure and certain."

The girls embraced and then took turns sitting by the bedside of the white-haired woman they'd known and loved their whole lives.

Ruth returned to the waiting room after spending more than an hour at her grandmother's side. There was no change. Friends and extended family members came by every so often to lend support, though only the immediate family was allowed in the patient's room. The staff was in constant attendance and there was comfort in knowing she was receiving such excellent medical care. The disturbing odors and sounds of life-preserving machines penetrated Ruth's being and to gain some relief, she often took brief walks around the floor and reception area.

As she headed toward the elevator to return to the floor, she heard her name called and turned to see Aunt Esther and her husband, Martin, heading her way. The women embraced, holding on longer than normal, and then Martin put his arms around Ruth. "I'm so sorry, Ruth. How are you holding up?"

Ruth took a step back and gave a faint smile. "I'll be okay. It's Mamm I'm worried about. She's had a miserable cold herself and then this."

"Yes, it must be terribly difficult on my poor sister," Esther said softly. "They've been so close all these years." Her eyes glistened when tears welled up. Esther's eyes were bloodshot and her lids were swollen. "Ruth, what about Daed's funeral? Has it been decided yet as to when and where?"

"Mark and Abram made arrangements. Most of us in the district use the same funeral home. Actually tomorrow we start the vigil at home. I dread it. Poor Mamm, she won't even be there." Ruth put her hands over her face and her body shook from the grief. Esther held her again and the two wept silently. Martin looked on, his eyes turned down.

Finally Esther gathered herself together. "I'll stay as long as you need me. Has the notice gone into the local newspaper?"

Ruth nodded. "The immediate family will try to be present during the visits, but someone has to stay with Mamm. We can't let her pass…you know…alone."

"It's that serious? They don't offer any hope?"

"There's always hope, I guess, but it doesn't look like she'll make it. The longer she remains in a coma, the worse her chances are."

"Let me go to Mary now."

They walked over to the room and Ruth watched Esther make her way to the bedside of her mother. Mary looked up and rose when she saw her sister arrive. "Danki for coming so quickly, Esther."

Esther ran her hand over her mother's hair. Part of her cheek was wrapped in bandages and her neck was in a brace. One of her legs was broken in two places, but the head wound was the most serious of her problems.

After a few minutes, Esther joined Ruth again in the hallway. "What about Daed? Will there be a viewing?"

"I haven't seen him yet. He'll be moved to the house later this evening, but the undertaker suggested we not expose his face to others. There was obvious damage."

"Oh, Lord. This is so difficult on everyone. He was such a good man," Esther said, choking on her words.

Martin came over and put his arm around her. "How does your mother seem?"

"Not good. She hasn't reacted to anything. I talked to her, but there was no response."

"She may still know you're beside her, honey. Hearing is the last of the senses to leave a person."

"You sound as if it's all but over."

"I didn't mean it that way. No, we must continue to pray for her healing."

"I've never prayed so much in my life," Ruth said.

"That's about all we can do at this point. That, and keep Mary from falling apart," Esther said.

"She's strong, Aunt Esther, and strong in her faith. She knows sometimes God takes our loved ones and we must accept it."

"I know. I know." Esther patted Ruth on the shoulder. "When you have the visitation, I can stay with my mother. After all, no one knows me anymore anyway. That's the least I can do. Besides, I need some time alone with Mamm."

"Danki. We'll discuss it with everyone tonight. We're all meeting at the house to have prayer and talk about the arrangements. Hannah's watching Nathanael and Fannie's little ones so Fannie can go over and clean the sitting room. Not that it really needs it. You know how clean Mamm keeps the house."

Esther smiled. "Sometimes it just helps to do something. What about the funeral itself? When is that?"

"Day after tomorrow. I'm not going to worry about the meal after the funeral. I know our friends will prepare enough food. They always do."

"I hate to even discuss this, but does daed have a white outfit to wear?"

"Honestly, Aunt Esther, I have no idea. My brothers will handle that end of it. They didn't clean him before he was taken to the funeral home, however, because it was an accident and…well, it was too much. The funeral director advised them to let his staff handle it. He's been so gut with all of us, they just allowed him to make that decision."

Martin suggested they move to the waiting room to get out of the way and they followed him down the hall. It was a long day. A difficult day. The care and the love they received from so many of their neighbors and extended family as they came by to check on Oma's condition gave them each the strength to bear the pain. That and the love they felt emanating from their Savior, who never leaves nor forsakes His children.

40

Chapter Seven
Holmes County, Ohio

Some of Carrie's friends arrived around seven o'clock. Belinda knew only about half of the group, but she was treated like one of the gang immediately. Of course, no one realized that hours before she was the typical Amish maiden. Her heart danced and her palms were damp when she became the center of attention. Dan, the college student who was considered a womanizer by his colleagues, hung around her like a moth to a kero lamp. Ginny pouted at his dismissal of her when he spent his entire evening trying to impress Belinda.

"So where do you plan to go to college?" he asked after he sipped from his bottle of beer.

"I…I probably won't go."

His brows went up. "Really? Don't you have some fabulous ambition in that pretty head of yours? Like being a lawyer or a veterinarian or something exciting?"

Belinda giggled. "Nee. No. I want to get married and have a big family is all."

"Is all? Where are you from? You sound so cute." He leaned back and stared at her.

"I've lived in Lancaster County all my life."

"Where do you live?"

After she explained how to get to her farm, he grinned over and asked, "Can I come by to see you—like tomorrow night?"

"I don't think so. I don't think that's a gut, I mean good, idea."

"You sound like the Amish people I buy apples from." He laughed and took another sip of beer.

"I guess I should tell you something. You see, I'm really Amish."

"Sure you are. And I'm really a little girl in guy's clothing."

"No, really. It's just that I'm going through my Rumspringa and so I can dress like this."

"Whoa! You're gorgeous. I think you're pulling my leg."

"Sorry?"

"Just an expression. I think you're kidding about being Amish." He ran his hands through his long black hair.

"Ask Carrie, she'll tell you I'm not lying."

"Well, let me ask you this. Can you go on a date with me? I really like you a lot." He moved closer and ran his forefinger along her profile. She moved back and took in a breath.

"Sorry, did that frighten you?" His brows rose.

"I just don't like to be touched like that—from a stranger."

"I don't want to be a stranger. You're fascinating, maybe even more so now."

"Why is that?" Belinda stirred her ginger ale with a straw and looked over at him, questioning with her eyes.

He shrugged. "You're off limits in a way. More of a challenge."

"I don't like the sound of that," she said with a crooked smile. "I'm not up for grabs."

"I didn't mean to sound that way. I respect you, Belinda. I won't do anything dumb, honest. But I do want to see you more. Of course, I have to go back to school Sunday night."

Time to get on safer ground. "Tell me about yourself, Dan. Where do you go to college? And what courses are you taking?"

"I'm going to Temple in Philadelphia. Pre-med. I'm a junior."

"You're going to be a doctor?"

"Hope so. My grades are pretty good. I'm starting to check out med schools, but I'd like to stay on the east coast."

"You must be pretty smart."

He grinned and reached for a handful of potato chips. Belinda looked over at two of the girls dancing with their boyfriends. Someone had turned the music up and it was so loud, she had trouble hearing him.

"Can we go in the kitchen to talk?" she asked him. "It's so noisy here."

"Sure, but wouldn't you like to dance first?"

"I'm not sure I know how to dance to this kind of music."

"I'll show you. It's easy." He popped the rest of the chips in his mouth and left his bottle on the table. Then he reached for Belinda's hand and guided her over to a vacant spot in a dark corner. She really wished she were home where she felt totally safe. This looked like it could be tempting. Her mind said one thing, but her body spoke differently. She felt his arm go around her waist as he reached for her right hand. "Just follow me," he added as he glided across the carpet. Somehow she was able to manage without making an utter fool of herself. She felt awkward and childish trying so hard to follow. Carrie smiled over at her once and she attempted to look relaxed—one of the crowd.

Dan's warm breath reached her neck and she felt a thrill pass over her. Oh my. Next he moved her closer to him and she was nearly pressed against his body. This was really going too far. Just when she prepared to break off the dancing entirely, Carrie's brother, Jeff, tapped Dan on the shoulder. "Think it's my turn, buddy," he said with a forced smile.

Dan stepped back, his mouth turned down and his brows creased. Belinda saw this opportunity to move away from the amorous young man and she reached for Jeff's extended hand. Dan looked over at her, shrugged, and moved over to another fair damsel, who was helping herself to a veggie dip.

"He looked a bit too involved," Jeff said softly into her ear. "I came to save you."

Belinda moved back slightly and smiled up at him. "I probably could have handled him, but dank…thanks, anyway."

"You're a pretty good dancer, considering…"

"Considering? That I've been sheltered?"

"Yeah. Something like that. Are you having fun?"

"I think so."

Jeff let out a laugh. "Think? You don't know?"

"It's so, so different from anything I've ever been to, it's just a little scary, to tell you the truth."

The music stopped and they stood for a moment while one of the girls changed the CD to softer, slower music. Jeff took up his position again and this time Belinda fell right into step with him. She noted Dan was now dancing in the next room with a girl she'd never met before. They were practically kissing and she breathed a sigh of relief that Jeff had arrived when he did. She definitely felt safer with him.

"Do you think you'll leave the Amish?"

"Nee. I mean, 'no' not really. It means giving up too much. Like your whole family, you know. I love them too much to walk away."

"But how can you go back to no cars or electricity and everything else that entails after tasting this life?"

Belinda wondered herself how she would be able to, but she didn't want to seem too indecisive. "I guess I'll have to wait and find out."

"How long do you have to make up your mind?"

"There's no set time frame, but once I'm baptized, I can't go back to doing stuff like this."

"I see. So then it's a permanent decision."

"Pretty much. If you do leave after you're baptized, you can be shunned."

"Oh, yeah, I heard about that. I actually know someone who was shunned. I didn't know her personally, but I heard through a friend. It was tough on the girl."

"Hey, everyone," Carrie yelled out. "I just got a call from my mother and they're coming back tonight!"

"Oh, great!" "Yipes! Wait till they see this place." "That stinks!'

"So, please, everyone stop and help me clean up or I'll be in big trouble!"

Her friends went into work mode and the vacuum buzzed away while trash was removed and stuck in the back of someone's truck to be disposed of off-site. Belinda hand-washed the glasses while Ginny dried and put away. Within the hour, the place was spotless. As Dan left, he stopped to give Belinda his phone number, which meant nothing to her since she didn't have access to a phone unless she was at Carrie's place. Not to be rude, she took the card anyway. "I'll see you next time I'm home, unless I see you sooner. I might drop by before I go back to school."

"Yeah, okay," she answered, not ever expecting to see him again.

Jeff was winding the wire of the vacuum around the plastic holders on the side, and was within earshot. After everyone else left, he asked if she still wanted to stay overnight or would prefer to go home. Carrie made the decision for her, insisting she stay. Since her parents weren't expecting her back until morning, Belinda relented and Ginny remained behind also. The four of them watched a movie. When her parents arrived an hour later, there wasn't a word said about the previous disaster. They finished the movie and then Jeff winked over when he made his way to bed around midnight.

The three girls chatted until three in the morning and then slept on the floor of Carrie's room on sleeping bags, leaving the luxurious bed to Carrie's dog, Whitie, a Pomeranian with a face sweet enough to kiss. His stiff hair amused Belinda when she petted him and he actually smelled fresh like Ivory Snow. A far cry from the animals on her farm.

Chapter Eight
Lancaster County, Pennsylvania

The funeral drew more than three hundred Amish, some coming a distance with the use of paid drivers. Most however, were neighbors and family. It was a solemn event and the Bishop spoke softly, reading from the Old Testament. There was no eulogy. There never was for the Amish. Humility required a simple service. The day was kind with blue skies and warmer temperatures and the family made note to thank God for his grace in providing them with some relief from the frigid temperatures and winter storms.

Family and close friends returned to the house for a simple luncheon served by women close to Mary and Leroy.

Mark stood off to the side, holding a paper plate with small amounts of salads and two beet-soaked hard-boiled eggs; he remained unmoving. His stoic gaze did not go unnoticed by Ruth, who made her way over to her brother's side. "You're not hungry?"

"Nee."

"Mark, what is it? Are you worried about Oma?"

"I was selected by the family to view the opened casket. It was my decision to allow others to view it or not. As you know, I decided it would not be wise."

"I see. There was too much injury?"

Mark set his plate aside and wrapped his arms around his midsection. He nodded.

"Then you made the right decision."

"I'll never forget the sight of him. It's so difficult to forgive the driver after seeing my dawdi so injured."

"It was an accident. The driver was upset, from what I learned. It wasn't intentional."

"Jah, but the speed. The marks on the road…"

"Still, it was a terrible accident. We can't hold hate."

"I don't hate. I'm just unable to forgive right now. I just keep hoping Oma makes it. Mamm will be devastated if…"

"I know. I'll pray for you to be able to forget what you saw and to be able to forgive."

"Danki. I'm going to leave soon. I need to tend to the animals."

Ruth nodded. "It will be easier after more time passes."

Jeremiah looked over from his place at the door where he greeted their visitors. When he saw his brother-in-law and his own dear wife looking so distraught he joined them and Mark shared his feelings.

"Jah, it would be hard. So hard. At least he died immediately and never suffered, Mark. We must be grateful for that, anyway."

"You're right. I will keep that in my mind while I think it all through. So I guess you two miss your little one."

Ruth smiled weakly. "Jah, and I'm sure my sister-in-law is ready for our return by now. Nathanael can be demanding. Just like his father," she said taking her husband's hand. "We should go. The crowd is thinning out now. Mamm is going back to the hospital with Ernie in a few minutes."

"She's exhausted," Mark said. "Look at her. This has been so difficult for her. Oma just has to make it."

"Whatever the Lord's will, will be done," Ruth said, lowering her eyes."

While the family attended the service, Esther presided by the bedside of her mother. She had been moved from intensive care into a regular unit since there was little left to be done. If she was to progress, it would be through her own battle. The doctors seemed more encouraged and there was discussion about placing her in a nursing and rehabilitation center. Mary insisted she could handle her mother at home, but the staff was skeptical. Esther was impressed that Katie stood by her mother's choice, even though she would need to give up teaching in order to aid with the nursing care. Family came first. It always did.

Esther sat beside her mother and read an old *Good Housekeeping* magazine, glancing over frequently to look for any change. When her mother began to stir, she set the magazine aside and pulled her chair closer. The woman in the next bed had a steady stream of visitors, some rather noisy, but her mother seemed unaware of her surroundings. Esther took her mother's hand and leaned over speaking to her in the Pennsylvania *deitsch* of her childhood. Her mother's eyes opened slowly and she looked up at her daughter and smiled.

"Essie, you came." The words were faint and Esther bent forward to hear.

"Of course, Mamm. Where else would I be with you here in the hospital?"

"I'm glad you're here. I miss you." Then she closed her eyes and seemed to be asleep.

Esther let out a long breath. "I miss you, too, Mamm. So much," she said softly. "Please don't leave me."

Esther wiped her eyes on a tissue and felt a hand on her shoulder. Martin had returned from the gift shop. He squeezed her slightly. "Is she any better?" he whispered.

"She spoke to me. She knew it was me."

"That's wonderful, Esther. Things are looking up."

She looked at her husband and smiled. "Yes, I believe they are. For the first time I have real hope." He nodded.

They heard footsteps and Mary appeared at the door. She looked at Esther and Martin and attempted a smile. "There you are. I had trouble finding her new room." She nodded as she walked past the roommate and went over to her mother's bed, which was near a large picture window.

"Mamm called me 'Essie,' Mary. You know how long it's been since I've heard that name from her lips?"

"Oh, my. Years, I'm sure. I'd even forgotten your nickname."

"Yes, years. She knew I was here."

"Then she's ready to come home with me. It's just a matter of time before she'll be just fine again." Mary stroked her mother's hair away from her face. "Mamm, it's me—Mary."

Again her mother searched the face with the voice directed at her and smiled. "Mary."

"Mamm, we're going to try to take you home in a day or so. Would you like that?"

She didn't seem to hear, so Mary repeated the question, again receiving no reply.

"She'll be happier at home. I know she'll get better faster with her family around her." Her prediction sounded hollow.

"Mary, she's a long way from being able to be in your home. Besides, can you manage by yourself? I mean, your back has never been strong and from the polio…"

"I'll be fine. Katie will be there to help."

"Katie plans to be married in less than a year."

"Well, maybe they can live with us for a while if Mamm isn't all better by then."

"We could provide monetary assistance to help with her care. Maybe you could get someone to come in and—"

"Esther, no offense, but we don't need your money."

"You know I can't very well give up my teaching and move back to—"

"Mercy, I wouldn't expect you to. Besides, you're married now. Nee, I just mean money isn't an issue." Mary's lips turned down.

"Maybe not, but your health is."

"Esther, I'm stronger than I look. I think Mamm will be on her own in a few weeks anyway. She's making remarkable progress, don't you agree? I mean it wasn't that long ago we didn't even think she'd make it. Now look at her."

Esther looked over at her mother and aside from saying a few words and being out of the coma, it didn't look like much progress had been made. "Well it's got to be your decision. I'm afraid I gave up any say a long time ago—when I left."

"Don't. I wasn't trying to make you feel bad. Honestly. Everyone has to make his own way in life. I chose to remain. You didn't. It's a simple fact. I want you to be part of the decision, but it's my responsibility to take care of her and money isn't a factor."

Esther nodded and turned toward Martin, who had stood back. His eyes were tender while he waited for Esther. She met his eyes. "We'll go back to the house now, Martin. I'm exhausted."

"I know all about that," Mary remarked with a decided edge to her tone.

Esther's brows drew together. "Of course. That was thoughtless of me."

"Sorry. I didn't mean it the way it sounded. We're all worn out. Even the kinner are out of sorts."

"I can come back later this evening, Mary. That way maybe you can get a good night's sleep for once."

"We'll see. I still have this phone. Your number's in there, right?"

"Yes. Anytime you want me to take over for you, just call."

"See? It will be easier on everyone when she's at home with me. We won't have to run back and forth."

"Maybe." The sisters hugged, more automatically than with real emotion, and Martin leaned over and kissed Mary's cheek after Esther left the room. "Leroy wants to come back tonight with Wayne. I'll drive them over when they're ready."

"Danki, Martin. You're very kind. I'm glad my sister has you in her life."

Martin gave a slight smile. "That makes two of us. She's a wonderful woman and loves you all very much. Please understand this has been difficult for her too."

Mary nodded. "I know. I'm sorry I've been on edge."

"Understandably. We'll be visiting frequently while your mother is in this condition. We don't have to stay with you—"

"Don't be silly. I want you to stay with us. I love my sister, Martin. I admit to feelings of anger in the past, but I'd like to have a better relationship with her. Maybe this will come about now. Strange how even through bad times, gut things can happen."

He nodded and went out to join his wife. Esther had her head in her hands and he could see her tears. He held her closely for several minutes and then they headed back to the home where the parlor lay empty. Their father was at rest and hopefully, the family could move on again.

Chapter Nine
Holmes County, Ohio

Belinda wrapped herself up in her shawl and headed out to the barn to find her sister. Nellie spent too much time playing with the cats and there was baking to be done. She found her sitting on the cold barn floor with three young kittens in her lap. "Nellie, Mamm's upset with you. You're supposed to help me with the baking."

"I was gonna come in now anyway." She kissed the pure black kitten on his forehead and laid all three on an old blanket her mother had given her. "I'm keeping the black one in the house if daed will let me."

"He's cute, but he probably has fleas by now."

"I can comb them out."

"Where's Daed?"

"He went to the auction up the road. There's farm equipment for sale."

As they headed back to the house, a car drew up to the front drive and slowly came around the circle toward the back.

"I wonder who's driving that cool-looking car?" Nellie asked.

Belinda shrugged as they walked closer. A young man got out of the car and Belinda was shocked to see it was Dan from the night before. He looked even better with his suede jacket and well-fitting jeans. His head was bare and his hair shone in the bright sunlight. He removed his sunglasses and extended his hand when the girls approached. Belinda shook it lightly and introduced her sister.

"She's a beauty just like her older sister," he said with a crooked smile.

Nellie let out a giggle and pulled her shawl closer. Belinda noted a flush on her cheeks.

"So what brings you here?" Belinda asked as the three walked toward the kitchen entryway.

"To see you, of course. I told you last night I'd try to stop by, remember?"

Nellie looked over at her sister with brows narrowed. Belinda ignored her and smiled at Dan. "I didn't think you really would."

"Well, I need to go start the rolls for tonight. I'll tell Mamm you have company."

"I'll tell her myself. It's too cold to stay outside. Come in and I'll make tea or coffee or something, Dan."

When they got inside, Grace and Gideon looked up from a history book they were reading together. Belinda introduced her new friend to the surprised family members. She was secretly relieved her father was not home. He would not be happy to see an Englisher paying her a visit. Especially a male Dan's age.

"Here, take a seat, Dan," Grace said, a smile working its way slowly across her face. After all, she had been taught good manners at home. A visitor in your house was treated with respect.

"Thanks, Mrs. Glick. I can't stay long, but I just wanted to say good-bye to Belinda before I head back to school."

"Oh, you're a college boy?"

"Yep. Pre-med."

"Which do you prefer, Dan," Belinda asked, heading toward the stove. "Tea? Coffee?"

"Whatever you have is fine."

Grace took her coffee mug, which was half-filled and sat across from her visitor. "Have you known my daughter long?"

Belinda took a mug off a shelf above the counter and filled it with the hot brew from the stove. She felt her heart palpitate rapidly. Why the third degree?

"Just met her last night. She sure had me fooled about being Amish. Wow! She could have passed for a movie star!" He grinned over at Belinda, whose heart just dropped to her black shoes.

"Well now, that's very interesting," her mother said, scowling into her mug. She took a sip and peered over the edge at Belinda, whose face was now the color of fresh-squeezed tomato juice.

"I didn't know you Amish could dance so well," he started, but after checking Belinda's expression, he added, "I mean some of you, I've heard…you know, can dance."

Belinda shook her head and poured cream into a small pitcher. She set it next to Dan with a thud. It wasn't lost on him. "So, you have a nice farm here," he remarked, changing the subject.

"Danki." Grace's stare went beyond her guest and landed on a plain white wall. Belinda sat next to him while Nellie began the process of starting the dough for rolls. Yeast permeated the cozy kitchen, but Belinda's heart felt anything but cozy. She hoped he'd drink his coffee quickly and exit, before anymore came out of his mouth.

"Yeah." Dan looked around the room, his eyes resting on the coal stove. "Nice stove."

"Mmm." Belinda's mother remained indifferent.

"So," he tried again. "Do you folks like horses a lot?"

Nellie giggled and shot a glance at her sister, who rolled her eyes toward the ceiling.

"Jah. We like them," Belinda finally said. "They work real gut. Mules, too."

"Oh, yeah, I guess so." He gulped down the rest of his coffee and stood up. "Guess I'd better leave. I have to pack yet."

Belinda stood up and reached for her shawl. "I'll walk you to the car."

Her mother scowled, but then forced a straight face and nodded. "*Machs gut.*"

"Uh, same to you," he muttered as he grabbed his jacket from the back of the chair and headed out. Once they reached the car, he let out a long breath. "What did she say?"

"Just good bye," she said with a grin.

"Whew. Sorry if I said too much."

"Too late now. What were you thinking?"

"I thought they knew what went on when you're at your friend's."

"But the part about the movie star—"

Dan laughed out loud. "But you did look like one."

"And today? Do I still look like one?"

"Well, not quite, I guess. You're still pretty, but the thing on your head hides your beautiful hair. Why on earth do you dress like that?" He pointed to her plain gray frock.

"All Amish dress this way. Don't you know anything about us? Goodness, you live in Pennsylvania. Even in our county!"

"I never paid any attention—"

"Well, why start now?"

"Look, Belinda, I really liked you last night. I just wanted to get to know you better. Is there anything wrong with that?"

Belinda's heart softened. Goodness, he was a handsome sort. And his eyes! "Well I guess there's nothing wrong with being friends." She extended her hand. He reached over to shake it, but then held on and covered her hand with his other one. "So I can see you again?"

"I guess, but only at Carrie's, okay?"

"If that's the way you want it, sure."

"It's the way it has to be."

After he took off, Belinda headed back toward the house. Nellie's head popped away from the front room window, but not before Belinda spotted her. My goodness, now she had spies. What next?

Grace looked up from meat she was cutting for stew when Belinda came through the kitchen door. She was not happy. "So, miss, what do you have to say for yourself?"

"I don't know what you mean," Belinda answered, vying for time.

"You know very well what I'm asking. Movie star? Dancing?"

"Mamm, it's my free time!"

"Jah? But free to do what? Turn into a fancy girl, doing things you shouldn't? I don't mind you seeing some English girls your age, but a college boy?"

"It's not serious in any way. Good grief, we hardly know each other."

"Then why did he come by?"

Nellie had stopped working on the dough and stood watching the exchange. She blinked her eyes several times to prevent tears from flowing. Belinda looked over at her sister and felt a stab of guilt. Nellie was worried, too. Maybe she should stop playing with fire and stay home like other obedient Amish girls. She should make herself like quilting and sewing and weeding in the summer. Absolutely. Her heart spoke otherwise.

"I guess he just wanted to say good-by before going back to school. He's going to be a doctor."

"Oh, my. So now that's important. My daughter wants to date a doctor. What next? Wedding bells? Or maybe you can just live together like the English do. Who knows? Maybe you can bear his child?"

"*Mamm*! How can you talk like that? Don't you trust me at all?"

"I did. Until this morning. You knew we wouldn't approve of that behavior. I think we've been too lenient with you. I'm going to speak to your father the minute he gets home." Grace turned back to her chore and took her meat cleaver and chopped off a large hunk of meat, causing the sound to reverberate off her wooden cutting board and nearly deafen her daughters. Her mouth was a grim line and her furrowed brows concerned Belinda, who had never seen her mother this angry.

"I wish you wouldn't talk to Daed," she said, her voice cracking. "Why upset him? I'm not going to date guys. I just have fun at their parties. But, if you don't want me to attend, I won't. I just don't want to give up my friendship with Carrie. I really like her and she's a gut person. She really is. You even like her *mudder*. You told me yourself. I know they go to church and—"

"Belinda! How can I trust you now? I can't avoid speaking to your father. He has every right to know what his daughter is up to."

Belinda's anger seemed to come from deep within. "Go ahead then! Tell him everything! Maybe I will go to Hollywood! You should see how pretty I looked! And maybe I will marry an English man—a really smart one who's rich too! That would serve everyone right! No one believes me—I didn't do anything wrong! But since no one trusts me, maybe I'll do what you think I'm doing! Yah, that's exactly what I *will* do!"

She stamped up the stairs to her room before her mother had a chance to respond. After slamming the door, she fell across her bed and cried tears of bitterness and frustration. She reached up and pulled off her kapp, grabbed the few hairpins holding the mass together and tossed them on the floor, allowing her long tresses to release themselves across her damp pillow case. She'd run away. That's what. They'd be sorry they treated her like a... like a tramp, for heaven's sake. All she did was dance a little and try to look normal! What was so wrong with that!

Downstairs, her mother slumped onto a kitchen chair and put her head in her hands, weeping as she did so. Nellie went over and sat beside her mother and patted her on the arm. "She doesn't mean all that Mamm."

"Oh, Nellie, I'm so afraid she'll leave us. I couldn't bear that. What can we do?"

"I don't think she's really doing anything bad."

"I bet she drinks." Grace raised her head long enough to blow her nose on several tissues from a box Nellie set beside her.

"Only one time, I think," Nellie said, hesitantly.

"See? I knew it! She even confessed that to you. Goodness, will you be next?"

"Mamm, you know that won't happen. I love being Amish. I don't even want to run around when I'm older. Don't worry about me."

"Honey, give me a hug. My heart is breaking." Nellie leaned over and she and her mother embraced and shared a good cry. When they slowed down, Grace looked up to see her husband, Jed, staring at the two of them.

"Mercy me. What has happened? Who died?"

"Oh, Jed, no one died. It's Belinda."

"Now, now. What about my dochder, Belinda?" He pulled a third chair over and placed his hands on their arms. "Take your time, Grace. Start from the beginning."

As she proceeded to inform him of their day and their final conversation, he nodded and refrained from interrupting her discourse. When she finally got to the end, she sat back and blew her nose again. Her eyes were puffed and red.

"So now you want to know what to do." He sat back and tugged at his beard. "King Solomon should be here."

"I think we just keep her home. The English have a name for it. Grounded, I think," Grace stated. Nellie nodded.

"Keep her locked up? A prisoner? Force her to stay Amish? Is that even something possible?" His brows rose.

"I don't know. Maybe not, but do you want to lose a dochder?"

"Now what a thing to say. Nee, but I can't force her and neither can you. That's why we allow Rumspringa in the first place, Grace. You know that. No one should be forced to remain in our community against their will. It would never work out. I trust Belinda will see the light, given time."

"We may not have time. I think she's smitten with this young college student. She seemed so impressed with him plannin' to be a doctor."

"Well, maybe she is, but that doesn't mean the young man is going to ask for her hand in marriage."

"That's what I'm afraid of." Grace looked over at Nellie and then suggested she go check for eggs in the chicken house.

"I did already this morning, Mamm, remember?"

"Go again."

Nellie's mouth dropped open as she reached for her shawl and headed out the door. When it closed behind her, Grace continued the conversation with her husband.

"You know how the English do things, Jed. They don't worry about marrying a girl. That young man would turn any young woman's head. I don't know if Belinda could resist him if he tried something."

"Oh, mercy, Grace. Certainly she wouldn't forget everything we've ever taught her about being a pure Amish woman just because some nice-looking boy shows her attention."

"You weren't here to see how she acted. She sure and certain looked fancy in her actions today!"

"Let me think about all this before I confront her. I can't allow her to talk to you the way she did, though. There have to be consequences. We can insist she stay home at least for the next few weeks. We have the right to do that. Maybe it will be punishment enough for our wayward dochder."

"I hope so, Jed. I sure do hope so."

Chapter Ten
Lancaster County, Pennsylvania

Two weeks later, Esther sat and listened while Mary tried to convince the medical team treating their mother that she could take care of Oma's needs. Up until now, the doctor had refused to even consider their request. The physician in charge tented his hands on his desk and leaned toward Mary as she spoke.

"Would you have help?" he asked.

"Oh, jah. We're Amish you know."

He smiled and nodded. "Yes, I'm aware of that, but your mother requires a great deal of care. She can do very little for herself. Do you have someone who could take over at night so you could get some rest?"

"I'm sure. Jah, my daughter will stay home to help."

"I see. And you're available as well?" he said looking over at Esther.

"I'm afraid not. I live in Philadelphia with my husband and teach at the university. I'm under contract and—"

"My sister will come help out on week-ends sometimes, that's for sure and for certain."

"Yes, I will, of course," Esther said, looking down at her hands.

"Have you ever nursed someone in this condition before?" one of the therapists asked.

"Nee, but I've helped care for a lot of sick people and even delivered a couple boppli."

The therapist smiled and wrote notes on her file.

"We would want to send a visiting nurse out to check on things and help if needed," the physician said while he stretched back in his chair. "You wouldn't object to that, would you?"

"Nee. That's fine. She'd be welcome anytime. Maybe not in the middle of the night, but—"

"You needn't fear that," he said with a smile. "We need our sleep also. I'll talk with one of the administrators this afternoon and call you—"

"I gave my phone back," Mary said, her mouth drawn.

"It's all right, Mary. I'll give them my number." Esther took out her professional card and handed it over to the doctor.

After a few papers were signed and lists of instructions given, Mary and Esther went down to the lunch room to purchase sandwiches before heading back to their mother's room. Esther carried their tray and walked ahead to the cashier to pay for the food. Mary opened her mouth to object, but then changed her mind.

They headed for a corner table and sat across from each other.

"I think it will work out, don't you?" Mary asked while she reached for a potato chip on her paper plate.

"It looks like they're willing to release her to you, yes. But if it becomes too difficult for you to manage, remember what I said. We have enough money saved to find a private nursing facility with a good reputation and—"

"Esther, I know all that and I appreciate your offer, but that's not going to happen. Not as long as I have breath in my body."

"I'm concerned about Katie, Mary. She'll have to give up her teaching job and then when it's time to marry, she'll want her own place."

"Katie and I have discussed it and she's fine with it."

"How about Josiah? Has he been informed of your plans?"

"I don't know about that. Katie hasn't mentioned Josiah." She took a small bite of her sandwich and looked down at her plate.

"Well it's important to talk to him about your plans."

"I trust he'd be fine with it. He's a gut man."

"Even good men sometimes expect to have their own place. You said he's been busy fixing up their future home."

"It shouldn't be forever. I really do think Mamm will be independent soon."

Esther reached across the table and placed her hand over her sister's. "Mary, be realistic. She can barely move. We haven't told her the truth about Dad yet, either."

"She hasn't asked. She talks about him, but she's never asked why he doesn't visit."

"That's because she's still confused. I'm not even sure she knows where she is." Esther let out a long breath and removed her hand. She attempted to eat more sandwich, though her appetite had decreased.

"I know. I know. But she will be clearer headed soon."

"God only knows how she will react to the news about Daed. It may even push her back into her coma." Esther leaned back in her chair and wrapped her arms around herself. Her brows furrowed.

"That's ridiculous!" Mary scowled at her sister.

"Is it? You know how close they were. Maybe her will to live will be gone."

Mary's scowl turned to sorrow. "Oh, Esther. I never thought of that. But she has her family—all of us. Surely, that would be enough."

Esther shook her head. "We'll have to wait and see. You should be preparing your response. I'm surprised she hasn't asked one of us yet about him."

"I don't think she remembers anything. While you were in the lady's room earlier she asked me again where she was and then asked why. After I told her she just closed her eyes and went back to sleep. That's about the tenth time we've been through this. It's frustrating. Sometimes I'm afraid it's more than sleep."

"The nurses don't always seem to know either. We'll just have to take it a day at a time." Esther ate only about half of her portion and set her plate aside. "Let's finish up and get back on the floor. If she goes home in the next day or so, we'll still be here to help, but Martin has to get back to work and I'm expected to teach Monday."

"It's okay, Esther. I hadn't figured on your staying anyway. I appreciate you coming here again, I really do, but I know your real life is back in Philadelphia."

"We will continue to come frequently. You know that."

"I do and I understand it can't be every week-end." Mary stood and collected their paper products and threw them in the trash. They walked together to the elevator. When they reached the floor, Esther braced herself again for the smells and sights.

Hospitals were not something she enjoyed visiting, but no one did really. She said a brief prayer when they entered her mother's room.

Standing by the bedside was the Bishop and one of the preachers. They nodded at the women as they came over to the bed. Esther shook his hand and explained who she was.

"Oh, jah, I remember you. So your mudder is going to make it, I understand. She seemed to recall who I was just now."

Esther and Mary looked over at their mother as she lifted her lids. She stared at the bishop and he nodded. "So, it was too bad you couldn't attend the funeral. So many came by to pay their respects. Your husband was indeed well-loved."

No one moved. A hush fell across the room. Only the sound of the machines continued to be heard. Esther reached for Mary's hand and they gripped each other for support. This was not in the plans. Not this. *Not done like this, Lord.*

Holmes County, Ohio

Belinda could hear her parents discussing something downstairs. It had to be about her and her 'wayward' behavior. Goodness, they should see what other kids do, if they think she's so awful. She even knew of an Amish girl from another district who had a boppli born out of wedlock. Nothing could be worse than that. Why couldn't they just let her have her fun and be done with it?

Belinda rolled over onto her back and stared at the ceiling. Then she turned her head to the side and observed her room and its plainness. It was boring just like her life. White walls. No pictures. Straight back chair. Barely any books, and definitely no television, music, or pretty lacy stuff. She contrasted her room with Carrie's. Maybe her's was a bit overdone, but it was so colorful and fun to be in. Her night spent with Carrie and her friend was so much fun and they didn't do anything so horrible. Mainly, they talked about guys in a general way. Nothing about sex. At least not detailed stuff.

And Dan. He was pretty cute. She had noticed the other girls seemed jealous when he paid so much attention to her. He smelled good too. Like a musky smell. Even his fingernails were clean—

not like so many of the Amish guys who had their hands in dirt all the time. So intelligent, too, to be going to medical school someday. Somehow the thought of living in a fancy home, wearing provocative clothing and paying bills over the Internet seemed rather ridiculous. She never wanted to really live that lifestyle. It was just sort of fun to pretend for a while. At least to consider that she had a choice. Her mother had been discussing her baptism as if it was going to happen real soon. No way. She knew this much. As long as she felt so enamored of living a different life, even if it was temporary, she couldn't very well take her kneeling vows. That was too permanent a decision. Once that happened, you were stuck in the Amish way of life—forever. Too final. Nee, she'd have to think it through and be very, very sure of her decision.

Her stomach rumbled and she realized she hadn't eaten since breakfast. The smell of beef and onions simmering on the stove made her mouth water. Somehow she'd have to make it down those stairs and face her father. She'd never been afraid of him in the past. She wasn't about to start now. In fact, she figured she knew how to 'smooth-talk' as Carrie called it and make him see things her way.

She stood and peered in the mirror. Her hair trailed down her back. Her swollen eyes looked back at her and she tried to smile and regain her self-confidence of the night before, but it didn't happen. She was scared. Not of her father, but of her own thoughts and feelings. Not only Dan's face came to mind, but Carrie's brother as well. Even Rebecca's brother. My goodness! Maybe she was a bit boy crazy. Merciful day. *Lord, protect me—from my own thoughts,* she murmured to herself while she twisted her hair into a tight bun and secured it under her kapp. Hunger won out. She made her way downstairs to her waiting parents.

Chapter Eleven
Lancaster County, Pennsylvania

Esther and Mary watched their mother while she struggled to comprehend the words of the bishop. Esther could almost see her thoughts forming, trying to get a grip on reality. Mary went over and took one of her mother's hands. Esther made her way around to the other side and laid her hand upon her mother's shoulder. The bishop looked from one to the other, his mouth dropped open, his eyes darted back and forth. "She didn't know?" he asked, nearly whispering the words.

Esther shook her head and returned her attention to her mother, who stared at her with questioning eyes. Then she spoke haltingly, one word at a time. "Is...it...true?"

Esther nodded, her eyes filling. "I'm so sorry, Mamm. He died in the accident, but he never felt a thing. It all happened so fast."

Her mother turned slightly to her other daughter. The neck brace prevented much movement, but her eyes took hold of Mary's. "You say so, too, Mary?"

Mary spoke through her tears. "Jah, it is so. It was a terrible night. The roads were slick. The driver, he...he didn't see the buggy at all."

"I see." She closed her eyes, but a flood of tears made their way down her cheeks onto the pillow and her loose white hair. Only her tears gave away her sorrow. She didn't call out or wail. She merely suffered her terrible loss in her heart. Her dear husband, her best friend, the father of her children, was gone. He would not return, but she knew where he was and she would one day be with him again. That much she knew and it was that knowledge that kept her from going mad. How could she go on without the love of her life? How could she put in twenty-four hours a day, day after day, year after year, without the sound of his voice or the gentle laugh when he re-told his stories for the umpteenth time, or held her in his arms to speak of his love in their special love language?

Could God do all that? Make her live on without her sweet husband? Could He take over and show her His love for her—somehow? Would He be her comforter and fulfill His promise of being ever present—never forsaking his children? She would think of this later. Right now she wanted to escape her thoughts—the truth. Even for a time. She slipped back into a light coma. It might be her saving grace.

Josiah stopped working on the house around four in the afternoon. It was getting too dark to work by natural light and his supply of kerosene was dipping rapidly. Besides, he needed to stop by and visit with Katie. She looked so strained ever since the day of the funeral. Her pleasant smile was only in his memories as she shared the grief with her loved ones. His sweetheart would definitely need his support during this time.

After putting his tools away in the spare room, he changed into another set of clothing he'd brought after sponge-bathing in cold water from the well.

He disliked being dirty and Katie had mentioned once that he always smelled good. He looked around at the work he had accomplished in the past week. It finally began to show. He had replaced the major beams under the first floor with the aid of his brothers. They also replaced some of the studs in the main rooms, which had been weakened by dry rot. When he purchased the small farmhouse, he couldn't see all the structural problems, which lay under the old wallboard. Fortunately, the older section, where the kitchen had been added years before, still had the original plaster walls and though they needed some work, most were substantial enough to remain. Only one section had crumbled and needed total re-doing. The living room was ready for paint now and Katie and he planned to work together once all the heavy work was done on the first floor. His brothers put in hours whenever possible, but it was difficult for them to spare much time since they had their own places and families. The kitchen was his next project, but it could wait. Katie was more important.

When Josiah pulled up to the Zook's farm, he drove around to the back where he noticed several buggies parked near the car belonging to Katie's Aunt.

Aenti Esther was a lovely woman and her humble demeanor impressed him. She seemed uneasy around the family, though, and he wondered if it was because she had left under difficult circumstances. Katie had explained she'd been upset about the community's decision to refuse the polio vaccination for the children years before. When Esther's younger sister, Mary had nearly lost her life to polio, she accused her parents of neglect. There were probably other factors, but that was all Katie had shared. There did appear to be a strain between Esther and Mary, but Katie and her two sisters, Ruthie and Emma, thought the world of their aunt.

Josiah knocked on the back door and Katie saw him through the window as she headed for the door. Her sweet smile made the trip worthwhile and when he stepped into the warm room, he was filled with love for this young woman who had accepted his proposal of marriage. He wanted so much to put his arms around her and maybe sneak a little kiss, but he held back. Her mother, as well as her aunt and sisters-in-law, were seated around the table in the kitchen while the men stood around the room behind them. Wayne was stacking fresh coal in the stove and nodded over at Josiah, who could hear children's voices coming from the front room.

After everyone greeted him, Josiah and Katie stood against a kitchen cabinet to watch the proceedings. When no one was looking he reached for Katie's hand. She looked over and smiled at him. Even in grief, she had a radiance about her that soared directly into his heart. Ah, that he would always love her this much.

"How is your mudder, Mrs. Zook?" he asked.

"She's back in a coma, Josiah, but she goes in and out of it so I'm not too worried. We were just discussing the arrangements."

"Should I leave? Is it personal?"

"Nee, as a matter of fact, you are part of this. Since you and Katie will be marrying next fall, this may concern you also." Mary cleared her throat. "So as I was saying, between Katie and me we can handle Mamm most of the time by ourselves, but if we can set up a schedule so maybe two afternoons a week, we can get time off, that would be ever so gut. We will probably have errands to run and things like that."

Everyone nodded in agreement.

Two afternoons? That's it? His Katie would be a nurse all those other hours? A woman in a coma needs constant attention. Could Katie handle all that work? Surely they didn't expect his lovely girl to put her life aside in the meantime. It could take years...

He heard Katie sigh and when he glanced over he thought he saw a tear forming. He held her hand tighter, hoping to encourage her somehow.

"We'll bring meals for you," Hannah said.

"And we can take turns with the bathing to help out," Fannie added.

Mary nodded and looked over at Leroy. "We'll have to set up her bed in the second sitting room."

"Jah. That can be done quick as can be."

"We'll help, Daed," Abram said. "We can get Oma's furniture tomorrow and set it up."

"You'll have to take out a couple chairs to make room," Mary said. "But try to leave the sofa so Katie or I will have a place to sleep."

Josiah listened intently while he pictured poor Katie's life. But what choice did his darling have? Family must stick together. Maybe her *mammi* would improve quickly, at least enough to be somewhat independent and then Katie's mudder could take over *all* the care. Or was that a fantasy on his part?

"Josiah?" Mary was looking directly at him.

"Sorry, did I miss something?"

"I just asked if you had any comments."

"Nee. I'm not even part of the family yet. Whatever you decide, I'll be just fine with it. My Katie is worth waiting for."

Mary smiled over at him. "Jah, that's for sure. After you marry, you could take a bedroom and live here till my mamm is living in the dawdi haus.

"Mamm, why couldn't we live in the dawdi haus until she's ready?" Katie asked.

"What do you think, Leroy? Would that be all right?"

Leroy shrugged. "I don't see why not. It would give them more space and it's attached so if you needed Katie in the middle of the night or something, she'd be right there."

"We have time to think this through. I know you are working hard on your own house, Josiah, so hopefully, you'd be able to move in there right away. We just need to consider every possibility." Mary had control of the conversation and it seemed to give her strength to make plans.

"We'll need supplies, Mamm," Katie said. "Like a wheelchair and all."

"Not right away, Katie," Mary said. "She hasn't been able to sit yet, being as she's in a coma so much. The nurses are going to show us how to turn her every couple hours to prevent blood clots and bed sores."

"I'll be here to help turn her, Mamm," Wayne said as he took a place against the wall.

"Oh, jah, we'll be needing you and your muscles, sohn," Mary said, smiling over at her youngest son.

"I can't help with the other stuff, though," he said, a blush rising up his neck.

"We wouldn't expect you to, dear. Nee, Katie and I can handle the rest."

Mark had been silent, but now he brought up a sore subject. "Mamm, you know they won't release her until she's able to eat on her own. She's still being fed intravenously. It may take awhile to get her to that point."

Mary looked down at her lap and pleated her apron slowly with her hands. "Jah, it may be a few days or even a week or more perhaps, but we'll need some time to get everything ready anyway."

Hannah nodded. "I can pick up the bed pads and adult diapers at the wholesale outlet. I'm going to be near there Tuesday."

"I'll bring over extra towels and cloths," Fannie said.

"That's not necessary," Mary stated. "Mamm has a lot of linens."

Esther asked what was on many of their minds. "And what about their home? You'll need help clearing it out, won't you?"

"I can't think about that now," Mary said, practically glaring at Esther, who moved back in her chair.

"I was just going to offer to help when the time came."

"I doubt we'll need your help, Esther. There are so many of us here."

"I just want to do something," she said, softly. Martin took her hand.

Leroy cleared his throat. "I'm sure we'll need you at some point, Esther. Danki for your offer."

"I'll make a list of chores and pass it around so you can put your name down," Mary continued. "We have some time yet, so think about what you're able to do. It's not going to be easy. I'm not fooling myself about that, but with all of you willing to help, it can be done."

The children's voices were gaining in volume and Hannah heard her eldest cry. "If it's okay, I'll take the children home. Mark can stay, but I need to get the little ones down."

"I think we're done," Mary said. "We can get together in a couple days and go over anything that needs discussion, if that's okay with everyone."

People nodded in agreement and several people began separate conversations.

Martin broke his silence. "I just want to mention that Esther and I will be leaving tomorrow. We both have to return to work, but we can come back next weekend to help out."

Leroy smiled over and nodded. "That would be gut."

Mary turned from her husband and looked over at Esther. "That's okay. We have it under control. We don't want to put you out."

"It wouldn't be putting me out, Mary. I want to be here to see my mother, even if you don't actually need me. Certainly you can understand that."

"You've been gone a good many years without seeing them."

"Please, don't speak like this to each other," Leroy said, stepping in.

Martin straightened his posture when he rose from the table. His mouth was drawn. "Esther loves her mother. Just because she made the decision to leave years ago, her feelings must be considered." He looked directly at Mary.

"I'm sorry. Of course they should. I don't know what got into me." Mary turned toward her sister and reached out with her arms.

"Forgive me, Esther. I hope you'll come often. Our home is always open to you."

Esther moved toward her sister and they embraced. "It's okay, Mary. I know you're under a terrible strain and the burden is always on you. Sometimes I feel such guilt."

"Nee. Please don't. You were so different from me. You always talked about going on in school and learning about the world. You would not have been happy remaining Amish. Mamm knew that. I was so young at the time that I didn't understand why you left. Actually, I was too sick to even care in the beginning. Then later, maybe I became angry you left because I saw how upset Mamm and Daed were. They wouldn't even let me talk about you. It was hard, Esther, on everyone, but in the end, I know your decision was right—for you."

Mark came over and touched Esther on the arm. "We're all glad you're back in the family, *Aenti* Esther, and we look forward to getting to know you and Martin better the more we see you. We'll always have room for you in our home, too."

"Thank you all." Esther wiped a tear with the back of her hand. "You're too kind to this wayward Amish girl." She smiled through her tears.

It took awhile to say good night since they all embraced each other. The children seemed delighted to have more family around and gave Esther and Martin huge hugs before they headed out.

After most of the people left and it was just the immediate family, Josiah and Katie sat by themselves in the sitting room that was to be turned into the hospital room. Josiah put his arm around Katie and kissed the side of her cheek.

"You're okay with all this?" she asked him.

"Why wouldn't I be?" he asked in return. "Katie girl, I'll wait as long as it takes to have you for my wife."

"Well, we can be married when we planned to, unless you think we should wait longer." Her eyes questioned his as her brows came together.

"Nee. I can't wait any longer than this winter. I'd marry you today if I could. Do you think you'll be able to take instruction for your baptism though? It sounds like you're going to be stuck here most of the time."

"Stuck? I don't like that word, Josiah. It's where I want to be. Well, sort of." Katie looked down at the floor.

"Honey, look at me." She turned her eyes toward him. "I love you with all my heart. I know this is hard on you, but I also know you have no choice. We're Amish and this is what we do. We care for each other and do what has to be done. We can stay in your bedroom when we marry or live in the dawdi haus. Whatever you want. In the meantime, I'll turn our own house into a home fit for my princess." A kiss sealed their evening and Josiah left a few minutes later.

He went to bed that night with restored hope for their future, relieved that his Katie was now able to smile again. Jah, life goes on. God is gut.

Chapter Twelve
Holmes County, Ohio

Belinda held on to the railing and walked quietly down the stairs in her stocking feet. Her mother was scooping stew into bowls from a white pottery tureen. The four of them turned their heads toward Belinda when she pulled her chair out from its place at the table next to her sister and proceeded to sit down.

"We've already blessed the food, dochder," her father remarked with a solemn face. She obediently lowered her eyes and silently said her own prayer, adding a request for God to keep her father from being too angry. She feared it was too late for a response to that request.

Grace took the ladle and removed more stew from the tureen and handed a bowl over to Belinda.

"Danki."

"Mmm. Gideon, pass the bread please." Mary said.

Silence. The only sounds came from spoons grazing the sides of their bowls and the crunch of the fresh crispy bread as people chewed. Belinda found it difficult to swallow. She kept her attention on the food before her.

"Do you plan to take pumpkins this week to market, Grace? Didn't someone request them last time?" Jed looked over at his wife as he swiped the fresh bread into the gravy left in his bowl.

"Jah. I'll take a few small ones. They take up too much space on the counter."

"Keep them behind the stand maybe." Her father motioned for the breadbasket again and removed the golden end.

"Can I go help?" Belinda asked her mother, not daring to look at her father yet.

Grace glanced over at her husband. "What do you say, Jed?"

"I say, we'll think about it."

Silence again.

71

Nellie stopped chewing and looked over at her mother. "I'll help."

"Jah, you always do, little one. Danki."

Finally, the meal was over and Belinda and Nellie rose and began to remove the dishes to take to the sink to be washed.

"Belinda," her father said, "we will go in the other room for a few minutes alone."

"Jah, Daed, but shouldn't I help Nellie first?"

"Nee. We'll talk first. Then you can help your schwester." He pushed his chair back and walked into the next room, Belinda trailing behind. She could feel perspiration forming under her arms and her heartbeat accelerate. She couldn't remember seeing her father look so stern before. Mercy, you'd think she'd committed murder!

"Sit, Belinda. We need to talk."

She obeyed and he sat across from her, placing his hands on his knees. His mouth twitched slightly when he began. "You owe your mudder an apology."

"Okay." She began to rise, but he lifted one hand and pointed toward the seat.

"We're not finished, dochder. Your mudder was very upset about the way you talked to her. She said you even shouted. Is that any way for a gut Amish girl to behave?"

Belinda shook her head and looked down at her lap. She folded her hands and held them motionless on her apron.

"She also told me about your English boyfriend."

"He's not my boyfriend. I hardly know him."

"Well, your mudder doesn't lie and she said he told her some things that did not make her happy. Like you dancing and wearing stuff on your face like the fancy people."

"It was just a little make-up, Daed. All the girls wear it."

"Not Amish girls."

"But, I'm in my Rumspringa. I can do that. You should see some of the girls when they're—"

"We're not talking about other girls, Belinda. We're talking about my dochder. Do you want a bad reputation with our young men? Do you think they'll want to marry you if you lead a wild life for even a little while?"

"I'm not wild, Daed." She felt her anger rankle and heard her own voice rising. She took two deep breaths and looked up at him, straining to show some sort of respect in her demeanor.

"You're not allowed to go back to this friend's place. We've decided you've abused our trust. We thought you just wanted to make a few English girl friends and that was all right, but now this. Dancing and even drinking. My goodness, we can't allow that."

"Believe me, I've heard a lot worse."

"That's quite enough. You may go help your schwester now. And I don't want you putting ideas in her head, so keep your thoughts to yourself. Your mudder will get her apology first, before you clean up. Understood?"

"Jah, but Daed, can't I just go see Carrie on week-ends and I won't stay overnight?"

"Nee. If you want to see your friend, she can come here to see you."

"You don't trust me!"

"You've damaged our trust. Now go talk to Mamm and then help Nellie *redd-up.*"·

Belinda felt rage, but she was still the daughter of an Amish man. She would respect him, even if it killed her. And she would apologize—but not see her friends? That she would not promise. After all, it was her right!

Grace looked up from the stove where she was wiping down spills from the dinner. A frown crossed her mouth.

"Mamm, can we talk a minute?" Belinda made a great effort to calm herself before apology time.

Jed and Gideon made their way out to the barn to check the animals. Nellie grimaced over at her sister while she scrubbed the Dutch oven soiled from their stew.

Grace pointed to the kitchen chairs and she and Belinda sat down. "Jah? And what do you have to say for yourself?" Grace leaned back and crossed her arms, maintaining her scowl.

Belinda cleared her throat and silently repeated, 'humble thyself' three times before speaking. "I'm sorry. *Sehr* sorry for talking to you so angry-like. I didn't mean to."

"You made me *schlimm*, dochder."

"I'm sorry I made you sad, Mamm. Truly I am. It's just no one understands, is all."

"We understand more than you think. I wasn't always as old as I am now, for goodness sake. I remember noticing the boys and all, but I stuck with the Amish boys. That's what you have to do. Otherwise…"

"What if I decide to leave the Amish?"

"See? That's been our greatest fear. Some can handle their time of freedom, but you, young lady, have let it get a hold of you."

"I'm not saying I'm going to leave, but I have a right to, if I want to. Everybody knows that."

"No one from my family has ever left the Amish."

"Maybe you just don't know about it. Everything is so hush-hush."

"Belinda, why do you put us through so much pain? I wish you were more like Rachel. She never even wanted to try her wings. And look how happy she is now that she's married to Reuben."

"Rachel was always different from me. She's content just working all the time and quilting with her friends."

"Is there anything wrong with that?"

"Nee, not for her and most of my friends. Mamm, I don't know why I'm so restless. I wish I could be satisfied. Really."

"Jah, but you're not. Well, you have to obey your father and me and for now you will stick close to home."

"But Carrie—even Daed said I can still see her."

"But not at her house. We talked about it."

"Can I at least go to market with you so we can still be friends?"

"Oh, jah, I guess. You wear me down, Belinda. I have white hairs from you. Gut thing you weren't twins."

Belinda grinned in spite of herself.

Grace's lips turned up. "Come give your mamm a hug and we'll try to forget all this loud talk from before."

Belinda knelt beside her mother's chair and hugged her around her waist. Oh, my, could she ever really leave her family? Her heart swelled with love.

"Now, you'd better go help Nellie before we have another Hollywood scene," Grace said, her mouth turned up now in a tender smile.

"Too late, Mamm," Nellie called out from her place at the sink. "I'm finished."

Belinda rose and reached for a dishtowel from a rack on the wall. "You didn't dry yet. I'll do it. Sorry about that," she added, as she reached for the wrought iron ladle handed down from her great-great-someone.

"Wanna play Monopoly tonight?" Nellie asked.

"If Gideon wants to."

Grace shook crumbs from a placemat into the garbage. "Oh, I forgot to tell you both. Rachel and Reuben plan to stop by this evening. He rode over earlier to tell us."

"I bet she's in a family way," Nellie said matter-of-factly.

"I wouldn't be surprised," Belinda remarked. "I know Rachel was hoping to be having a boppli by now."

"Goodness, we'd be *aenties,*" Nellie proclaimed with a look of approval.

"And I'd be a *grossmammi,*" Grace said with a grin.

"Now don't make plans yet," Belinda reminded them. "Could be they just want to visit."

No sooner had she spoken, than they heard a buggy coming down the drive. Nellie ran to the window. "Speaking of the devil…"

"Nellie! Don't ever say that! That's horrible!" Grace joined her at the window and watched her eldest daughter and her husband tie the reins to the hitching post. "I guess they don't plan to stay long since they're leaving the buggy in the front."

Nellie opened the front door and greeted her sister and brother-in-law. The look on their faces did not speak of happy news. Belinda searched her sister's eyes for a clue, but realized she would have to wait to learn the reason for the long faces. It wasn't like Rachel, who always took the cheery side of things, to have such a frown.

Chapter Thirteen
Lancaster County, Pennsylvania

According to the nurses, it would be at least several days before Mary's mother would be allowed out of the hospital. She remained conscious continuously now, which was a great relief to the family, but she needed therapy to help her become strong enough to return home.

Each passing day, Mary tried her hardest to console her mother on the loss of her beloved husband. The tears never seemed to cease. Mary wondered how a body could hold so much extra moisture. She patted her mother's eyes frequently with tissues, swallowing her own grief to remain strong for her mother.

Mary held her mother's hand almost the entire visit, trying to soothe her with words of her father's arrival in heaven and the fact he had not suffered in the accident. Gradually her mother accepted her loss and her tears became less profuse. "You'll have to start eating, Mamm. That way I can bring you home."

"I don't care."

"Of course you do. You want to be with family who love you and will take gut care of you."

"It doesn't matter…any…more."

Mary held back tears. "Jah, it matters. We all need you, Mamm. You can't give up you know. It wouldn't be fair to us."

"You have each other."

"It's not the same. We need *you.*"

"Nee. I'm just an old woman. I'd be a burden. Better the gut Lord takes me now."

"Mamm, please." Mary's dam broke and she allowed her tears to flow. Her mother's mouth dropped open. "Honey, don't cry. Jah? Okay, I'll try to eat something later. I promise."

Katie had been sitting on the other side of the bed listening the whole time. When her Oma agreed to eat, she let out a sigh of relief. "Danki Oma. Jah, Mamm is right. We all need you. Don't forget, you have to come to my wedding."

"Oh, jah. I forgot about you becoming a bride. Nice young man, your Josiah. Hard worker your Mamm tells me."

"And don't forget Emma's going to have a boppli."

"Goodness, I forgot that too. My, my. There is a lot going on in this family. I guess I should hang around a little longer, jah?" The hint of a smile appeared, though her eyes were glassy from unshed tears.

Katie leaned over and kissed her. They had removed the neck brace after they took another MRI and decided she was in no further danger of damaging her upper spine. Her hair was straggly and Katie pushed it off her forehead while she adjusted her grandmother's spectacles. "We need to get you a shampoo when you come home with us."

"Dear Katie, are you going to be my nursemaid, too?"

"Jah, you bet." Katie's cheek dimpled when she grinned.

"But what about your teaching?"

"Becky's looking for someone to help out. Right now she's managing okay, but that's because six children are home ill from the flu. There's been a lot of sickness this winter. I'm glad it's nearly spring."

Mary rose from her chair and went to look out the window. "I guess our driver will be here soon, Mamm. I was hoping your supper tray would arrive so I could help feed you."

"Maybe they ain't bringing one today, since I hardly look at it. What a waste."

"I'll talk to nurse Helen about helping you. She's almost as concerned as we are."

"Tsk. All this fuss over me. It would be better if..." She turned her head and closed her eyes.

Katie choked back her own tears while she walked over to the large window and looked out at the dreary landscape. At least the snow had all melted and it was mid-March. Some of the trees were budding and she had spotted yellow crocuses by the barn that very morning.

"I hear the food cart coming with the meals. Katie, stay by the window and tell me when you see the driver. In the meantime, I'll help Oma eat something."

Katie stood watch and soon the nurse's aid brought in the trays for the two women. Oma had a new roommate who spent most of the time sleeping. Aside from loud snoring on occasion, it was a relief not to have the constant flow of traffic from her original roommate's visitors.

Mary put the head of the bed up so her mother could eat. "Oh, look at this," Mary said, lifting the cover off the plate. "A fine piece of meatloaf and carrots with mashed potatoes. Now ain't that a pretty sight?"

Her mother pushed her glasses in position. "I'm not hungry. I bet the potatoes are fake, anyway."

"But they look gut, just the same," Mary continued while she placed the paper napkin under her mother's chin. She spooned a small amount of potato into her mother's mouth.

"Just what I thought. Fake as can be. I can't eat any more, dochder."

"Mamm, I think I see our driver," Katie called over.

"Oh, shaw. Just when we were making progress."

"Now Mary, I can probably do it myself. Just cut the meat up first, honey."

Mary cut it in small pieces and then they said their good-byes and left the room. When she and Katie passed the nurses' station, she asked if someone would look in on her mother to make sure she got enough food down. A young aide nodded and smiled. "I'll try, but your mother is a stubborn lady, I'm afraid."

"Jah, you can say that again," Mary said, smiling back.

Once they arrived home, Katie made her mother go upstairs to rest while she fixed the chicken for dinner. She noticed her mother's limp seemed worse, probably from all the extra stress and work since the terrible accident. When Katie put water on the back of the stove to boil for the noodles, she heard a horse on the drive and then she saw Josiah appear at the kitchen window as he headed toward the back door. Her heart took its typical leap at the sight of her fiancé and she motioned for him to let himself in.

"Hallo, Katie," he said, placing his hat on a hook.

"There's kaffi left from before," Katie said, wiping her hands and reaching for a clean mug from the cabinet.

"I'd better not have any more. I drank a full pot this afternoon, just to stay awake. I finally decided to stop working before I had an accident. Besides, I wanted to come see you. How's your mammi today?"

"She seems a little better. I wish she didn't cry so much, though. Her heart is broken. At least she's eating a little."

He beamed and came over to her. "That's wonderful-gut to hear. How about a kiss for your husband-to-be?" His arms surrounded her and he leaned over and pressed his lips gently on hers.

"Hey you two," a voice said, coming from the next room. Wayne walked in with a huge grin.

"Wayne, why were you so quiet?"

"Was I? Gee, sorry Katie. Next time I'll play a bugle."

"You don't know how," she teased.

"So what's new, Josiah? And don't say, 'New Jersey,' 'New York,' and stuff like that."

Josiah laughed. "Nothing much. I'm working on the floors now. The wood's coming up real nice. Wait till you see, Katie. The boards are about six inches wide."

"Oh, lovely," she said when she checked under the pot lid to see if the water was boiling yet. "You'll stay for supper?"

"I guess if you have enough."

"We always have enough for guests," she said, smiling over.

"I'm gonna go change," Wayne said. "Think I can trust you two love birds to be alone for a couple minutes?"

"Don't tease so much, bruder. I heard you looked real cozy-like at the last sing with Becky," Katie remarked as she added salt to the simmering water and measured out some homemade noodles.

"Becky's a nice girl, but we're not in love."

"Maybe *you're* not…"

Wayne's neck turned scarlet. "She's not in love with me. Goodness, we don't know each other enough to be serious."

"Whatever happened to that other girl you seemed interested in?" Josiah asked while he filled a glass with water and sat at the table.

"That's been over a while now. Too bossy for me."

"Like my Katie?" Josiah asked with a wink.

"Now Josiah, you'd better watch yourself. We're not married yet. In fact, except for my family, no one even knows about us. So I could pull out anytime."

Wayne grinned. "Uh, oh. I'm leaving. Looks like a challenge," he said heading for the staircase.

Once they heard his bedroom door close, Josiah stood again and picked up where he'd left off. Katie stepped back and let out a whistle. "Josiah, we better slow down. You give me the shivers kissing like that."

He laughed and poked her under the ribs, causing her to giggle. "Just want you to remember who you belong to, is all."

"I promise not to forget."

"So when do you think you'll be able to bring your mammi home?"

"Mamm thinks in a week or so. We have everything set up here at home. They want her to have more physical therapy so she'll be easier to handle."

"Jah, and the way she's improving, maybe we'll have more time together than we figured."

"That would be ever so nice."

Mary came down, gave Josiah a hug. "You staying for supper?" she asked.

"If there's enough food," he said.

"We always have extra for friends," Mary said before she turned to ask Katie if she needed help.

"Nee. Everything is fine. Josiah, would you go tell Daed we're gonna eat in about fifteen minutes?"

"Jah, sure." After he left, they heard Wayne head down the stairs. He had a fresh shirt and clean trousers on and Katie thought he looked quite handsome—for a bruder. She set the table and then they all sat down together to eat. After the main meal, Katie spooned out some fresh tapioca pudding into small dishes for everyone.

"If you cook like this after we're married, I'll get mighty fat," Josiah said as he patted his full stomach and pulled back from the table.

"Not the way you work," she said as she reached for her father's dish and added a fresh dollop of pudding.

"My Katie knows I like tapioca better than ice cream," Leroy said elevating his spoon for his second portion.

Mary looked over at her spruced-up son. "Why are you all dressed up tonight?" she asked.

"I'm gonna head over to a friend's house when we're done here."

Leroy looked up from his dessert. "And who would that be?"

"Just a friend, Daed," he said, looking away, licking his lips.

"I bet I know who," Katie said with a lopsided grin.

"Okay. So it's Becky. We like to play Canasta."

"Jah," his father said with a smile. "You need to get all redded up to play cards."

After everything was put back in order, Katie put on her shawl and went out with Josiah as he prepared to leave.

"I'll try to stop by tomorrow, Katie. I'm going to stain the floors on the first floor though, and I may be too beat. I hope you can get over the next day or two to see how everything looks."

"Oh, I want to, Josiah. You know that. It's just been so hard..."

"I know, honey. I understand. Now give me a kiss and I'll be on my way."

She put her arms around his neck and stood on tiptoe to kiss him. He always smelled so clean, even after working all day.

When she returned to the house, her parents commented on how happy they were that she was marrying Josiah. Jah, she was a fortunate young woman to find herself loved by such a splendid Amish man.

Chapter Fourteen
Holmes County, Ohio

Belinda's older sister, Rachel, came into the sitting room with her husband and they all sat down. Nellie squeezed next to Belinda to make room for her mother.

"You look worried, dochder," Jed said before he placed his pipe between his teeth and pulled in a deep breath.

"We have to tell you something. First off, I'm in a family way."

Nellie jumped in. "I knew it! Wow! That's great."

"Well, we were happy, but…"

"But?" Grace's brows rose and her mouth formed a rigid line.

"There are complications. I've seen the midwife three times now, but she's concerned that the baby isn't growing much."

"In fact, not at all in three weeks," Reuben added, his eyes cast down.

"Oh." Grace waited a moment before asking, "What does she think is the matter?"

Rachel put her hands over her face and began to sob. Grace rose and went over to her eldest daughter and knelt beside her. "Honey, it will be okay."

"Nee. She thinks the boppli is dead. She couldn't get a heartbeat and I haven't felt any movement."

"Oh, dear God in heaven," Grace said softly, pulling back slightly. "If so, we must accept it as God's will."

"Mamm, why would he will our baby to die? Why?" The tears continued to flow.

Belinda glanced over at her brother-in-law and noticed his eyes were glassy and his mouth trembled slightly.

Jed laid his pipe aside and rested his elbows on his knees. He studied his daughter. "Rachel, we have no right to ask our maker these questions." His voice was so gentle, Belinda choked up herself.

"I know. It's just ever so painful."

"Jah, and it doesn't help to say you're young and all that," he added. "It's not time to talk about your long term future."

"Is there anything you can do?" Grace asked her daughter.

"Nee. Just wait is all."

"Wait for what?" Nellie asked, her forehead creased.

Grace looked over and placed her index finger over her puckered lips. "Hush."

Nellie looked over at Belinda who shrugged and shook her head.

"There's nothing anyone can do, I'm afraid," Reuben said finally. "We just thought you should know."

Mercy, how awful. My poor sister.

"Jah. We can pray the midwife is wrong, too, can't we?" Grace asked.

Reuben nodded. "That's what we're doing. We pray a lot and we also ask for strength to get through this. We know we're young and all and we will probably have many boppli, but it's still hard. We were so excited."

Belinda looked over at her sister. "I think if we keep praying hard enough—"

"Danki. Maybe so. There's no harm in asking," Rachel said wiping her eyes with a hanky. "So we are on our way to tell Reuben's family. We'd better go now. I'm so tired—I just want this to be over with. She placed her hand over her slight protruding abdomen and gently stroked it.

"Rachel, may I ask—how far along are you?" her mother asked.

"This is my fifth month."

"And I had no idea, though I suspected."

Rachel stood and Reuben took her by her hand and led her toward the door. "I'll let you know when…"

"Jah. Of course," Grace said as she reached for her son-in-law and held him close. "It will be okay. It will take time, but God heals our broken hearts."

"Jah, He does. We really know that, Mamm, but right now…"

"Right now, you can't see. I know. Bless you, Reuben."

Jed came over and placed his arm around his daughter. "You okay, dochder?"

"Nee, Daed. Nee."

"Oh, my child," he said enveloping his first-born in his own arms. "We lost a baby before you came into our lives. Stillborn."

Everyone looked shocked, including Grace. "Jed, I've never told anyone."

"Tonight, it should be told, Grace. Rachel and Reuben need to hear how one can get through these tragedies and come out all right."

"I guess you're right. Jah, it was a terrible time for us, but look now—we have four wonderful children."

Rachel looked from her mother back to her daed. "Danki. I think that does help to know."

After they left, the family sat down. They remained silent for several minutes, each struggling with their own personal thoughts. Then Gideon let out a loud long breath and gained everyone's attention. "I'm never getting married," he stated emphatically.

Jed smiled over at his thirteen-year-old son. "We'll see. I have a feeling one day you'll notice the girls and fall head over heels in *lieb.*"

The comment helped break the heavy aura of sadness ever so slightly. Belinda wiped her eyes and the three young ones resumed their game of Monopoly.

When she retired for the night, she got on her knees and prayed for the unborn child in her sister's womb and then prayed for strength for the whole family.

The next morning, Belinda put on her old boots before helping her father and brother load their wagon for market. Mid-March brought warmer temperatures and the only reminders of the blizzard of February were the remaining piles of gray-covered snow behind the barn where the sun rarely shined. The mud was almost more annoying than the snow had been, Belinda thought while she and her brother lifted a wooden crate of onions to her father who was standing on the wagon bed. The only reason she looked forward to Wednesday was the knowledge she'd most likely see her friend Carrie. Even though she was not allowed to visit her anymore, they could talk and just maybe she'd be able to sneak out at night again. After all, the English were different, but they weren't bad. At least *her* friends were nice. She couldn't speak for all the English—that was for sure.

"That should do it." Her father shoved the last case toward the back of the wagon and jumped down. Gideon climbed into the driver's seat and moved the wagon toward the road.

"Wait. We'll go on ahead, Gideon," his father called over. "The women can follow in the buggy. We may as well get started. Tell your mudder we're heading over." Belinda nodded and she and Nellie walked back to the house.

Grace was putting on her bonnet, but her eyes were troubled. "Maybe I should go to Rachel today instead of market."

"It might make her sadder, Mamm, to have someone else around," Belinda said. "You know how she is. She likes to be alone sometimes."

"Jah, and of course Reuben will be with her. You're right. It may be several days before anything happens. It's just hard on everyone, but especially poor Rachel."

"All we can do is pray, Mamm," Belinda said, touching her mother's arm. She nodded and they headed out to the waiting buggy.

It was only four miles on back roads, but it would be slow going even with two mules hitched up to the wagon.

Once everyone arrived, the family set up their stand moving almost automatically. It was a busy day. Customers wandered through the enclosed building, stopping occasionally to make purchases. A popcorn vender's machine pumped out fresh popcorn making Belinda's mouth water. She ate her liverwurst sandwich during a slow period and then re-arranged the bins, replacing produce where it became necessary. Her apron pockets were filled with change and folded bills. Her daed would be pleased at how much they would put away at the end of the day.

Around four, she spotted Carrie arrive with her brother, Jeff. They both waved at her. Finally, she was able to take a break. She walked over to Carrie, who joined her, and they meandered around the inside of the building until they found a vacant bench to sit on. After telling Carrie about her sister and the baby, they were silent for a few moments.

Carrie finally sighed and changed the subject. "I heard Dan stopped by your place. He seems to like you a lot, Belinda."

"He's a nice guy, but too worldly for me."

"What does that mean exactly?" Carrie asked, twisting a long strand of hair around her finger.

"You know. He doesn't really understand our ways. I'm a little afraid of him, actually."

Carrie laughed. "Rightly so, I'm afraid. I think he's tried to make out with every girl he knows. Watch out. He's quite the charmer."

"Jah, I noticed."

"So we're having a party Saturday night at Kim's house. You have to come. She lives right next door to me. Remember I pointed out her house when you were over?"

"Jah, I remember. I don't know. Maybe."

"You have to. There'll be about twenty of us. You know most of them."

"Will Dan be there?" Belinda wasn't sure why she even asked. I mean, she couldn't care less, right?

"I don't know. He shows up when he wants to. You never know with him. It's gonna start around nine. Come anytime. In fact, come early and have supper with my family first and then I'll fix your hair in a new do I found in a magazine."

"Oh, dank…thanks, but not this time." *Not any time probably.* "I'll try to get over to Kim's though, if I can."

"It's gonna be casual. You can wear your jeans. Do you want to borrow a top?"

"Nee. I have the sweater I bought, but thanks anyway."

Nellie came charging through the aisle, looking frantic as her eyes searched from side to side. When she spotted the girls, she headed right over. "Mamm needs you pronto. She got a bunch of people waiting. Hurry up. She looks mad."

"Goodness, I haven't been gone that long."

"I know, but you should stay within sight. That's what she said."

Belinda and Carrie rose and headed back, Nellie scooted ahead of them. "So hope to see you Saturday. You know my brother can take you home whenever you want," Carrie said. "I'm leaving early today. I have a ton of homework. I just wanted to tell you about the party."

"Thanks, Carrie, I'll do my best to get there."

She moved behind their table and waited on the next person in line. Her mother glared over at her once, but said nothing.

When they got home, Belinda peeled potatoes for supper while her sister washed fresh kale. Grace was upstairs taking a break and the men were in the barn preparing for their busy planting season. The ground was still too wet to work, so they spent time cleaning up their equipment in preparation.

Nellie looked over at her sister. "What do you and Carrie find so much to talk about? You're so different."

"Not really. Just because we dress different?" She cut the potatoes in sections for boiling.

"Not only that. I bet she fools around with guys and everything."

"What do you know about 'fooling around' little schwester?"

"Not much, just what I hear from my friends."

"I see. Well, don't believe everything you hear. Carrie's not serious about anyone. She just likes to dance and have fun."

"Does she smoke?"

"Nee."

"Bet she drinks, though," Nellie added, almost under her breath, while she laid the wet vegetation on a clean linen towel. "What am I supposed to do with this stuff now?" she asked pointing to the mound of kale.

"Mamm will cook it. She knows how Daed likes it."

"Jah, with lots of garlic, I bet. He likes garlic with everything."

Belinda was glad the conversation had changed. She dreaded telling her sister about Saturday night. She knew how it would upset her, but what choice did she have? She could sneak out or run away. Those were about her only options, short of staying home all the time and dying of boredom. Literally, 'dying' of boredom. Nee, she had to get out and she'd just have to trust her sister to keep quiet.

As Belinda set the table, she heard a buggy on the gravel drive and looked out to see her brother-in-law get out of the vehicle. He walked slowly over to the kitchen door and let himself in. His expression was somber and Belinda knew without asking. The news was not good.

Belinda and Nellie stood waiting for him to speak. "She lost the baby." He wiped his sleeve across his eyes and took a deep breath.

"Oh, I'm so sorry," Belinda said, as she went and wrapped her arms around him. Nellie sat on a kitchen chair and began to cry. Grace came into the room from the sitting room.

"I heard, Reuben. What a shame." Belinda moved back and her mother took him in her arms. "How's our Rachel doing?"

"Not real gut. The midwife left a while ago, but I wanted you to know. I stopped to tell my folks, but now I need to head home."

"Can I go with you, Reuben?" Belinda asked.

"Maybe I should go, too," Grace added.

"Maybe just Belinda right now," he said softly, turning to Belinda. "Rachel asked me to bring you back."

Grace nodded. "Jah, go Belinda. I'll wait till tomorrow and then spend the day with her. What about the baby?"

"I have to tell the bishop later. We'll bury the boy right away. No ceremony. Just us and the bishop. That's the way Rachel wants it."

"Then that's the way it will be," Grace said. "I'll go tell Jed and Gideon. They're in the barn." She went over and patted his arm. "Time will heal your pain, sohn. We will be praying for you both."

"It's not fair," Nellie said through her tears.

"We don't question, Nellie. It was God's will. The dear boppli is with Jesus now—in His arms, so you mustn't keep crying, honey. Come with me to the barn. Maybe that tiger cat had her kittens. She was acting funny this morning."

"It's not going to help, Mamm. I know what you're trying to do." Nellie reached for a tissue and blew her nose. "Give my schwester my love. I'll go over with Mamm tomorrow."

"I will, little one," Reuben said, patting her on her head. "I know the gut Lord will bring us kinner. It's just real painful right now, is all. Real painful."

Chapter Fifteen
Lancaster County, Pennsylvania

Katie and her mother walked down the hall to Oma's room. They entered to find her propped up on a large leather armchair having her lunch.

"Look at you!" Mary said, leaning over to kiss the top of her mother's head. "And you even have your hair tidied up."

Oma smiled and nodded as her daughter stepped back to allow Katie to greet her grandmother. "What kind of soup is that, Mammi?" Katie asked, dropping her shawl over the end of the bed.

"I think it's vegetable, but everything is cut so tiny I'm not sure what kind they put in. I've been sitting up over an hour," she added, breaking open a cellophane package containing two salt covered crackers.

"My, that's ever so gut," Mary said, grinning widely.

"Jah, and I took a couple steps."

"Really? I guess the plastic cast keeps it from getting worse." Katie glanced over at a walker folded up by the side of her grandmother's bed.

One of the aids came into the room to collect the empty trays. "Still workin' away on it? Take your time." Shanice was a pleasant black girl who took her job seriously, often helping feed the ones who couldn't feed themselves. Mary felt good knowing that when she was on duty, her mother would be well taken care of.

"So, Mamm looks pretty gut, don't you think?" Mary said to Shanice.

"Remarkable. We're very proud of her. She walked from the bed to the chair."

"Was it painful, Oma?" Katie asked.

"Well, not too bad. It feels so gut to be sitting up like a regular person."

"We're hoping to take my mother home in a couple days," Mary said as she handed her mother a dish with green jello.

"I don't want that, Mary. It looks awful."

Shanice laughed. "Can't blame you for that. If you're still hungry, I have cookies in the back."

"Nee. I have to watch my waistline," Oma said with a crooked grin.

After she left the room, Oma announced she needed to use the bedpan. "I'll buzz for someone. Maybe they'll let me walk to my own bathroom over there," she nodded toward a closed door.

"Now, Mamm, you can't do everything at once."

"Well, I want to be strong enough to go back home to my place."

Katie and her mother exchanged glances.

"Mamm, you know that's not going to happen. Maybe in time you can live in the dawdi haus attached to our home, but to—"

"We'll see. Now leave for a while and let me go potty."

They passed another aide after they stepped out into the hall. "We may as well go get a cup of kaffi. This will probably take some time," Mary said to Katie.

"I'm hungry, too. Can I get a salad?"

"Of course. You're so thin, Katie. You aren't still dieting are you?"

"Nee, but I always watch what I eat now. I feel better weighing less."

"I'm glad, dear. I'm thrilled with Oma's progress, aren't you?"

"I have to admit, I'm surprised. Goodness, it wasn't that long ago, we thought we might lose her."

"Jah. God is gut. She's ever so much more like herself. Even when she mentions Daed, it seems she's accepting her situation, though she still cries a lot."

"But she can't live by herself. I can't believe she thinks she could go back to her farmhouse. What are we going to do with it?"

"We may sell off the house with a half acre and leave the rest of the land for family. It's not that far, and we can keep the barn and all the equipment."

"Becky loves the kitchen in Mammi's farmhouse. She thinks it's sweet. She was in there with me last week when I went to get her Bible for her."

"It is nice. I think your brother is sweet on Becky, speaking of 'sweet', Mary said after they reached the cafeteria. She reached for a tray and pushed it along the rail. "Get yourself a salad, Katie. I'm going to buy a muffin. They're so big, we can split it."

Katie nodded and removed a small chef salad from the refrigerated section. They added two cups of coffee and paid the cashier. Then Mary led her daughter to a small table away from the other diners and they sat across from each other.

"I know Becky likes him. She has for a long time."

"She never let on," Mary said while she cut her blueberry muffin in half and pushed the plate between them.

"I didn't even know till recently. It would be ever so nice if they marry some day, don't you think?"

"Jah, I like Becky a lot. She's a very friendly girl."

"Healthy too. They could have a bunch of boppli for you to spoil."

Mary laughed. "And spoil them, I would. Do you think Josiah wants a large family?"

"Oh, jah. We both do. It's ever so much fun to grow up in a large family."

"I'm sorry we didn't have more children," Mary said looking down at the muffin. She broke off a small piece.

"I didn't mean to say I was unhappy in my family. I love my whole family so much, Mamm. After all, I have two sisters and three brothers. That's nothing to sneeze at."

"Katie, that's such a funny expression. Why would someone sneeze?"

Katie laughed. "I have no idea, Mamm." She bit into her half muffin. "These taste gut, but not like homemade."

"I think they put too many things in them so they never get stale."

"Probably."

"I need to talk to the head nurse today and clear things for Mamm to come home. Maybe they'll let her go tomorrow. What do you think?"

"I'd be surprised. This is really her first day out of bed. Her leg must be healing well, or they wouldn't let her walk at all." Katie took another mouthful of salad.

"The nurse told me it was a clean break and would heal well with care. It really doesn't seem to hurt her that much. She still gets headaches though."

"Did the doctor say how long they would last?"

"He didn't know. Time, I guess, is the healer." They ate in silence for several minutes and then Mary laid her napkin aside after finishing her muffin. "Well, I guess we should go back soon. Whenever you're done with your salad."

Katie took her last bite and they cleaned their tray off before heading upstairs.

When they got back to the room, they found Oma sound asleep. She had a sweet smile on her face.

"I don't want to wake her. Stay with her, Katie, and I'll go talk to the nurse about our plans."

Katie picked up a magazine she'd borrowed the day before from the waiting room and flipped through the pages. She heard someone come through the door and looked up to see Emma and Gabe walk in with a handful of daffodils. They greeted each other. When Oma opened her eyes, Emma went over and kissed her cheek.

"You look wonderful-gut, Mammi," Emma said.

"Jah and so do you. Having babies seems to agree with you," she added with a grin.

Emma smiled. "I feel real fine. We're so excited."

Oma looked over at Gabe. "You ready to start all over again?"

He nodded. "Oh, jah. I can't wait."

"The men have it easy," Oma said, clucking her tongue. "You don't even have to get up at night with the boppli."

"Jah, but we have to make sure they have shoes and clothing and food on the table."

"Mine rarely wore shoes. Just in the winter when they went out, but they sure could put the food away. Oh, jah, those were happy times." Her eyes filled and over-flowed. She reached for a tissue and covered her eyes. "My darling husband. He loved his family so. He'll never meet your boppli."

Gabe's eyes softened and he went over and patted her hand. "Someday, he will, God willing. But you have many more happy days coming. We're counting on you to spoil our little one," he added.

Her eyes brightened slightly as she wiped them with the hem of her sheet. "I intend to do just that."

Mary came in and greeted her daughter and her husband. "Gut news. We're taking Mamm home in two days. He said it was a miracle and I said. 'Oh, jah, God is in the miracle business,' and he looked real funny at me, like I was speaking *fernhoodled* English."

"He's the one confused," Oma said, nodding her head. "Sometimes doctors think they heal all by themselves."

Gabe agreed. "When it's the gut Lord who does the healing."

"Emma nodded, "but God's given them the talent to help out, we can't forget that."

"Jah, and the brains," Katie added.

"If you two are staying for awhile, we may leave early," Mary said. Our driver mentioned he had to run errands after he takes us home. I don't want to take advantage of him. He's been so reliable."

"Jah, we'll stay a while. We came over the back way in our buggy. It takes longer, but it's a pretty drive," Emma said.

"And a lot safer," Gabe added.

"We never should have been on the road that night." Oma said softly. Conversation stopped and everyone turned toward her. "My dear husband would be alive today except I wanted to visit my friend Elsa. We'd planned it for days and he didn't want to disappoint me. She was sick you know."

Mary looked over at her daughters. That was one of the unanswered questions. Everyone had wondered what on earth had taken the elderly couple out on such a treacherous night. Now they had their answer. Poor Oma. On top of the pain of losing her husband and injuring herself, she also had to contend with the guilt of being the one who suggested the ride. The Lord would have to do more than heal her fragile bones. It would take far more to mend her sorrow and guilt. And one other thing, Oma did not know her friend, Elsa, had also left this world—the same day as her husband.

Holmes County, Ohio

Reuben dropped Belinda off at his front door before taking the buggy to the back. She let herself in. All was silent. She called her sister's name, but received no answer. Then she walked quietly upstairs and knocked on Rachel's bedroom door.

"Come in," Rachel said softly.

Belinda went over to her sister. The room was darkened with drawn shades and she could barely make out the slim body of her older sister. She smoothed back the loose hair from Rachel's forehead. "I'm so sorry."

Rachel wept bitterly and reached for Belinda. The girls held each other closely and tears fell from Belinda onto her sister's hair and shoulder.

"It was a little boy. He was so tiny. I felt sick, Belinda. It was horrible and the labor took two hours. All for nothing. My darling boppli is dead."

"I know. I know." Belinda's voice broke as she felt her sister's pain in her own heart. Until Rachel's marriage, they were very close—sharing all their thoughts and feelings, but once she was married, Rachel had been pre-occupied with her life with her new husband. It had hurt Belinda, though she never spoke of it to anyone. It seemed that was about the time she became restless and discontented with her own life. Perhaps the void left by her sister's absence was one of the reasons she became so absorbed in the English way of life. Though she was heartbroken for Rachel, it felt good to be needed.

Rachel went on speaking through her sobs. "The bishop is coming soon. I held my boppli for over an hour, but he was so gray and cold. It was horrible."

"He's with Jesus now." Belinda's voice cracked.

"I know. That's what I try to tell myself."

"It's true, Rachel. Someday you'll see him again and he won't be dead. He'll be alive and in a wonderful-gut place."

"You believe that, don't you? I mean, really believe it."

"Oh, I do. Remember what the Apostle John said in Revelation 21?"

"Read it to me, Belinda. I need to hear it again. Please." She pointed over at her Bible sitting on her bedside table.

Belinda went first and raised the shades to allow the sunshine to pour in. Then she sat down on the bed and turned to the third verse. "And I heard a loud voice from the throne saying, 'Now the dwelling of God is with men, and he will live with them. They will be his people, and God himself will be with them and be their God.'" She looked over at her sister, who was riveted to each word. "Now this is the part you must hear, schwester." She lifted the Bible closer and continued. "He will wipe every tear from their eyes. There will be no more death or mourning or crying or pain, for the old order of things has passed away."

"Jah. I remember now. It's a promise."

"And God doesn't break his word."

"Danki, Belinda. I know that and I'll put those words in my mind and keep them there. My dear boppli is happy now."

"Jah." Belinda leaned over and held her sister again.

Reuben came in the room with a tray of hot tea and he'd even brought three cups and saucers from their cupboard. "How's my darling *fraa*?" he asked, attempting a smile on his weary face.

"I'll be okay, Reuben. It will take time."

"I know, Rachel. Believe me, I'm hurting, too." He placed the tray on the wide windowsill and came over to the bed. Belinda stood up to give him a chance to be near her sister and she went to pour the tea, while Reuben helped his wife to a sitting position and placed his own pillow behind her. "It's your favorite tea. Chamomile."

"Danki. What would I do without you—and my family," she added, looking over at Belinda.

"Hopefully, you'll never have to find out," Belinda said, smiling.

"Honey, the bishop will be here in a couple hours. Do you want to stay up here?"

"Nee. I'll be with you, husband. We're in this together."

"Do you want me to stay, too?" Belinda asked.

"Don't be hurt, please, but I don't think so. It's going to be difficult, but I want it to be just Reuben and me. Do you understand?"

"Of course."

They each drank some tea and remained silent for a few moments.

Reuben took advantage of Belinda staying with Rachel and excused himself to check on the animals.

"Nellie told me you've been in trouble with Mamm and Daed, Belinda. Is it true?"

"Jah, they're so strict with me. Now I can't even go see my friend Carrie. It's not fair."

"They just want to protect you. That's what parents do, you know."

"But they don't trust me anymore. They think I'm gonna do something crazy. I'm not. You know that."

"I had a friend who said the same thing, but she ended up acting just like the English."

"I remember her, but I'm not like that. I love to dance and stuff like that."

"And dress like them?"

"What's the harm? It's fun, Rachel. Didn't you ever do anything during your Rumspringa?"

"I guess I put on lipstick a couple times. Oh, and I did try on a fancy dress in a store once with my friends. I just didn't care, is all."

"I wish I was more like you, Rachel. I know Mamm and Daed did, too."

"Oh, Belinda, just watch yourself. I don't want anything to happen to my dear schwester."

Belinda took hold of her sister's hand. "I'll be careful. I promise. Is there anything I can do to help you, Rachel? Anything at all?"

"Just continue to pray for us. I know God is with us and will lead us through this valley. It's just getting through this grieving right now. I just keep picturing him…" She put her other hand over her eyes and shook her head. "I need to picture him with Jesus. That's what will get me through this."

"Jah." Tears streamed down Belinda's face and she wiped her face with her free arm. "I guess Reuben should take me home if the bishop is headed over soon."

Rachel looked over and nodded. "I hope everyone understands why we need to do this part alone."

"I'm sure they do. Everyone has to deal in their own way."

"Jah. I hear Reuben downstairs. Danki for coming, Belinda. I love you."

"I love you, too." She leaned over and kissed her sister on her damp cheek and headed downstairs. When Reuben took her home, they barely spoke. There just wasn't much to say. Platitudes were unnecessary.

The whole family was saddened by the death of Rachel and Reuben's son, but as always, they looked upon His death as the will of God and believed totally in the resurrection and the life hereafter, so they knew they would one day meet their little relative and all would be well.

Chapter Sixteen
Holmes County, Ohio

Belinda's thoughts turned to the week-end. Saturday finally arrived. Belinda pulled out the bundle with her English clothing and sniffed them. Still clean. A bit wrinkled, but that's the style anyway. The only make-up she owned was a brown pencil for her brows and a tube of bright red lipstick. She shoved them in the wad of clothing and replaced them in the closet.

The day dragged. She and Nellie made donuts for Sunday church service. She counted and they had over five dozen. It was a big job, but it helped the time pass. Then she used the carpet sweeper on the rugs downstairs and mopped around the edges. Grace seemed please with her spurt of energy and commented on all she had done.

"I'm glad to help, Mamm."

"Now that's what I wanted to hear. I appreciate it when you are like this, Belinda. Maybe in time, we can let you have a little more freedom."

"Jah? Danki," Belinda said, feeling a dread at the deception she was about to commit.

Belinda checked the sitting room clock every fifteen minutes. Would this day never end? Finally, around half past eight, her father excused himself and headed for bed. Gideon and Nellie followed a few minutes later, but her mother sat reading a history book about the Anabaptists. Belinda pretended to be reading a novel, but she couldn't keep her mind on the words. She yawned a couple times, hoping her mother would take the hint. Finally, Belinda asked her if she was going to bed soon.

"I took a nap earlier so I'm not real tired yet." Her mother turned a page and raised the wick on the lamp, drawing it closer. Then she looked over at her daughter. "Why don't you go up, Belinda? You look tired yourself."

"I guess so. What time do you think you'll go up?"

Grace laid her book down, keeping her finger in her place. "Why? What does it matter?"

"Oh, it doesn't. I just wondered, is all."

"When I'm tired." She picked up the book and returned to her paragraph.

After a half hour, Belinda said good night and headed up the stairs. Nellie was already asleep when she came in the room after washing up and brushing her teeth. She took her shoes off in the hall and quietly changed into her English clothing. She removed her kapp and let her hair flow loose, brushing it several times to bring out the oils to make it shine. Then she put a toot with her make-up by the door and slipped into bed to wait for her mother's footsteps on the stairs. It was already close to ten. Of course things didn't usually get exciting until late evening at the parties, anyway. She couldn't wait. Just thinking about their dance music gave her a thrill. Would she ever be satisfied to live the Amish life again?

Finally, around half past ten, she heard her mother go into the bathroom and then a few minutes later, she heard the bedroom door close behind her. Belinda waited another few minutes before turning the doorknob as silently as possible. Nellie turned over, but remained asleep. Belinda took the bag, picked up her shoes, and headed down the stairs. It was so dark, she had to feel her way down the staircase to the kitchen. Without thinking, she closed the door behind her without leaving it unlocked, but blew a sigh of relief when she remembered the hidden key under the brick.

It took half an hour to walk the distance to Carrie's house and that was a fast-paced walk. There was only a half moon in the cloudless sky, but it gave enough light to keep her from tripping.

Whenever she heard a car coming, she hid behind a bush until it passed. Once she got to Carrie's neighborhood, she saw a group of cars parked along Kim's drive and even on the lawn area. She stopped long enough to fluff her hair a bit and add the lipstick. She wished she had borrowed Carrie's shoes or told her to bring them, since she'd totally forgotten how clunky her own looked. She even considered going barefoot, but that would definitely draw attention to her feet. By now everyone knew she was Amish, so perhaps it didn't really matter. She was pleased to be accepted by such a sophisticated crowd.

Before knocking on the door, she removed her warm shawl and rolled it into a ball. After knocking loudly several times, Kim opened the door and asked her to come in. "I'm so glad you could make it, Belinda. Dan was just asking about you."

"Dan?"

"Dan Stewart. You know—the pre-med student you danced with all night," she said, giving a crooked grin.

"Oh, that Dan. Sure. That's nice. Is Carrie here yet?"

"Oh, yeah, somewhere. Make yourself at home. I spiked the punch if you want some. My folks probably won't come home at all tonight, so you're welcome to spend the night, if you want."

"I can't, but thanks for inviting me." Belinda prided herself on not saying 'danki.' She was giving up some of her odd expressions intentionally.

"There you are. Carrie said she thought you'd show up eventually." A deep male voice sounded behind her, and even without looking, she knew it was Dan.

She turned and smiled. "I couldn't stay away."

"Love your shoes," he said with half a smile.

"Oh, my. They are horrible, aren't they?"

"No, they're cute. Come on, I'll get you a drink." He took her hand and led her to the dining room where there was a punch bowl, paper cups, a cooler on the floor with cans of beer and sodas. A group of people stood around talking. Some of the kids were familiar to her. She saw Jeff talking to a guy she didn't recognize and he waved over and smiled. Two other girls greeted her, but there were several people she'd never met. Her heart beat quickly and for a split moment, she wished she were home.

Dan dipped out a glass of punch and handed it to her. It was delicious. Fruity and bubbly. She took a couple pretzels and chewed one while she looked around. There was music, but no one was dancing yet. The decibels were raised to the point where she had difficulty hearing everything Dan was saying, but she caught a couple words like 'beautiful,' 'interesting,' 'fun,' and some others, which she couldn't quite make-out. Finally, she leaned over. "If you want to talk, we'd better go where it's quieter."

"How about upstairs?"

Her heart nearly leapt from her chest. "Oh, no way!"

Dan laughed heartily. "I figured. Okay, they have a library in the back. Come on, I'll show you." He led her by the hand into a mahogany paneled room with stacks of books and two computers. An enormous television rested against a wall with Civil War prints on either side. There was a leather sectional and two other comfy chairs—and no one else in the room. "How's this?"

"It's beautiful and I can hear you at last."

"Wait right here and I'll get you a refill." He took the empty cup from her hand and disappeared. She looked around at the decorating. There were family photos on the wall taken at various places—all very exciting. Apparently they'd gone on a cruise and there was a picture of the whole family sitting around a long table. They were in formal attire and Belinda pictured herself in the middle of the scene, wearing a gorgeous red satin gown with matching satin shoes. "Looks like fun, doesn't it?" Dan's voice startled her when he returned with a larger glass filled to the brim. "Better drink some before it spills," he warned.

She took a sip and it was so tasty, she took another and another. "Oh, I'd better sit down." She sat on the sofa and he sat next to her, so close she could feel his leg against hers. She should probably move away, but for some reason, she didn't want to. My goodness, he was a handsome guy. He touched her hair and ran his finger down to the end. "You're beautiful, you know."

"No, not really," she replied, taking another sip.

"Yes, really," he responded. Then he put his hand behind her head and drew her over to him, cupping her chin with his other hand. Before she had time to realize what was happening, his lips were on hers. She wanted to pull away, but didn't. In fact, she found herself responding and though it frightened her, it also excited her. His mouth moved to her neck and then her ear and she closed her eyes and everything began to spin. Oh, mercy.

"Please, let's just talk," she murmured as a thrill went through her body. He ignored her request and went back to her lips, moistening his first.

The door to the study opened. Dan pulled back and looked over, annoyed to see Carrie's brother, Jeff, standing at the entryway. "Yeah, what do you want?" he asked with his eyes glaring at the intruder.

"Thought maybe Belinda might want to dance with me. She likes this kind of music." Belinda could hear dance music in the background. She moved away from Dan, relieved at the interruption. She realized she wasn't strong enough physically or emotionally to have stood up against his approach.

"Jah, I like that song." She nearly lost her balance. "Oh, dear."

Jeff reached her arm and began to steer her toward the door.

"Hey, wait a minute. Belinda, where do you think you're going?"

"I...I think I need to go with Jeff."

"Really now. Like you weren't enjoying—"

"Dan, the lady prefers dancing—with me. I'd advise you to leave her alone. I saw you take the large glass of punch into her. You know she's not used to drinking."

Belinda stood watching the two converse, but her head continued to spin. Should she have gotten angry for the interruption? After all, it should have been her decision to stay or go with Jeff, but somehow she realized even through her fog, that things were definitely moving too quickly between her and Dan.

"So go ahead, Belinda. Get your dance in. I'll see you later." Dan rose and pushed past Jeff, who stood with his arms folded. Once Dan was gone, Jeff turned back to Belinda. "I hope you're not upset with me."

"Nee. No. I guess not."

"Belinda, that guy is out for one thing only. Hasn't anyone told you about him?"

"I don't remember. He was okay before."

"Well, he was not okay tonight. Please, don't be alone with him again. Believe me, you'd end up sorry."

Belinda held onto his arm, feeling she might even kutz. What a horrible feeling. She didn't even taste the alcohol in the punch. The fruity taste had taken over. "I think I'm gonna throw up," she said, leaning into him.

"Uh, oh. Let's get outside. There's a patio out the door here. Come on." He moved her swiftly to the end of the room where a pair of doors led out. Unlocking it quickly, he got her to the grassy area just in time. He even leaned over her crouched body to keep her flowing hair from getting soiled. She moaned between heaves and finally relaxed slightly. Then she took a tissue from her jean's pocket and wiped her mouth.

"I will never, ever, drink again. That was so horrible," she said weakly as Jeff helped her to her feet. There was a settee on the brick patio and he led her there to sit, removing his jacket to place it about her shoulders. She shivered and clung to the coat, wishing she'd never left the comfort of her home.

"Feel a little better now?" Jeff asked, softly.

"Jah, but I don't know why people drink if that's what happens."

"It's a lot worse when you've never drunk before. He knows you're Amish. I can't stand the way he was planning to take advantage of you."

"You think he was actually gonna...?" She couldn't even frame the thought, much less the words. *Oh, danki, God, for sending Jeff in before anything happened.*

"I don't doubt it for a moment. You have no idea how many girls have been fooled by him. I even worry about Carrie sometimes, but I think she's on to him."

"She's too smart to let a guy take advantage of her. I wish I was that smart."

"It hasn't got anything to do with smartness, Belinda. It's the difference in cultures. I'm sure Amish guys would have more respect for girls."

"Jah, that's true." Belinda felt uncomfortable and looked for a way to change the subject. "It's pretty out here," she said, glancing at the holly bush next to the house. "But it's awfully cold."

"Let's go back in now. Stay near me, though, till you want to leave. I'll drive you back anytime you say. Did you walk over?"

"Oh, it's not that far."

"But in the dark? You should've called me. I'd pick you up."

"Jeff, we don't have phones."

"Oh right. I forgot. Well next time, we'll make plans and I'll come by for you."

"My parents would die if they knew I was here." They stepped back into the study and sat together on the couch—the same one she sat on with Dan, but this time she felt perfectly safe.

"They don't know?"

"Nee. I've been grounded."

JUNE BRYAN BELFIE

"Sorry. Maybe they have a point." His mouth turned up in a grin.

Belinda felt heat rise. "Why? I'm old enough to know what I'm doing!" She stiffened her back and held her head high.

"You weren't prepared for Dan, were you?"

"Maybe I just don't want to go so far, but I'm sure I could have stopped him when I was ready."

"Right." He shook his head. "Belinda, you're so naïve. It's nothing to be ashamed of. You can't just go from one world to another, without knowing what you're getting into. It's dangerous in our world."

"Then why do you stay in it? Why not become Amish like me?"

"It's not that easy. You know how hard it would be to leave your life-style. The same would hold true for me, I think."

"Tell me about yourself, Jeff. Why aren't you in college?"

"I wanted to take a year off first and work. To get a taste of reality, I guess you could say."

"And then you'll attend college?"

"I'm thinking about it, but it all depends. I love to do landscaping. I'm working for a guy now, but it's been slow because of the weather. The big season is coming up though and I can't wait. We're designing several properties. If I do go to college, I'll probably take horticulture, garden design, that sort of thing. I'd like to go locally so I could continue to work part time."

Belinda nodded. "I bet there's a lot of money in it."

"If you own your own business, but that would take a few years. I have to learn a lot first. My boss is really a good guy. He takes his time explaining things to me and I've learned a lot already from him. I may just stay on and learn the business from him. Time will tell."

"Do you have a girlfriend?"

He smiled over at her. "Not at the moment. I was going with a girl until a few months ago."

"What happened?"

"You're sure not afraid to ask questions," he said, smiling. "I just decided she was not the type I wanted to marry."

"Goodness, so many people don't even get married now, I've heard. That's a disgrace. They even have boppli."

"Boppli?"

"Sorry, I mean babies."

"It's not the way it was intended. God wants the family to be intact."

"We don't get divorced either," she said proudly. "Marriage is for life."

"It should be that way. The Amish have a lot of strong points," he added, resting his elbows on his knees. "I'd like you to teach me more about your ways. Would you?"

"Sure. You really are interested?"

"Not that I'm gonna change into Amish," he said, "but I find it interesting. And I like the fact that people are modest and not promiscuous?"

"What does that mean?"

"Uh, you know," a blush formed on his neck as he continued, "running around with a million guys or girls."

"Oh. I see. No, we don't run around like that. I want to stay pure for my future husband."

"That's why I came in when I did, Belinda. I wasn't trying to be nosy, but I guessed you were getting in deeper than you realized."

"I see that now. I do appreciate your concern, Jeff." She liked her friend's brother. He was special in some way. Jah, she'd enjoy teaching him the Amish way of life, though she knew he'd never be able to follow it. Not after living in such a rich style. "I think I'd like to go home now, though. Do you mind?"

"Of course not. Let me bring the car over."

"I can walk with you to your car. I'm steady now."

"Okay, don't you have a coat?"

"I left my shawl next to the table in the hallway. It's black, has a fringe and—"

He grinned. "I imagine it's the only shawl here. Wait while I get it."

The ride took about five minutes. She asked him to leave her at the foot of the drive for fear of waking her parents. He smiled and said good night. She stopped half way up the drive to wave back as he turned the car around.

When she got to the back door she reached over and moved the brick to retrieve the key. Dear heaven! There was no key.

Chapter Seventeen
Lancaster County, Pennsylvania

Some of the staff at the hospital stood outside to say good-by while Oma was moved from her wheelchair to the back seat of a limo, driven by their driver. Edward was a man in his sixties, who augmented his income by faithfully providing rides for his Amish community for reasonable fees and he knew the whole family.

Oma smiled broadly at the nurses and aides who had been so faithful and kind to her during her stay. After pulling away from the curb, she sat back and let out a long sigh. "I'll miss some of my new friends."

Mary smiled over. "Jah, everywhere you go, you make new friends."

The ride from the hospital seemed longer than usual. Mary sat with her mother in the back while Leroy rode up front with Edward. She kept checking over to make sure her mother was comfortable.

Once they got to the house, the whole family was waiting to greet her. Smiles, laughter and tears filled the warm farmhouse and Oma wiped her eyes frequently, though the tears were no longer just from her grief. Some were shed at the joy she felt from being home with her loved ones again.

Friends had supplied them with a wheelchair, which had seen much use throughout the community over the years. Oma sat in the corner of the sitting room and listened to the banter and laughter of her children and grandchildren. Though at one point she had wished the good Lord had taken her home, she now realized what she would have missed. She looked over at Emma, her belly expanding with new life. Her countenance was radiant, revealing her excitement and her love of life. Then Oma glanced down at the young children—her great-grandchildren, as they played together, creating farm buildings with Legos. Jah, she would like to see them grow up a bit more. And Katie, sitting next to her Josiah, holding his hand and smiling up into his eyes as though he was the only person in the room. Nee, she would not have wanted to miss that. *Danki, Jesus, for giving me more time with my family. I know my Amos is in gut hands and enjoying every minute with you and his own parents and bruders up there. Tell him to be patient. I will be there soon, but not just yet.*

"Mamm," Mary's voice was beside her chair and she looked up.

"Jah?"

"Do you want anything to eat?"

"Nee. Not now, but soon I'll need to rest. My body ain't so strong like it was."

"Of course. I've been thoughtless. I'll take you right into the room we've set up."

"Not yet, Mary. Let me soak up all this fun first. I'm so glad to be with my loved ones again."

Mary leaned over and kissed the white hair tucked neatly under her mother's kapp. She looked like her Mamm again, though scars would remain forever along her cheek and neck. But she was alive and Mary was ever so grateful.

After a while, people started leaving. Ruthie and Jeremiah were the last, but before they left, Ruthie placed baby Nathanael on Oma's lap for a brief time. He gave a sweet smile as well as a drool. Oma cooed and kissed the top of his head. "He's a handsome *buwe*. You must be proud of him, Jeremiah. My, he looks just the way I picture you looked. I can't remember exactly, but you were a screamer, if I have the right boppli in my mind."

"Jah, that's what my mamm used to tell me. She said I cried about everything, but our sohn rarely cries."

"Then he took after Ruthie. She was the sweetest of all."

Mary looked over at her mother and shook her head. "You just don't remember her colic then. My, my, she had strong lungs."

Ruth laughed and reached for Nathanael, who was beginning to squirm. "We'd better get him home before he makes a liar out of his daed," she said, placing him over her shoulder. Jeremiah went to the front door and brought the car seat in so they could strap the baby in place. Even buggies needed protection for the boppli. In fact, more protection. Ruth was nervous about being on the road after the terrible accident that took her grandfather's life. They said their good-byes and left.

Wayne and Leroy took off for the barn, which was their custom, leaving Mary and Katie to watch over Oma. She looked so tired, her eyes half-closed when they wheeled her over to the bedside and helped her into bed. "Danki. I guess I'll take a little nap now. It's been quite a day."

"Jah, a gut one, but tiring. I'm sure and certain of that," Mary said, caressing her mother's arm. "We'll leave your door open and just call if you want anything at all."

"I smell something gut. What's for supper?"

"Goose. Our own Patty."

"My, I feel like the prodigal sohn. Goose, no less. My favorite. But poor Patty. You had her more than a year."

"Jah, well it was her time."

"We all have our time, dochder. I'm thankful now, that my time ain't quite yet." She closed her eyes and went right to sleep. Mary drew her shades and tiptoed out of the room.

Katie smiled over at her mother as she joined her daughter in the kitchen. "Gut start, Mamm. She seems so much happier already."

"Jah, nothing like home, Katie. Don't you forget that."

Katie thought about her own future home and for the first time she believed it might not be too long before her mammi would be in the dawdi-haus and Katie would be living as a *fraa* to the most wonderful-gut man she knew.

Things went well that whole first week home and Oma gained strength each day. A therapist stopped by every few days to guide her as she attempted to be more independent. She was even able to work on a quilt she had begun before the accident. Wayne set-up her frame next to a window in the room she stayed in and she worked nearly an hour a day on her colorful quilt. Katie sat with her sometimes and worked on her own mending or read out-loud from the Bible.

One morning, Mary suggested Katie could return to teaching for the rest of the season, since she felt her own back was strong enough to handle her patient now.

Katie was excited at the thought of teaching again. She missed seeing the kinner and felt badly that Becky had help for only a couple of days a week from one of her sisters. Then she had become ill herself, leaving Becky alone once again.

Friday, Becky came by after school was dismissed. Katie noticed bags under her friend's eyes. They sat at the kitchen table while Mary remained with her mother in the next room.

"Mamm thinks she can manage without me, Becky, so I can come back to teach till school gets out for the summer."

Becky's eyes widened and a huge smile danced across her face. "Oh, Katie, could you? It's been so difficult this past week. I have a full classroom now and the Bender boys have been giving me a terrible bad time."

"You didn't mention them acting up again. I thought we had them straightened out," Katie said.

"They were okay at first, but lately it's been a real trial. They won't listen to me and the other kinner are starting to follow their example."

"Then of course I'll come help. As long as my mammi stays as gut as she is, my mudder can handle it alone. And Daed is always around in case anything happens."

"Your mamm's limp seems bad, Katie. I noticed it today."

"Oh, jah? I didn't even see it. Maybe Emma or Ruthie can help out then. They offered to before, but we didn't think we'd need them."

"Maybe it would be a gut idea to suggest it." Becky reached for a cookie sitting in the center of the table.

"Oh, jah, have a cookie," Katie said with a grin.

"Goodness, you'd think I lived here," Becky said, laughing.

Wayne came in the back door and looked over at the girls. "Have enough of those left for me?" he asked, pointing to the fresh chocolate chip cookies remaining on the plate.

"Sure. There are more cooling," Katie said. "Come sit with us."

Wayne hesitated before chucking his hat on a peg and removing his work jacket. He washed his hands and then sat across from Becky, taking a seat next to Katie's place as she went to pour kaffi for her brother. Katie returned to her seat and set his mug next to him.

"*Wie geht's?*" he asked Becky while he stirred sugar in his mug.

"Things are gut," she answered. "How about you?"

"Real busy planting."

"It's getting nice and warm." Becky tilted her head and gave a sweet smile. Katie was wishing she wasn't there. She felt like the proverbial third wheel.

"Jah." He took a sip and then put the mug down and helped himself to two cookies, crunching one between his teeth.

"I'm ever so glad to see your mammi doing so well."

"Me, too."

"Katie says she can help me at school." Becky nodded toward Katie who just watched their exchange, trying to read her bruder's expression. She knew he liked her best friend, but she was looking for hints of more.

"That's gut."

Why on earth was Becky so crazy about her bruder? Goodness' sake, he certainly didn't act very exciting.

"I need to take medicine into my patient," Katie said, as she rose from the table and poured a glass of water.

"I'd better go back and help Daed," Wayne remarked, standing abruptly. "He's grooming the horses. See you later, Becky."

"Jah, Nice to see you again, Wayne."

After he left, Becky swooned. "He's so wonderful. I can't believe it."

Katie rolled her eyes toward the ceiling. "Oh, jah. Wonderful. Especially when he teases me about my cooking."

"At least he doesn't call you fat anymore."

"How can he? Look at me!" Katie said proudly, turning a complete circle while pulling in her stomach—nearly spilling the water.

"Tsk. Such pride from an Amish *fraulein*," Becky said grinning. "I'd better head home. I have to help with supper." She went over and touched Katie's arm. "Danki, for being willing to come back so soon to teach. I really, really appreciate it. And of course, if your mamm needs you, I will totally understand."

"I'm actually looking forward to teaching again. I could use something normal in my life. Between the funeral and Josiah's

110

problems earlier with the guy from Philadelphia, and now Oma...
Well, I could use a break."

"Remember I warned you about those brothers. Bring your
helmet."

"And my whip?" Katie said, giggling.

"Jah, that too."

Becky left and Katie took the medicine into her grandmother's
room. She could never be a nurse, she thought. Too confining. Jah,
school will be a pleasure after all this.

Chapter Eighteen
Holmes County, Ohio

Belinda held the brick in her hand and frantically searched the ground below. Where could it be? They always left a key hidden. Then she recalled slipping it in her own apron pocket the week before after returning from church service before the others. It was probably still in the pocket. She could picture the apron hanging in the kitchen, alongside Nellie's.

None of the screens would lift from the outside, so entering through a window was out of the question. Perhaps, she could get Nellie's attention by throwing pebbles at the window, though she knew her sister was a deep sleeper.

She gathered a handful from the drive and went around front to their bedroom window. The first three stones missed the pane completely and merely tapped the siding. The fourth met its target, but was barely audible even to Belinda. That surely wouldn't awaken Nellie. After a half dozen more fruitless attempts, she went to the back yard and sat on the stoop. It was cold and she felt goose-bumps form on her arms. When she pulled the shawl closer to her body, she was glad she had warm jeans, though they certainly weren't warm enough in thirty-degree temperature.

What were her options? Okay, she could walk back to Carrie's. They would be up till the wee hours, but how embarrassing. She really didn't feel like walking that far again—especially since it was getting colder by the minute. The barn would be warmer. The odors wouldn't bother her. She was used to the animal smells and didn't find it unpleasant the way some of her friends did. Straw was scratchy though. And then what? Her father would be furious finding her the next morning. Mercy, her options weren't good at all. Maybe she should knock hard enough to be heard and take the consequences right away. At least she'd have a warm bed to sleep in. The thought of her father's words at finding his wayward daughter standing in English clothing in the middle of the night—way too ghastly. She'd sleep in the chicken house if she had to, and when her father and brother went into the barn to milk the cows, she'd sneak in the back door and no one would be the wiser.

She made her way through the screened door to the chicken house, causing quite an up-roar when she bumped a ledge where several layers were nesting. Oh, the smell! Worse than the barn, that was for sure. She looked around the eight-foot square building and decided her father's wrath would be easier to handle. "All right, girls, I won't intrude," she whispered as she shut the door behind her on her way down the path, back to the barn. Perhaps she could still avoid being seen in the morning, if she picked a spot in the barn away from the milking stalls. When she walked into the barn, she caught sight of one of their lanterns next to a box of wooden matches. She lit it and made her way up the narrow ladder to the hayloft. There would be no reason for her father or Gideon to climb up to the loft. While they milked the cows, she'd climb down, get back in her room and change into her Amish clothing. There would be no time for sleep, but she still had a few hours now before milking started.

Stalks of hay poked her at every turn and she thought she might freeze to death from the cold. The warmth from the animals wasn't enough to give comfort. Perhaps she did sleep briefly on occasion. While awake though, her mind skipped through the events of the evening. Dan was so handsome, but he was probably trying to take advantage of her. According to all her friends, he was a Romeo, which she discovered was not a complimentary term. Yet Carrie's friends all seemed to take turns 'falling in love' with him or at least attracting his attention for a couple weeks at a time. Belinda wondered how far these English girls went to attract a man. Surely, they didn't give up their virginity just for the sake of a fun time. How awful that would be. They certainly must have more respect for themselves than that—and yet, she had felt tremendous attraction and excitement at his attention and my, those kisses. It was a good thing Carrie's brother stepped in when he did. Perhaps it was the punch that lowered her resistance to Dan's charm, but whatever it was, her heart beat rapidly at the thought of what could have happened. *Danki, God, for sending Jeff in to save me. Don't let that kind of temptation ever come to me again, because I don't know...*

Jeff's smile came to her mind. He was not as handsome as Dan, but he was definitely cute. His chin had a dimple and he had thick blond hair, much like her own. He seemed to like her, though more like a big brother than anything else. Of course, he would be protective of his sister's friends, treating them like his own. Still, he was very sweet to care that much about her and be so protective. There was no love lost between him and Dan, she was certain of that. The tension could be cut by an axe when they were together.

She finally drifted off and when she awoke she saw the sun had begun to rise. Goodness, that meant it was late and sure enough, she could hear her father and brother talking below her while they worked together. Apparently, the milking was already done and she wondered whether they were about to return to the house. It was her responsibility to cook them breakfast and here she was, unable to even return to her room without being seen. Oh mercy. What now?

Jed and his son, Gideon, finished their chores and headed back to the kitchen. "It looks dark inside, Daed. I wonder what happened?"

"Maybe Belinda forgot to set her alarm, sohn. I won't be pleased if there is no breakfast prepared."

"Jah, me neither, Daed. I'm starving."

They opened the door to discover an empty kitchen. Then they heard footsteps coming down the stairs and Grace appeared. "My goodness, where's Belinda?"

"She must've slept in today, Grace. That girl is in trouble more than not these days."

"Ach. Maybe she's sick. I'll go check and then I'll cook up some scrapple for you."

"We'll wash up and cut the bread," Jed remarked, his jaw set in a straight line.

"Nellie's still sleeping, too, I guess," Gideon said as he headed toward the sink to wash up. His father scrubbed his hands first and then reached for the towel to dry his hands.

"Jed," Grace shouted down, "Come quick. Belinda isn't here and Nellie's crying. I don't know what's happening!"

Jed and Gideon tore up the stairs and went into the bedroom. Jed put his hands on Nellie's arms. "Stop fussing, Nellie. Tell us where your sister went."

"I...I don't know, Daed. Honest. I woke up and she wasn't here. I thought she was downstairs, but I went to check and she wasn't. I'm so scared. Where could she be?"

"We'll have to find that out, dochder." Jed turned to Grace, who had her arms crossed about her chest. Tears ran down her cheeks. "Don't worry so, Grace. I'm sure there's an explanation."

"Like what? She wasn't allowed out. Do you think she ran away?"

"Look in her drawers. See if anything is missing."

Nellie sniffed loudly. "I think I know what happened."

They all turned their attention to her. "I bet she went to Carrie's house."

"What, and sneak out without telling anyone?" Grace's eyes darkened and she scowled at Nellie.

"I...I wasn't gonna tell anyone, but she's done that before."

"Mercy! What gets into that girl!" Grace looked over at her husband, who stood, hands on hips, anger welling out of every pore.

"She's gone too far. Do you know where this Carrie girl lives?"

"Jah. I can show you, but Daed, don't be too mad at her. She doesn't do anything so terrible."

"And how do you know that, dochder?" He asked now glaring at his youngest daughter.

"She told me herself."

"Oh, and we're to believe it? Gideon, go hook up the buggy. Nellie, get dressed and we'll head over."

"I just hope she's there," Grace said, her voice faltering. "If not, where could she be?"

"Not too far, that's for sure. None of the horses are missing and it's cold outside."

"But her friends have cars and—"

"Don't get ahead of yourself, Grace. I'm sure she's fine. At least that's my prayer."

Grace followed her husband and son down the stairs while Nellie began to dress. When they walked into the kitchen, the door from the outside opened and in walked a bedraggled Amish girl in English clothing—tear-stained and shaking. It was not a pretty scene.

Chapter Nineteen
Lancaster County, Pennsylvania

Becky and Katie dusted off the tops of the desks and the bookcases in the schoolhouse. Friday arrived none too quickly for the young teachers. The children had been picked up or had headed home on foot or bikes, leaving the girls with some peace and well-deserved quiet.

"I warned you about the Bender boys," Becky said, shaking her head, as she bent down to dust the rungs on her chair.

"I wonder what's going on in their home to make them so difficult in school," Katie remarked.

"As far as I know, nothing to raise eyebrows. Their mother had twins about a year ago, but that's nothing new."

"How many kinner do they have now?"

"Mercy, I can't keep up. I think around fourteen. We have seven of them in school!" Becky walked over to the door and shook her dust cloth and then folded it and put it away in a closet.

"The girls are adorable. Well, this is the last year for the older boy and then Eli will have only one more year."

"Thank the Lord," Becky said, letting out a long sigh. "Do you have to rush home?"

"Nee. Not really," Katie answered while she folded her cloth and sat down at the desk. "Let's relax. After all, it is Friday."

"Only two more months. I'm glad it's finally April," Becky said. She sat in one of the older student's chairs and tucked a loose strand of hair under her kapp. "Katie, how come Wayne hasn't been at the last couple Sings?"

"I thought he was. I don't know. I know he hates to sing."

"Well, nobody really goes for the singing. You know that."

"He's been kinda quiet lately, come to think of it. He won't open up to me. Maybe you can get him to talk."

"Hard to do, especially if I never get to see him."

"Becky, don't give up on him. I think he still likes you." Katie looked over and studied her friend's expression. "Want me to ask him?"

"Oh, mercy no. I'll never chase a guy, Katie. If he's cooling off, even though it may break my heart, I have too much pride for that."

"Pride?" Katie smiled over. "We're not supposed to be prideful."

"You know what I mean. Maybe it's self-respect then. Anyway, I still love him, but I'm getting tired of hoping."

"You two seemed to be really hitting if off. Did you say something that would have made him upset?" Katie crossed her arms and sat back in her chair.

"Not that I know of. I might have seemed annoyed when I saw him talking to Margaret last time we were all together."

"Did you say something to Wayne about it?"

"Just that I thought she was stupid-looking and he shouldn't waste time talking to her."

Katie's eyes widened. "Becky! You didn't! That's a terrible thing to say."

"I guess I was wrong, but she is stupid-looking. No matter what's being discussed, she's always grinning. Even when I mentioned your mammi being in the hospital."

"No way!"

"Jah, see what I mean?"

Katie nodded. "But you still shouldn't say something like that, Becky. You know better. Maybe Wayne thought you were jealous."

"I was."

"But you just said—"

"Yeah, but she's still pretty and—"

"Not as cute as you are and you don't have to worry about her with Wayne. I know for a fact that she's after Abe."

"Poor Abe."

Katie started to rise. "Why don't you stop at the house with me. Maybe I can work it so you and Wayne are alone together and you can talk."

Becky's mouth turned up. "Really? Danki, Katie. What would I do without you?"

Wayne was working in the fields with his father when they arrived at the farm, but he waved with one hand while holding the reins to the working mules in his other. They were pulling the seeder in straight rows in the field next to the house. Becky and Katie watched while the mules plodded along the ground, heads nodding as they moved their powerful bodies.

"I guess our plan won't work, Katie. He still has a ways to go out there."

"He'll stop soon. He and Daed usually stop around four unless it's harvest time. You can stay for dinner."

"I don't think I should stay. My folks would worry if I didn't show up. Should I make fudge? He loves my fudge," Becky said when she entered the home behind Katie.

"If you won't be in the way." The girls removed their boots and went into the kitchen where Mary was stirring bean soup. The aroma filled the air while the beans simmered gently with a ham bone from last night's supper.

"Hallo, girls. How are you young *maedel* today after a long week?"

"Gut," Becky answered. "It's been a rough week with some of the students."

"Jah," Mary responded. "Katie told me."

"How's your mamm doing, Mrs. Zook?"

"Pretty gut. Go see for yourselves. She's in her room working on her quilt."

The girls went and spent several minutes chatting with Oma and then went back to the kitchen to see if Mary needed help.

"Nee, I'm fine. I'm gonna take a break though, so Katie, I'll leave you in charge. Keep an eye on the soup for me. I made wheat bread earlier and we can have potato salad from last night, too."

After she left, Katie set up the ingredients for fudge and Becky measured out the butter. Wayne came in and his brows went up. "Smells mighty gut in here. Whatcha making, Becky?"

"Your favorite. Fudge." Becky smiled over at him.

He went to the sink to wash up. "Make plenty."

"Jah, I am. Did you finish the field you were working on?" she asked.

"Pretty much. I missed one area near the edge, but it can wait till tomorrow." He reached for a towel and dried his hands.

"Oh, goodness, I forgot something. I have to go help Oma for a couple minutes." Katie removed her outer apron and glanced over at Becky, who turned a light reddish color on her cheeks. "Don't worry, I won't be long," she added.

Wayne nodded and reached for a mug.

"Do you want fresh kaffi?" Becky asked.

"Nee. This is fine. I like it strong," he said, smiling over at her. "So it must be easier at school now with my schwester there to help."

"Ach. You can't believe it. So much better now."

"I'm surprised my mammi is doing so gut. She's a strong lady."

"Jah, we Amish women are strong. I can do just about anything."

He grinned. "Oh, jah? Can you plow a field there, Becky?"

"I could if I had to, I betcha."

He laughed. "That I'd like to see."

"Well, I really meant lady stuff, like cleaning and cooking and quilting and things like that."

"Oh, and I suppose making boppli."

"Wayne! What a thing to talk about!"

He grinned and headed for the shelf with the tin of cookies. "That's what you meant."

"Did not!" Her hands became clammy and she wondered where this whole conversation was headed. Instead of waiting to find out, she excused herself and went into Oma's room, pretending to be looking for Katie. When she returned, he was gone, but he'd left a note: *Beck—don't forget to fill a toot with fudge. Wayne.*

Becky was so annoyed, she put one small piece in the toot before leaving. "That will show him!" she said, holding her head high as she headed for her buggy.

Holmes County, Ohio

"Nellie, Gideon, go to your rooms please. Belinda you stay right here." Jed's forehead was furrowed, his mouth rigid. Grace stood behind him, wringing her hands, eyes glued on her daughter.

Belinda stood facing her parents with a firm jaw. Inside she was cowering, but she forced a brave persona. Her father pointed toward the sitting room and turned to lead the way. Belinda and her mother took seats on the sofa and her father remained standing. He placed his thumbs under his suspenders and stared at his daughter for several moments before clearing his throat. "All right. Where were you?"

"I went to see Carrie." Her voice was barely audible.

"Were you given permission?"

"Nee." A tear trickled down a cheek and she wiped her eyes with her sleeve.

"So you deliberately went against our wishes."

"I guess you could say that, but—"

"I don't want to hear your excuses, Belinda."

"Jed," Grace said softly, "perhaps we should let her talk. Maybe there was a gut reason."

"I'll handle this, Grace." He continued to stare into his daughter's eyes. She wished she'd never left the house. This was more than she could bear.

"I don't know how we can raise you to be a gut Amish woman when you disobey our wishes at every turn."

"Daed, I just wanted to have fun," she said, haltingly.

"Fun? You can have fun with your Amish friends during the daytime. Nee, you had to sneak out on a cold night, dressed like…like a tramp—"

"All the English dress like this. That doesn't mean they're tramps. Carrie is a nice girl. Even Mamm likes her mother and—"

"We're getting off the subject. I'm not sure what we're going to do about you, Carrie. We may have to send you to stay with relatives away from these people who have turned you against us—"

"No one's turned me against anyone, Daed. I like being Amish. Really. I just get so bored sometimes and they play music and dance and have fun."

"Yah, and we have Sings, don't we?"

"That's not the same."

"What's different? Because you don't drink alcohol at Sings? Or worse things?"

"I never saw anyone do anything bad like drugs or stuff," she said, more boldly now that her father's voice had softened ever so slightly.

"They drink, I bet. And things I can't mention."

Grace put her hand on her daughter's and they turned to each other. "Belinda, we're afraid you might do something serious."

"I know what you're thinking, Mamm, but I won't ever. Not till I'm married."

Her father paced the floor and returned to his position in front of them. "Have you allowed men to kiss you?"

Whoa, she hadn't expected such a direct question. Belinda had been raised to never lie. Here was her opportunity to test her truthfulness. She looked from her mother to her daed and swallowed before answering. "Maybe." So it wasn't exactly a lie—and not exactly the truth. Of course, she knew in her heart it was a non-answer.

"I want an answer." He stood, arms folded, staring at her.

"Okay, I guess so, but that's all we did."

"You may go to your room now. I don't want you talking with Nellie about this. Especially about the parties you've attended."

"Daed, just one thing, please. Why did you say I could go on my Rumspringa if you didn't want me to try my wings?"

"We wouldn't have permitted it if we'd known how you'd behave. Your schwester, Rachel, never found it necessary to sneak around at night and get herself kissed by strangers. Nee, she just liked staying out a little later with her Amish friends and maybe wear lipstick once or twice. We assumed it would be the same with you."

"But we're so different. Rachel's always been content with everything. You know that and I've always been restless. You know I'll come around when it's time."

"We don't know that, Belinda, but your mudder and I will discuss this whole situation and tell you in a day or so what we've decided to do. In the meantime, you will not leave the premises and there will be extra jobs for you, including mucking the stalls and weeding the herb and vegetable gardens, without Nellie's help."

"Jah. I understand."

"Now you may go and wipe that stuff off your lips."

Her hand went to her mouth, surprised there was any color left after such a horrible night. She headed upstairs, washed her face, and climbed into her bed for a brief rest.

Belinda couldn't get warm. Her body continued to shake even when she covered herself with her quilt plus the one off Nellie's bed. Nellie didn't say a word, but sat on her own bed, keeping her eyes glued on a book. Belinda knew she had really disappointed her younger sister, which hurt her more than upsetting her parents. She tried to talk to Nellie about the weather, but Nellie just kept her head down and sniffed loudly every so often.

"So what are we going to do?" Grace asked her husband when he took a seat next to her.

He put his head between his hands. "I don't know, Grace. I wish I had an answer."

"Maybe she could live with your sister, Deborah, and her husband."

"That wouldn't be a gut solution, Grace. They live in the next district. If her English friends drive, they could pick her up and drive her places. Nee, it would have to be farther away. Maybe your brother, Gabe, could take her for a few months—at least until she gets over all this foolishness."

"His fraa is in a family way, right?"

"Jah, but that wouldn't matter, as long as she ain't sick with it. Gabe is a gut man. He would see to it that our dochder would be well provided for and get to services on Sunday."

"It's a lot to ask of him, Jed. A lot to ask of anyone."

"I'd do the same for him, Grace. It wouldn't be for long. She'll smarten up quick, I betcha." He snapped his suspenders and looked down at the rug.

"I wish I felt that confident. I don't see many options though, so maybe you should write to him. We'd have to send her with a driver. The bishop doesn't like people to fly."

"It's not that long a drive, I guess. I've been out there several times. I'll write tonight and send it speedy-like."

"I hope this is the right answer. Can we force her to go?"

"We have no choice." He slumped over and put his head back down.

"She threatened to run away, you know."

"It's talk, Grace. You know how dramatic she gets."

"Jah, true, just the same..." Grace left off the rest of her thought and twisted her kapp ribbon.

"Well, make a list of things you want done around the house, Grace, and we'll keep our young dochder busy. So busy, she'll be too tired at night to go anywhere. In the meantime, don't put a key out. Apparently, she's used it other times to come in at will."

"I hope we're not doing the wrong thing, Jed. I don't want to push her away."

"Honey, we do the best we can. The rest is up to the gut Lord. He's in charge, after all."

"Yah. That's for sure and for certain." Grace nodded and got up to put the coffee pot on. A good brew always helped, especially served with fresh apple crisp. Later, she'd make a list of chores. Maybe those windowsills would get a coat of paint this spring. Something good may yet come out of all this. *Lord, be with us.*

Chapter Twenty
Lancaster County, Pennsylvania

Emma stopped by the house to give her mother a break. The children were both in school and her chores were done. She sat with Oma and chatted about her life with Gabe. Oma was able to walk with a walker from her room to the sitting room now and she sat in an upholstered chair near the window, sewing the hem on a dress Mary was making for Katie.

Mary was working in the garden, something she enjoyed doing and found little time for now that she had her mother to care for. This April day was near perfect. The cloudless skies had never appeared bluer and she drank in the warm fresh grass aroma giving a verbal prayer to God thanking Him for his amazing creation.

After weeding several rows of lettuce, she stood up and rubbed her sore back while she looked out at Leroy and Wayne seeding a field. The fresh onion grass added to the familiar scents and then she headed toward the house, stopping first to gather a few red tulips for her mother's room. After placing them in a vase, she set them on the windowsill and settled into a rocker to be near her family.

"So, Emma, you look so gut. How do you feel?"

"Okay, though I'm tired a lot. Gabe makes me lie down every afternoon before the kinner get home."

"That's smart. Jah, I remember feeling tired when it got closer to the end."

Oma looked over at her granddaughter. "When's the boppli due again, Emma?"

"Around the middle of June."

"You look ready now. You're pretty big," Oma said.

"I know. I'm having trouble sleeping at night already."

"Oh, jah, the gut Lord gets you used to bad nights." Oma smiled over at Emma. "And how is that wonderful husband of yours?"

"He's just perfect. We got a letter from his sister in Ohio, yesterday."

"Oh jah?" Mary asked. "That's nice. Everything okay?"

"Nee. Not really. In fact, they're having a lot of trouble with one of their dochders. They've asked us if we can take her for a few months till she gets her head together."

"Oh, my, and with the baby coming? What did Gabe say?"

Emma shrugged. "What can he say? It's his niece and he wants to help out if he can."

"Do you know what kind of trouble she's getting into?" Mary's brows puckered.

"Well, apparently she's been sneaking out at night to go to parties with some Englishers. They're afraid she'll get a big head and want to yank over."

"That's a big responsibility for you two, ain't it?" Oma asked, setting her sewing aside.

"It is and I'm not really looking forward to it, but what can I say?"

"Maybe she'll be a help with the boppli when it comes," Oma suggested.

"Or maybe she'll just be in the way," Mary added, clucking her tongue. "I think Gabe better re-think his responsibility in all this. How well does he even know the girl? He's been in Pennsylvania for several years now."

"He used to go back more before we met," Emma said. "He said she used to be very sweet, but always inquisitive and excitable."

"I guess you should at least attempt to help the girl. Maybe she just needs to mature a bit more," Mary said.

"Jah. That's what Gabe thinks, too. Anyway, it's been decided that on Saturday, Grace will call Gabe on the barn phone at the Gingrich's at noon. He okayed it with Benjamin first. They'll discuss details then about time and place."

"They'll get a driver?" Oma asked.

"That's the best way. Buses are almost as costly and this way she can't get off at a different stop and run away."

Mary's hand went to her heart. "Mercy, she's threatened to run away?"

Emma nodded. Her mouth was drawn.

"I'd be scared she might run away from your place if she ain't happy," Oma said.

"It's a chance we take, but Grace and Jed said they wouldn't hold anything against us if it happens. All we can do is our best."

"Jah, that's all anyone can do. She can come stay here if it doesn't work out, Emma. Now that we have two empty rooms."

"Danki, Mamm, but don't forget Wayne."

"Oh, jah, you're right. A handsome boy like our sohn and a wayward girl? Not gut in the same batter."

"I think we'll manage just fine. I'd better leave now. I have to finish off the bread for tonight and the kinner will be home soon."

"Jah, and you need to get a rest in," Oma stated.

Emma kissed Oma and her mother and then went out and walked over to her buggy. She waved to her brother and father working in the field and then climbed in the buggy, clicked her tongue to alert the horse and returned home. On the way, she felt queasy and mild pain radiated through her back. Probably doing too much work around the house. Spring was housecleaning time and she enjoyed freshening up her home, but perhaps she needed to pull back just a bit. Jah, her boppli was more important than shiny floors. She smiled and patted her protruding tummy.

Holmes County, Ohio

Belinda was exhausted after weeding the entire family vegetable garden by herself. She saw Nellie watching her from her place on the porch while she sat shelling fresh peas. When Belinda looked over, Nellie quickly focused on her chore. In the past, they did these things together and it saddened Belinda to see the fissure her behavior had caused in her family. Thoughts of running away were only fleeting now. She had decided she'd tow the line and behave as a correctly raised Amish girl should act.

She missed her friends and wasn't even allowed to work the market now. She decided to write to Carrie and try to explain since it seemed rude to just not be in touch with her. She'd been such a good friend and she missed her terribly. She also missed Jeff, though she refused to dwell on a man she knew was not of her world. Perhaps when she wrote to Carrie, she'd mention appreciating Jeff's support during a difficult time. She wouldn't mention that he may have saved her from something terrible happening. It was difficult to even admit to herself that she was being carried away. My, what little strength she had.

After cleaning up, Belinda went into the kitchen and asked her mother for her next chore.

Grace looked up from the counter where she was rolling out pie dough. "I guess you can help Nellie with the wash. She just went down in the cellar now to take the clothes out of the tub."

"Goodness, am I allowed to talk to my schwester now?" In spite of her attempts to sound otherwise, it came out sounding like sarcasm. Grace glared at her.

"You must earn our trust again, dochder. So far, I believe you've been trying, but don't push me."

"I was just asking a simple question! Why is everyone so touchy? I'm bending over backwards to be the kind of daughter you want—even though it kills me sometimes!"

"Don't raise your voice at me, young lady! I'm sick of you and your temper!"

"Ooooooohhh." Belinda marched past her mother and headed for the basement steps, stepping as heavily on each step as her slight hundred and ten body could manage. She heard her father's footsteps above when he entered the kitchen. She made her way over to Nellie to help her run a sheet through the wringer.

Nellie looked over at her and frowned. "I could hear you shouting from down here. Daed was just outside the house. I saw him through the basement window, Belinda, and he sure didn't look happy. I think you're in for it again."

"Oh, I've had it with this family. I can't please anyone! I wish I had somewhere else to go."

"Why don't you just behave? Then everything would be gut again."

"I'm trying, Nellie, but they're not making it easy on me. I try not to complain, but I'm beat from all the work. It's not fair, is all. Lots of maedel take this time to have fun."

"They don't all sneak out at night and go to kissing parties," Nellie remarked, her eyes burning into her sister's.

"Even you? I thought you'd understand. I can't wait until you're my age and then we'll see how you behave!"

"Belinda," her father's voice came booming down the stairs. "Come up here. Now!"

The girls exchanged glances and Belinda dropped her end of the sheet and nearly ran up the stairs.

"Jah, I'm here."

He nodded toward the sitting room. "I have to talk to you."

She followed him in and Grace slipped into the room behind her.

"This won't take me long. I've been in touch with your Onkel Gabe. He and his fraa, Aenti Emma, are willing to have you come and live with them."

"In Pennsylvania?" Belinda's mouth dropped open.

"Jah. Lancaster County. You know, you've been there."

"I barely remember it." Tears came down un-bidden while Belinda looked from her father to her mother. "You want to get rid of me, too?"

"Oh, Belinda," Grace began, reaching for her daughter's hands. "We ain't getting rid of you; we just want what's best for you."

"And that means tossing me out of my home and sending me to live with strangers? Well, practically strangers."

"Just for a while. Till you get over this…this…"

"What? Get over what? Wanting to be a normal teenager like ninety-nine percent of the kids in this country? Is that so hard to understand? I'm not leaving the Amish, or let's say, I *wasn't* leaving the Amish, but now? I don't know! Maybe I just will!"

"Listen to you," Jed broke in. "See how you're acting? Like a spoiled kinner! You don't make any sense at all. We just hope you won't make things hard on your aenti and onkel. She's with child, you know, so you'd better behave and help all you can."

"What if I won't go?"

"You have no choice, Belinda," her daed said. She saw not just anger, but sadness as well. She really had made a mess of things. So maybe people would be nicer to her in Pennsylvania. Maybe she'd be freer to explore the other world. Now, she was more sophisticated and could handle the men issue better. Jah, much smarter.

"Okay. I'll go. And maybe I'll just stay there forever and raise my boppli there and you won't even have to come see them." She turned and left the room, stamping her way up the stairs to her room. Her sister would just have to hang the sheets by herself. She'd have to get used to it anyway!

Chapter Twenty-One
Holmes County, Ohio

Things were tense the rest of the week. Belinda did her chores without a word and even though she did them poorly on occasion, nothing was said. Nellie's eyes were red and swollen most of the time and when her father asked about it, she blamed her sniffling and discomfort on allergies.

Belinda felt helpless in her situation. She tried to be optimistic about her move, but inside she trembled when she thought of leaving everything that was familiar to her. It wasn't only leaving her family, but her home, her lovely farmland, her friends. She even dreaded not seeing Jeff again. His tenderness toward her and his genuine concern touched her beyond words. No one had ever been so watchful and protective—not counting her parents of course. They were way *too* watchful as far as she was concerned. It's funny. Dan was not even part of her thoughts. He was definitely just trying to see how far he could go. She supposed she was even more of a challenge because she was Amish. He said as much. He had been tempting though. Goodness, what a relief Jeff came in when he did. Oh, my. She thought she had problems now!

She couldn't very well write a special letter to Jeff. That would be much too forward. Besides, he probably treated all his sister's friends the same way. She was sure it was just his nature to be brotherly to all of them. Or maybe not.

After Belinda finished cleaning the horse stalls, she took a bath and then was allowed to take off the rest of the afternoon—at least until four when supper had to be prepared. That gave her two hours to herself. She decided to write to Carrie and hopefully, she'd read it to Jeff.

Dear Carrie,

I'm writing this letter because I won't be able to see you again. At least for now. My parents are real mad at me. The night of the party I forgot to leave a key to the house outside, and I ended up sleeping in the barn. (Lots of fun) The next morning my father caught me in my jeans and all and knew I'd sneaked out. They simply won't understand I just need to have fun. I'm so sick of it. I may actually leave the Amish. I'm real confused. Anyway, they're making me go live in Pennsylvania with an aunt and uncle I barely even know. I'm so mad, but I don't have a choice. I'd run away, but where would I go? But if they're mean, I'll have to run away. I just hope they are nice and will let me go out and make new friends.

Did Jeff tell you about Dan? Boy, he really was getting fresh with me. He thinks he's so cool. (In a way, he is, but not as cool as he thinks.)

Jeff really saved me from that jerk. I like your brother a lot and I appreciate what he did. That's why I left without saying good-bye to anyone. I hope Jeff explained I wasn't just being rude.

Mom won't let me even go to market with them, so this is the only way I figured to get in touch with you. I'm glad I had your address and I will write to you from Pennsylvania. I leave next week, I think. They keep changing the day for some reason, so I'm not sure exactly. I'm going to pack my jeans and sweater somehow.

Thanks for being such a good friend. I will miss you. Say hello to Jeff and I'll miss him too. He is like a brother.

Belinda read that line over and then erased it. *"He is a good friend, too."*

"Jah, that sounds better," she said aloud as she signed it and slipped it into an envelope. She went downstairs, placed a stamp on it from her mother's desk drawer, and tucked it into her apron pocket. If she hurried, she could still catch the postman. It was good timing. The truck was just headed up the road toward their mailbox. She waved while she waited. Joe Kelly, their postman, drove up to the box, gave her a hearty greeting and handed her their mail. She gave him her letter to post and explained she was leaving temporarily. He wished her well and rode on. Jah, she'd even miss her mailman.

Belinda was dying to read the letter from her uncle, but she took it in and handed it to her mother, who stuck it in her pocket and nodded. "Start the potatoes, Belinda. You can mash them when they're ready."

"Aren't you gonna read the letter?" she asked her mother as she reached for a large pot and began filling it with water.

"Later."

"When am I going away?"

"We'll discuss that later too. Maybe the letter will give a final date. I know your daed plans to talk to Gabe tomorrow at noon on the phone at the Gingrich's barn."

Belinda glanced over at her mother who began peeling carrots. She thought she saw a tear, but her mother's eyes were glassy a lot lately.

"Will you miss me, Mamm?" Belinda asked, turning off the water and moving the pot to the counter where her mother had laid a dozen potatoes.

"You know I will." She sniffed and turned her head away from Belinda. "What about you? Think you'll miss your family?"

Out of nowhere, Belinda broke down completely. She held onto the counter edge and wept. Then she felt her mother's arms around her and the two embraced, her mother speaking love words in the *Deitsch*. Words Belinda hadn't heard since she was a youngster.

After a few minutes, they separated and her mother handed her tissues from her pocket, saving some for herself. "Maybe it won't be too long, Belinda. Your daed is sad, too. We all love you, you know. We just want what's best for you."

"Jah, I know you do. Maybe you're right. Maybe I've been too wrapped up in trying to be cool and keep up with my friends. I wish I wasn't the way I am, Mamm. Really. I'm scared a little too. I never even met Onkel Gabe's fraa. Maybe she's mean."

Grace managed a faint smile. "He wouldn't marry someone mean. He had his kinner to think about. Gabe is a kind man, Belinda, and you'll meet lots of his new family there. And maybe a nice young Amish man will take your fancy."

"Maybe. I doubt it though. Besides, they may be afraid to hang out with me since I was sent away from my own home."

"They won't know why you're there. Gabe could have asked you to come to help with their kinner when the boppli's born. You could be like her helper."

"Boppli are cute, but when they get older…"

Grace laughed. "Jah, when they become teens…"

Belinda looked over and smiled. "Jah, like me. Trouble, trouble, double trouble."

They grinned at each other and went back to their preparations for dinner.

After dinner, the family gathered in the sitting room. Belinda sat with Gideon and Nellie at the game table and they continued playing Monopoly. Gideon had six properties with hotels and Belinda had landed on them three times within the hour. She ended up mortgaging all her properties and still owed him money. "I guess I concede," she said, smiling over at her brother, who was stacking his money in piles.

"Jah, you're done."

Nellie put her head down and laid the dice down without rolling them. "I guess we're finished then. I'm almost out of money and besides, it won't be the same without Belinda."

Silence permeated the room. Then her father shuffled his feet and cleared his throat. "Got a letter from the family in Pennsylvania today and I got a driver lined up for Monday. He'll take you right to the farm, Belinda," he said directing his eyes at his daughter. "Tomorrow Gabe and me will talk on the phone to make final arrangements and set a time."

Nellie let out a sob and made her way quickly up to her bedroom. Gideon looked down at the board and began removing the green houses and red hotels, replacing them in the box.

"So I guess I should pack. It's only a couple days." Belinda made every attempt to sound casual, but her effort was lost.

"Belinda, honey, I wish it were different." Her daed rose and went over to the chair by the game board and took his daughter's hands, coaxing her to stand. Then he put his arms around her and patted her on the back.

"Oh, Daed, why don't we think about it some more first. I can try to be gut."

"Dochder, a decision has been made. Arrangements are set. I think in the end, it will be real gut for you. Maybe you'll appreciate what you have after being away. It shouldn't be too long. We can pay you a visit after Gabe's boppli is born."

"And if I'm gut again, can I come home with you then?"

"Let's not talk about it now, Belinda. This is real hard on all of us. You know that."

She shook her head. "Jah. I don't know why God made me the way he did. He put all kinds of ideas in my head. Not Amish ideas. I want to be like Rachel. Really I do. And maybe after a time away, I'll be gut like her."

"We will all pray for that to happen, Belinda. I sewed you a new frock to wear on your trip. I was going to surprise you Monday, but maybe you need something to cheer you up tonight. It's on a hanger in the closet by the front door.

Belinda walked over and took out a lovely, pale green dress with matching cape and apron. "Oh, it's lovely, Mamm. Danki." She went over and hugged her mother. Oh, how she wished she meant it. It was so plain and boring.

Three more nights in her own bed and she'd be off exploring new territories and living with relatives she barely knew. Belinda folded her dresses, carefully laying them in the family's one suitcase. She added her underwear and two nighties. Her English clothes were underneath, hidden under one of the dresses. It was mid-afternoon on Friday and the warmest day of the month so far. She loved the month of May with all the colors of the wild flowers and bushes. The lilacs were budding, just waiting to burst forth and so was the spirea bush next to the porch. Her heart ached while she added her kapps and bonnets and folded her spring shawl. She certainly wouldn't need her heavy wool one, since she hoped to be home by fall.

Belinda heard a vehicle on their gravel driveway and looked out her front bedroom window. It looked like Carrie's family car. Quickly, Belinda tucked stray hairs under her kapp and replaced her soiled apron with a fresh one she had previously packed. Then she headed down the stairs and out the front door. Her daed was standing, leaning against a shovel, talking with Carrie and Jeff when she reached them. The girls let out little screams of joy and hugged each other, rocking back and forth as they did so.

Jeff and her father looked on with huge grins. While the girls went off toward the horse corral to talk, Jeff followed Belinda's father over to the barn. Her brother, Gideon, joined the men after he rode in from school on his bike.

The girls waved to him while he parked his bike alongside the barn and he waved back.

"I can't believe you came by to see me," Belinda said, smiling over at Carrie, who petted one of their horses when he came over to the fence.

"It was Jeff's idea. I hadn't even thought of it till he mentioned it."

Why did Belinda's heart leap like that? For heaven's sake.

"I'm so glad you did. I felt awful having to write like I did."

"I'm sorry you got into so much trouble. I thought Rumsprig, or whatever you call it, allowed you to party and stuff."

"Some parents allow it, but I guess what made them really mad, was my sneaking out and stuff. They didn't like the guy-kissing part either."

"How did they find out about that?" Carrie stopped patting the horse and rested against the fence, folding her arms.

"I told them."

"Why?"

"They asked me."

Carrie rolled her eyes. "Whoa! You're brave. My parents would have a fit if they knew some of the things I did."

"Carrie, you're not that bad."

"You don't know everything about me, Belinda. Better you don't. So can you write when you go to Pennsylvania and get letters back?"

"I don't see why not. It's not a jail. I hope."

"Oh, Belinda, maybe you should live with us," Carrie said.

"Don't be silly. My parents would never allow that and it wouldn't be right for your folks either."

"Well, if things don't work out, it's a possibility."

"You're such a gut friend, Carrie. I'll never forget you."

"You sound like you're gonna live there forever. Are you?"

"I can't think beyond today." She looked over as Jeff and her father walked over to the family vegetable garden and continued talking to each other. She was surprised her father gave Jeff the time of day, but she remembered Jeff was into gardening and landscaping. They appeared to be engrossed in their discussion. When the girls walked over to them, her father looked up. "Tell your Mamm, your friends are staying for supper."

If Belinda had false teeth, they'd be on the ground! Never, had her father invited Englishers to a meal. Only the driver had spent time in their home and that was just to get paid!

Chapter Twenty-Two
Holmes County, Ohio

"What fun," Carrie said, looping her hand through Belinda's arm and heading toward the house. "I never ate Amish food before."

"It's fattening, Carrie, though you don't have to worry. I can't believe it. Your brother must have mystical powers over my daed."

"Oh, Jeff makes friends wherever he goes. One of his best friends is a Mennonite, didn't he tell you?"

"Nee. Not that I remember."

"Oh, yeah, Jeff goes to church with him sometimes. Nice guy. I might even be interested in him except I think he has a girlfriend now. A girl from his church."

"We're not that different from the Mennonites," Belinda said when they entered the kitchen. "Of course, they're more lenient than we are. I'd love to have electricity, especially in the summer so we could use air conditioning. I hate it when it goes in the nineties."

"I don't know how you handle it. And not driving?"

"When are you getting your license?"

"Soon. Real soon. I can't keep counting on Jeff to drive me everywhere. Lucky he had off today or we wouldn't be here."

"He's landscaping?"

"Yes, and he loves it."

"Sit down," Belinda said pointing to a kitchen chair. "I'll go tell my mother you're staying for dinner."

"I hope she doesn't mind," Carrie said, while she looked around at the plain white walls and absorbed the wonderful smelling fresh blueberry pie, which sat on the counter to cool.

Belinda came down the stairs, followed by her mother and Nellie, who had busied themselves turning mattresses and re-making beds.

"Welcome, Carrie," her mother said, extending her hand. "It's nice to have you stay for supper."

"Thank you for having us," Carrie said as she shook Grace's hand. "Hi, Nellie. How's it going?"

Nellie grinned and nodded. "Gut. We sold out all our produce Wednesday."

"Really? Wow, that's really good," Carrie said.

"Jah, less work. We didn't have to take anything back."

"I hope you like shepherd's pie," Grace said when she went over to the stove to check the oven.

"I don't think I've ever had it," Carrie said.

"You'll like it," Nellie said. "It's my favorite and it's all made with left-overs."

Carrie grinned. "Then I'll love it too. I guess I should call my mother to tell her we won't be home for dinner," she added, reaching into her large purse for her cell phone. After she hung up, Belinda took her upstairs to her room so they could speak in private. Belinda set her suitcase on the floor and the girls sat on the bed. Belinda noticed Carrie looking around. She suddenly saw her bedroom for what it was. It was ever so plain and small in comparison to Carrie's.

"You keep it so nice and clean, Belinda," she said smiling over at her.

"Jah, it's not hard since it's so small."

"But it's plenty big enough."

"I guess so."

"How many suitcases do you have to pack?"

"Just the one," Belinda said, pointing to the medium size suitcase with the leather straps. "We don't travel much," she added.

"Oh, I guess your dresses don't take up much room," Carrie said. "Are you excited?"

"Nee, not really. I don't want to leave." Her throat felt restricted.

"I think it's kinda mean," Carrie whispered, leaning toward her friend.

"They don't mean it that way. They just want me to stay Amish, is all."

"But they're doing the opposite. You might find out you want to leave after being treated like this."

"Maybe. I honestly don't know what I want anymore."

"I think Jeff kinda likes you, Belinda."

"Why do you think that?"

"I can tell. He talks about you a lot and it was his idea to come here today. I wanted to, of course, but he's the one who suggested it."

"That's because he thinks of me as his sister," Belinda said, hoping she was wrong.

"Mmm. I don't think so. He wants to learn about the Amish ways, too. I couldn't believe he said that."

"He's probably just curious. Lots of people are."

"True, but his Mennonite friend, Joseph, got him some books to read."

"And he's reading them?"

"Yeah. Almost every night I see him pouring over them. He doesn't even like reading that much, so I was surprised." Carrie lay down with her head on Belinda's pillow. "I kinda like your room. It's so…I don't know, restful."

Belinda laughed. "That's what I do here." She plopped down next to her friend and put her arms behind her head. "I rest."

Nellie knocked on the door. "Mamm wants you to go get daed and all while I set the table."

"Okay," Belinda called through the door. "We'll be right down." While they made their way through the hallway to the staircase, Carrie asked for her address in Pennsylvania.

"I don't even know it myself yet, so I'll write first and you'll see the address on the envelope. Please write back right away, though. I have a feeling, I'm gonna be homesick."

"I'll write the very day I get your letter," Carrie said. "And once you're settled in maybe Jeff will drive me out to see you. I doubt I'll have to twist his arm."

"I'd love that."

Dinner went smoothly. Carrie sat between Belinda and Nellie. Jeff and Gideon sat across from them. The long harvest table had been made by Jed's great-grandfather from a large pine tree found on the original property and Jed spoke proudly about it while Jeff ran his hand along the smooth finish exclaiming his approval.

"It's beautiful," Jeff said. "I like to make furniture myself. I'm not this talented, but I'm learning."

"Jah?" Jed looked up from his meal. "Do you have a workshop?"

"In the garage. It's just a bench and a few tools. I made my mother shelves for her workroom."

Grace looked up from her bread, which she was smothering in fresh butter. "What kind of work does she do?"

"What doesn't she do?" he said grinning. "She paints metal and tin antique pieces; she sews; she—"

"She does scrap booking," Carrie added. "She's very good with her hands."

Grace nodded. "So she made all those nice stenciled items she sells at her booth?"

"Yes. Her room is filled with them," Jeff added. "I'm working on a cabinet now, but that's a lot harder than shelves. I hope to have it finished by her birthday in July."

"What a nice sohn," Grace said, nodding her approval.

"I can learn to make stuff, too, Mamm," Gideon stated. "Once school is done."

Grace nodded and patted her son's hand. "Jah, that will be real nice."

"Are you finished for the year soon?" Jeff asked, turning his eyes to Gideon.

"I'll be finished for gut in a couple weeks."

"Really? Wow, you're so young."

"I'm gonna be thirteen in August," he said rather proudly.

"Oh, yeah, I can see you're almost a teen," Jeff said, looking over at Belinda with a crooked smile.

Oh my, he is cute when he smiles.

The discussion leaned toward farming and gardening in general. After a few minutes, Jed leaned back in his chair and laid his napkin next to his plate. "So, Jeff wants to run his own landscaping business someday," he said, looking around the table.

"That's nice," Grace said as she rose from her chair. "I have more food here if anyone is ready for seconds," she said, glancing back at her guests.

"Uh, if you have plenty…" Jeff said, looking around at the others first.

"I'm stuffed," Jed said. "Grace, Jeff needs another portion. Just save enough room for my wife's homemade blueberry pie," he added, grinning.

"You bet," Jeff said when Grace reached for his plate. "This is really good."

"It is," Carrie added, "but there's no way I can eat any more. I bet my mother would like your recipe for this. Do you give them out?"

"Oh, for sure. I'll jot it down after dinner."

If it weren't for the clothing, her guests could have passed for Amish. The conversation was natural and pleasant and there was a definite connection between Jeff and her daed. Probably their mutual love of the earth and all of God's creation, thought Belinda.

After cleaning up, Belinda went outside with her friends. They walked around the yard and Jeff pointed out different weeds and gave them the Latin names. Carrie's phone went off and she waved them on once she started a conversation with the young man she was now dating. Belinda and Jeff walked over to the chicken house and stood outside the fence for a few moments and then went over to the horse pasture. Belinda looked out at the rolling hills stretched before them. It was all her father's land. She was silent.

Jeff leaned against the wooden fence and stared out. "You're going to miss this, aren't you?" he asked softly.

She nodded without turning her head.

"I'm going to miss you," he said.

She remained motionless and then nodded. "I'll miss you, too. I never thanked you properly for looking out for me that night."

"I was afraid you might get mad."

"Nee. I don't know what got into me."

"I think it was the punch, Belinda," he said turning his head to look at her. She turned her eyes to meet his.

"I never want to feel that way again. I was so dizzy."

"Dan takes advantage of girls. I was concerned for you. I know how moral you are."

"Am I? Why did I let him kiss me then?"

"I can't answer that. I hope it was the punch and not something more."

"I have no feelings for Dan," she offered. "None at all."

"Do you have feelings for anyone, Belinda?"

"I…I don't know."

He reached for her hand and she looked into his eyes. "I know we are from two separate worlds, but I feel a connection between us, which I can't even explain. From the first time I saw you, I…"

"So you don't think of me like your baby sister?"

"Baby sister?" He let out a laugh. He squeezed her hand gently. "Hardly. I wish you weren't going away."

"Carrie said maybe you'll come visit me after I settle in."

He released her hand and folded his arms across his chest. "Did she? Sure, why not. I actually know someone in Lancaster County. A guy from high school moved there last year. He got a job with *Sight and Sound*."

"Really? Oh, I'd love to go see one of their shows. Have you ever been?"

"No, but maybe if we come out to see you, I can take you to one."

"I'd love that, Jeff. But I'd pay my own way."

He shook his head. "No, it would be my treat. I have plenty of money now that I'm working and I put in overtime when it's busy."

"Jeff, we'd better leave now," Carrie said when she came around the corner. She slipped her phone back in her purse. "That was Scott. He wants to come by and I told him we'd be home by eight."

Belinda noted Jeff's mouth turn to a frown. "Well let's go thank your parents, first," he said to Belinda as they headed back toward the farmhouse. After saying good by to the family, Belinda followed them out to the car.

"Danki—thanks so much for coming by," she said, her voice faltering. Carrie reached over and gave her friend a huge hug and then got in the front passenger seat. Jeff stood a moment, his eyes questioning, then extended his hand for a shake. Ignoring it, Belinda moved over to him and surrounded him with her arms, holding him closely. She could feel his grip tighten about her waist. Then she drew back and turned toward the house. She twisted her head slightly toward the barn and noticed her father standing alone by the entry. He must have seen them parting. His expression gave nothing away about his thoughts. What on earth made her do something so bold?

Chapter Twenty-Three
Lancaster County, Pennsylvania

Gabe stacked his tools in a corner of the barn and pumped water into a trough where he washed off his hands before heading to the house. The heat penetrated his thin shirt and he removed the damp clothing from his upper body and splashed water over himself to cool off. Emma stood off to the side folding the freshly laundered clothing and placed them in her large wicker basket. Lizzy helped her mother by sorting out the socks on the picnic table under an old apple tree. She made a game of everything and Emma could hear her singing a song, naming the socks and pretending she was a "sock" teacher.

Gabe came over to Emma and put his arms around her."

"Stop it! You're soaking wet," she admonished him, grinning at the same time.

He laughed and dropped his arms. "I'm gonna take a shower under the outside spigot before going inside. Can you get me some clean pants?"

"Here," she said, removing a pair from the line along with a fresh shirt. "Fresh from the laundry. I just made some lemonade? Want some?"

"That sounds gut. Maybe we can sit under the tree for a while. Listen to Lizzy. I love to hear her sing."

Emma smiled over at her step-daughter. "Jah, she has a sweet voice. The Lord must love to hear her."

"Maybe not her sock song, so much," he said with a grin. While he went off to clean up, Emma went into the kitchen to get a pitcher and glasses.

Gabe came over after a few minutes in his dry clothing and Emma poured some lemonade for him.

"So are you ready for Monday when my niece arrives?" he asked after he sipped some of the cool liquid.

"Jah, I think so. I hope she doesn't mind sharing a room with Lizzy."

"How does our Liz feel about having another bed in her room?"

"She's excited, Gabe. I hope Belinda likes little girls. Teens can be so self-centered sometimes that they hurt people's feelings without even being aware of it."

"She won't get away with hurting my Lizzy. I won't put up with that. Jed seemed more concerned with her running around at night than anything else. We won't leave any loose keys around, that's for sure."

"I'm a little nervous about this whole thing, but I could use some help. My back has been acting up lately. Even now, it's bothering me."

"Don't try carrying that laundry basket then. Mervin or I can take it upstairs for you. You'll have to watch yourself, honey. I don't want anything to happen to you or our little one. I don't think I mentioned it, but when I talked to Jed earlier, he told me his oldest dochder, Rachel, just miscarried."

"Oh, I'm real sorry to hear that. It was their first, wasn't it?"

"Jah, they haven't been married that long. She's taking it hard though, according to Jed."

"It would be so sad." Emma laid her hand over her tummy. "I love our boppli already."

"Jah, me too."

Lizzy bunched all the pairs of socks together and hugged them to her chest while she made her way over to her parents. She dropped them into the basket and poured herself some lemonade.

"Danki, Liz. It's a big help to have you sort the socks," Emma said.

"And I'll help you when our boppli comes, too," Lizzy said after taking a huge sip of juice.

"Jah, you will be a wonderful help to me."

"Will that lady help you, too?"

"Belinda? I hope so. I hope she likes boppli," Emma said as she wiped her brow with a paper napkin. "Goodness, it's hot out today."

"I like it hot," Lizzy said. "At least when I'm home and not in school."

"So you're almost done school," Gabe said, resting his arms behind his head and placing one leg over his other knee.

"Three more weeks. I can't wait. Mervin said he'd take me fishing this summer."

"That will be fun. Are you excited about your cousin coming?"

"Yup. I made her a card saying hallo and put it on her bed."

"Now we don't know Belinda, so don't be disappointed if she takes a while to warm up to you," Gabe said to his daughter.

"Oh, she'll like me, Daed. Everybody does."

Emma laughed out loud. "My, my. Listen to you. Of course, you're right, because you are a special person and very, very nice."

Lizzy got up from the bench and went over to Emma to be hugged. "Will I always be special to you, Mamm? Even when you have your boppli?"

"Of course, Lizzy. Don't forget what I told you."

"About love being like the ocean? It just keeps getting bigger and bigger?"

"Jah, I never run out of love."

"That's gut. I'll see you later. I wanna go swing now."

She ran off and Gabe reached for Emma's hand. "*Mei lieb*. You've made my life so happy. God is so gut."

"He is." She leaned over and their lips met for a tender kiss.

"I want you to tell me if anything upsets you ever. It may not be easy having Belinda here, but you come first. If she's a problem, we'll just have to send her home."

Emma nodded. "I'll do my very best to make her feel welcome. The rest will be up to her. And now I want to start an angel food cake. I want to make a strawberry dessert with our fresh berries."

"Maybe she'll help you make jam," Gabe added while they walked toward the kitchen door.

"That would be ever so nice. It's too hot today anyway to make jam. Mervin said he'd help Lizzy pick more strawberries this evening when he comes home and it cools off."

"We have a ton this year. We could set up our stand again."

"As long as it doesn't have to be manned. It's too hot to sit up at the road for long."

"Jah, it is. So far, we haven't had anyone steal from us. People are pretty honest around here."

"Jah, I guess it wouldn't work in the city. Not from what I hear from the Englishers I've talked to."

"Nee. I could never live in a city. I thank the Lord everyday for this beautiful land."

"And for your fraa?" She asked, teasing.

"Oh, jah, and for her, too." He kissed her cheek and then reached for the laundry basket. They went into the house out of the hot sun.

Holmes County, Ohio

Belinda stuck her brush and comb into her suitcase along with her Bible and a notebook she used for addresses and birthdays. She also added extra paper and stamps, which her mother had insisted she take with her. Grace and Nellie stood and watched while she squeezed in a tin filled with oatmeal cookies for her aunt. "Now don't forget to write in a couple of days," her mother reminded her. "We'll be anxious to hear how things are going."

"I hope I have time to write, Mamm. Who knows? Aenti Emma may give me a ton of chores to do."

"I'm sure you can find the time—given you have twenty-four hours in a day, just like the rest of us."

Nellie sat down on the edge of the bed and folded her arms. Her mouth was turned down and she blinked frequently. "When do you think you'll be back?"

Belinda looked over at her mother and then back to Nellie. "That's not up to me. Ask Mamm."

"I guess it depends upon you, Belinda. When you're ready to settle down."

"Mmm. It may take a while," she said with sarcasm, not lost on her mother, who frowned and clucked her tongue.

"I don't know why you want to fool around with the Englishers anyway," Nellie added. "It's not like you can marry one of their guys."

"I'm not looking to marry anyone. Not yet, anyway. I'm way too young."

"Martha Ann Troyer had triplets before she was your age."

"Goodness, poor thing. I heard she just had her twelfth boppli last month. That's fine for someone else."

"Do you want your father to take your suitcase downstairs when you're ready, Belinda?" Grace asked.

"I can handle it. Danki." Belinda snapped the clasps shut and grabbed the handle. It was heavier than she expected, but she was strong from all her physical labor. She glanced around the room and wondered when she'd see it again. Plain as it was, it was home and she felt a sudden pang of sadness when she realized she was leaving her comfortable bed in addition to everyone whom she loved. How did this all come about? Was it worth it? She felt remorse, but set her mouth firmly and headed down the stairs, holding her head high.

Her daed came in the front door and nodded. "Is that it?"

"Jah. That's all I have."

"I packed you a lunch, Belinda," Grace said.

"Danki. I'll keep it in the car with me." Grace handed over the toot.

"The driver is here. I guess we shouldn't keep him waiting." He picked up the suitcase and headed outside where Gideon stood checking out the shiny black car—his eyes larger than donut holes.

Nellie and her mother followed them out and watched while the driver placed her bag in the trunk. He opened the back door on the passenger side and stood silently by. Grace placed the bag with the lunch in the back seat and stepped away from the car.

Nellie was the first to hug her sister and tears ran down her cheeks. "Don't forget me."

"Nee. Never." Belinda choked back her own tears. She kissed her sister's cheek and turned toward Gideon. A blush went up his neck as he allowed a sisterly hug and then backed away. "See ya."

Next Jed took his daughter's hands in his and looked into her eyes. "You be gut, dochder. Don't give your aenti or onkel any trouble and don't forget your old daed." Belinda broke down and began to cry.

"Oh, Daed, I'll never forget you or any of my family. I'll be gut. I promise and maybe I'll be home real soon."

"Jah, that would be the way I'd like it, Belinda." He embraced her then and she felt his body shake slightly. When she moved away her mother reached for her and wordlessly held her in her arms. She felt a tear on her neck.

"I'll write real soon," Belinda said, releasing her hold on her mother, and she walked over to the car. She slid into the backseat while her family stood watching and placed the seatbelt across her lap. Wiping her eyes with her shawl, she forced a smile. As the car went down the drive she turned and waved. Her father was holding her mother and she couldn't see her face anymore. She saw Nellie weeping and her brother had his back turned with his head down. It was one of the worst moments of her entire life—and she had caused it to happen. How selfish and heartless she felt as the farm went out of view and clouds drifted across the sky, blocking the rays of the May sun. She shivered and pulled her shawl closer, but nothing helped.

Chapter Twenty-Four
Lancaster County, Pennsylvania

"Here she comes," Liz called out as she peered out the front window. Then she scooted into the kitchen and grabbed Emma's hand. "I saw the car coming down the drive. I just know it's Belinda."

"Jah, it probably is, Lizzy. Let me change my apron. You can go out."

"I think I'll wait for you." Her smile turned down and Emma realized her daughter was shy about meeting her new relative.

They went out together and Emma saw Gabe and Mervin head out of the barn to greet her also. When the car stopped, Gabe reached for the door handle and Belinda got out. She smiled and nodded and everyone took turns hugging her—except Mervin, who just nodded. The driver opened the trunk and set her suitcase on the grass next to the drive. "Good day for a drive," he offered, waiting for his payment.

"Oh, here's the money," Belinda said as she handed him several bills neatly folded. "I gave you an extra five dollars," she added proudly.

"Thanks, Belinda. Guess I'll be off. Looks like Ohio here."

"Jah," Gabe said with a nod. "Not much different. I used to live in Ohio myself and sometimes I forget where I am."

The driver laughed and climbed in the driver's seat and took off.

"You must be hungry after your long trip," Emma said when they headed toward the house. Gabe trailed behind with Mervin, who had insisted on carrying the suitcase.

"Nee, Mamm packed me a lunch. I am thirsty though. Maybe some water?"

"I have sweet iced tea. Would you like some?"

"Jah, that sounds gut."

Gabe stepped forward and reached for the door. He held it open and Belinda walked in first. She stood in the kitchen and looked around. "I like your home. It reminds me of my house in Ohio. Your kitchen is a little larger though. Something smells gut."

Emma smiled over at her new guest. "We're having chicken and noodles and Lizzy helped me make angel food cake with fresh strawberries."

"Wow. That's really nice." Belinda smiled over at Lizzy, who was holding Emma's hand.

Lizzy nodded. "I like to cook. Do you?"

"Sometimes."

"You can help me make cookies when we run out," Lizzy added.

"That sounds like fun."

Emma reached in the refrigerator and took out the iced tea. "Why don't we all have some and Lizzy, you can put a plate of the oatmeal cookies out, too. Shall we sit outside? It's gotten cooler."

"I heard we're getting a cold front coming in," Gabe said while he reached for some glasses and handed them to Emma who set them on a large metal tray. She added the pitcher of tea and Gabe carried the tray out to the picnic table, which stood under two large maples next to the house.

"Lizzy, you can take your cousin upstairs first so she can see her room," Emma suggested before heading outside. "Merv, where did you put her suitcase?"

"I stuck it in Lizzy's room on a bed."

Belinda leaned over and whispered into Lizzy's ear, "I need to use your bathroom."

Lizzy grinned and took her hand. "Come on. I'll show you." They went up the stairs together and Mervin's eyes followed the pretty Amish woman as she climbed the staircase.

"Wow, she's pretty, Mamm. I wish I was older and not a relative."

Emma laughed and tussled his hair. "You just wait, young man. Your time will come."

After Belinda used the bathroom, she followed Lizzy into her room. "This is my bed," Lizzy said, pointing to the bed next to the wall. "And your bed is the one next to the window."

"Gut. I love to look outside when I get up. Of course, it's usually still dark out, but in the summer it's light early."

"Do you snore?"

Belinda laughed out loud. "Goodness, I hope not. My sister, Nellie, told me I do once in a while. Do you?"

"Nope. Never. Did you bring anything to sleep with?"

"Like a doll or something?" Belinda asked.

"Jah. I sleep with him," Lizzy said, pointing to her ragged bunny, which sat on her pillow.

"How cute!" Belinda went over and picked up the stuffed animal and squeezed his tummy. "He doesn't squeak."

"Nee. He just sits there. I have a teddy somewhere," Lizzy said as she bent over and reached under her bed. "I keep him here because my bunny gets jealous if I put him on my bed."

"Oh, I see. Would he get jealous if I put him on my bed?" Belinda asked, keeping a serious expression on her face. The gravity of the question demanded it.

"I don't think so. Anyway, I'll put teddy on your pillow just in case you want company. Are you sad because you aren't home?"

"A little. I'm glad I'll have company in my room. Danki for sharing, Lizzy. I want to be friends."

"Oh, jah. Me, too. Let's get cookies." She took her cousin's hand and they went downstairs together to join the others.

"Here, sit over here, Belinda," Emma said, pointing to a bench in the shade. "I've poured some tea for you and help yourself to cookies."

Everyone, except Merv, who sat on the ground off to the side, took seats around the wooden picnic table and drank tea.

"When is your boppli due?" Belinda asked.

"Soon, thank goodness. One more month to go. I figure about the middle of June."

"I bet you're excited."

"Jah, we're all excited. Especially Lizzy."

"Have you picked out names yet?" Belinda asked while she reached for a cookie.

"Nee. Your onkel and I can't agree on a name yet for boy or girl. I guess when the time comes..."

"Jah, then you have to decide," Belinda said with a grin. She turned to Merv, who hadn't taken his eyes off her. "Are you still in school?" she asked.

"Nee. I'm thirteen now," he said inflating his chest slightly.

"Oh, I see. You're a man now," Belinda said, with a wink.

"Almost. I help my daed. He needs me, don't you, Daed?"

Gabe nodded. "You bet I do. He's a gut helper, I'll tell you that."

"Well, he's strong, I can see that. I saw him pick up my suitcase like it was a feather."

"Jah," Merv said, sitting straighter, "it was like a half a feather."

Everyone laughed and he turned the color of the geranium on the kitchen sill.

"Do you need to rest before supper?" Emma asked her niece.

"Nee, I rested too much in the car. Let me help you when it's time to eat. I can set the table."

"That's my job," Lizzy said. "But you can help me. You can fold the napkins."

"I'm gut at that. Sure."

They spent an hour together chatting about the differences and similarities of the two counties and discussing their families. When Emma asked how Rachel was doing, Belinda's eyes became moist. "It's hard on them. This was their first. She's strong, though, and I'm sure she'll be able to have more boppli in the future."

"It's a shame," Emma said, lowering her head. "I can't imagine how I'd feel." She placed her hand over her protruding belly.

"I guess we'd better go milk the cows," Gabe said, rising from his seat. "Come on, sohn. Let's head over and herd the ladies back to the barn."

After the men left, the women cleaned up the table and prepared for supper. It was a good beginning. Emma felt more relaxed now that she had met Belinda. She wondered why such a pleasant young Amish girl had been sent away from her own home. Mercy, what kind of parents did this poor girl have, anyway?

Holmes County, Ohio

No sooner had Jed finished milking his cows than he heard a car on the drive. He looked up to see a young man get out of the driver's side after parking along the fence by the horse pasture. Jed's straw hat shaded his eyes and he recognized the young man to be Belinda's English friend, Jeff. When he came over to the barn, Jed extended his hand and received a strong handshake. He liked that in a man. Gut eye contact, also. "What brings you here, Jeffrey?"

"I found that book I was telling you about. The one that shows the soil restoration."

"Oh, jah. I remember."

"You can keep it as long as you'd like. I practically have it memorized." Jeff handed Jed the book and watched him flip through the pages.

"Danki. I'll look through it."

"So, how did Belinda make out? Was she okay about leaving?"

"I guess. It ain't something we wanted to do, you know."

"I'm sure it was difficult. I hope she'll like it in Pennsylvania."

"Jah, maybe she'll settle down a bit."

"Perhaps. She's a very nice person and you should know, she didn't do anything terrible when she was at our house."

Jed looked down and shoved a few stray pieces of hay with his foot. "We are of two worlds, Jeff. What may be gut in your world could be considered bad in our's. Do you understand me?"

"I think I do. Belinda is very special. I felt almost responsible for her when she was at our home."

"Almost like a sister?"

"Uh...I guess you could say that."

"Please, Jeff, we all like you, but we don't want you to put fancy ideas in Belinda's head. It would break my fraa's heart if our dochder left the Amish."

"Sir, I wouldn't try to do that. I respect your way of life. In fact, I have a Mennonite friend who is explaining his beliefs to me. We think very much alike. I even go to church with him. I'd like to learn more about the Amish way, too."

"Just out of curiosity?" Jed leaned against the portal and folded his arms.

"More than that. I've been searching for more… I guess you'd say, for more meaning in my life. I see how money isn't the answer and I'm not happy with the way our society is going."

"Nee? In what way?"

"In every way. People are getting lazy and wanting the government to do everything for them. Even my college friends think education should be free. Someone has to pay for all the freebies and it's always the hardworking people."

"In our world, we honor work. Jah, sometimes we complain, but I couldn't sit back and let someone else work my farm for me. It ain't right."

Jeff nodded. "Another thing is the morality in our society."

"There ain't none there, right?"

Jeff hesitated before answering. "I can't speak for everyone. We have a lot of good citizens who believe in God and live good moral lives, but when you look at the number of babies born into single parent homes, and people living together without being married… well, it's astounding. I don't want that."

"Jah, you're right. And abortion. That's murder. Call it what you want, but you can't take a life no matter what."

"That's got to be the worst, and unfortunately, a lot of girls don't know the truth about abortion. The press lies to them. Anyway, I'm getting pretty fed up on the way things are going. I'm afraid I sound like a preacher. That's what happens when I get started." He grinned and cleared his throat.

"That's okay, sohn, but what can you do about it?" Jed slipped his thumbs under his suspenders. This young man was interesting.

"I don't know. I guess, first off, I'll live my life in a Godly fashion. I've thought about going into ministry, but I love working outside in the soil, as you know. Figure I can make a difference to those around me. My father thinks I should go into law. I don't know. I wish I did."

"You're young. You can take your time deciding. In the meantime, how's the job going?"

"Good. I'm learning a lot and I love what I'm doing. In fact, I'm headed back to work now. I just wanted to stop by. I guess I'd better leave or my boss will wonder where I went."

"Danki for bringing the book by. Stop by anytime. I like to talk to someone like you. You know what's going on in the world and you have your head on straight—for an Englisher." He winked and slapped Jeff lightly on his arm.

After he left, Jed returned to his chores. Too bad the boy ain't Amish. Gut lookin' too. Could give the girl some handsome kinner. Jah, too bad.

He measured out some oats and headed for the horse stalls.

Chapter Twenty-Five
Lancaster County, Pennsylvania

Belinda had trouble sleeping. The bed was not as comfortable as hers at home and she wasn't used to sleeping with Lizzy, who tossed about most of the night, made some odd sounds and even coughed loud enough to wake up a rooster! While she lay awake she thought about her friends at home. How could one be homesick already? Goodness, it wasn't even twenty-four hours since she'd left. She wondered if Carrie was planning any more parties and then she tried to picture and name the new people she'd met. The memory of that awful night, when she had been so sick, came flashing through her mind. Then she pictured Jeff. He was sweet to care so much about her. He really had saved her, she was sure of that. Dan had such an influence on women. She'd been warned. Why did she think she, of all people, would have the strength to fight off his advances? The man was smooth. He really was. She suspected most of the other girls had not resisted his charms.

Oh, Lord, danki for sending Jeff to me in time. I don't know what I was thinking, allowing Dan to be alone with me, even after being warned. I'll never be so naïve again. Nee, I'll try to stay within the Amish community here and then maybe Daed will let me come home soon. Probably not till after the baby arrives, but that's only a month away. Please, God, make my parents believe in me again. Help me be strong enough to resist temptation. Danki for my family and keep them all well. Especially watch over Rachel and help her and Reuben to get over their sadness and give them another boppli, who will make it into this world and be strong and healthy. Danki for everything. Amen.

At breakfast the next morning, Belinda tried to hide her frequent yawns, but Emma looked over at her. "You look tired, Belinda. Did you have a poor night?"

"Jah, I'm afraid so. I'll probably sleep better tonight."

"You can nap if you want."

Lizzy looked up from her oatmeal. "Or we can make something for dessert together. Daed and Merv ate the rest of the cake last night before they went to bed."

"Wow! There was a lot to eat! Sounds like my brother and father. Gideon eats more than the rest of the family put together."

"How old is he?" Lizzy asked.

"He'll be thirteen in August."

"I bet he and my bruder would have fun together."

"He likes to fish and he hated school."

Lizzy grinned and clapped her hands. "See? Just like my bruder!"

Emma poured herself a cup of tea from the teapot and sat down to join the girls. Gabe and Merv were working in the fields. "On Wednesday night, we're all going to a birthday party at my parents' house, Belinda. It will be nice for you to meet more of the family."

"That would be fun. Who's having a birthday?" she asked.

"My youngest sister, Katie. She'll be nineteen."

"Oh, is she married yet?"

"Nee, but it won't be long. I'm not supposed to tell anyone outside the family, but since you're family, I guess it's okay. She's sort of engaged to a young man and they plan to be married this fall or winter."

"Most of my friends are getting married in the next few months, too," Belinda said. "My Amish friends, anyway."

Liz looked over at her while she drank a glass of fresh raw milk. "Do you have English friends?"

"Jah, a lot of them, too."

"Are they bad?"

Belinda laughed and reached over to pat Lizzy on the hand. "Not really. They live differently, that's for sure, but that doesn't make them bad."

"Is that why you came here? To get away from the bad ones?"

Belinda looked over at her aenti. "I'm not real sure why they sent me away. I guess they thought I'd leave the Amish if I was around the Englishers too much."

"Would you have?" Lizzy asked, focusing on Belinda's eyes.

"Maybe. I don't know."

Emma's mouth turned down. "Lizzy, you ask too many questions. It's none of your business."

Lizzy looked down and her lower lip jutted out. "Sorry."

"That's okay, Lizzy. You can ask me anything. Problem is, I don't have all the answers."

"No one does, Belinda," Emma said.

"What can I do to help you today, Aenti Emma?"

"Mercy, I have no idea. Do you like to paint?"

"Sure. As long as I don't have to climb a tall ladder."

"Nee. No ladder. Our sills in the sitting room need painting, and I've always got mending to do, but I can catch up in the evenings with that. And there's the canning. I've been canning asparagus all week. You have to use a pressure canner and it makes the whole house too hot, so maybe we'll skip that today."

"Painting sounds fine. I'm not great at it, though."

"I'll help you," Lizzy said. "I'm a pretty gut painter, ain't I Mamm?"

"I don't know if I've ever seen you paint, Lizzy," Emma said as she finished her tea and stood to clear the table.

"I did once a long time ago. Before my mamm died, I guess. I painted a wooden stick bright red so Daed could put a bird house on it."

"I know the one. Next to the pussy willows, right?" Emma asked.

Lizzy's mouth formed into a smile. "That's the one. It's still there."

"Then I guess you did do a really gut job." Emma patted her on the head. "I'll get the paint and sandpaper. You may have to prime in spots if the paint's worn down to the wood. I have primer, too. Lizzy, I think I'd rather have you do the dusting for me. It's too hard for me to bend down and do the chair rungs with my big tummy."

"Okay. I guess. I have to change my apron first and fix my hair. I'll be back."

After Lizzy got to the second floor, Emma and Belinda fixed up a corner of a table for paper and supplies. While Emma stirred the paint, Belinda started sanding the rough spots.

"I hope Lizzy doesn't get in your way too much," Emma said. "She's just so excited to have you here, but I know she can be a little annoying sometimes."

"She's fine, really. Nellie is older than Liz and she can talk too much and sometimes it drives me crazy, but Lizzy is really sweet. Please don't worry."

"I'm glad to hear you say that. She gets her feelings hurt easy-like, so I just wanted to warn you."

"And let me know if I say too much in front of her. Sometimes I don't think first. That's one of my problems." Belinda turned and folded the sandpaper and ran over another rough edge.

"Talking too much?" Emma took the stirrer out of the paint can and laid it on extra paper.

"Saying things my parents didn't like. It's hard being an Amish teen. Did you have fun during your Rumspringa?"

"I didn't do anything much. Stayed out a little later sometimes. That was about it."

"Mmm. I don't know what my family has told you, but I went to parties with my English friends."

"Your daed mentioned that."

"Did he tell you I sneaked out at night?" Belinda set the sandpaper down and wiped her hands on a rag. She looked over, waiting for an answer.

"Jah. We heard. Is that when they decided you needed to get away from certain friends?"

"I guess so. I admit I was having a ball. My friends weren't real bad, though my parents think anything is bad if it's not Amish."

"Was there drinking?"

"Jah."

"And?"

"I drank a little."

"See, I think that's what scares people. When you drink alcohol, you might do things you wouldn't think of doing normally. It's gotten a lot of people into difficulties. Sometimes heaps of trouble."

"I know. It almost got me into a problem. I didn't realize I was even drinking much, but wow! I even kutzed."

"Horrible. I hate to vomit. My poor sister, Ruthie, gets so sick when she's expecting. Thank goodness, I hardly know I'm pregnant."

"You're lucky."

"Here's a brush. Let me wipe down the area with a cloth and you can start painting." She folded a cloth and ran over the surface, removing the dust formed from the sanding. "Have you drunk anything since that night?"

Belinda dipped her brush and wiped off the excess paint before starting the sill. "Nee. Of course, I haven't been anywhere since then anyway, but believe me; I'll never drink again. There was a guy there and I think he was gonna get fresh with me."

"Oh, goodness. What did you do?"

"A friend came in the room and stopped him before he got too far."

"Thank God for that." Emma let out a deep breath.

"I know. I'll never, ever, let a guy kiss me like that again—until we're married, that is."

"Mmm. The Englishers are different all right. It's wrong. Totally wrong."

"I know. It's not God's way and I want to be more like God wants me to be."

Emma touched her on her arm. "I'm glad to hear all this. I'm beginning to understand better why my brother thought you should come for a visit. You were getting mixed up with the wrong people. I'm glad you're here."

"Danki, Aenti Emma. You guys are neat. I was scared at first to leave my family, but you made me feel right at home here."

"Gut. Now let me see where my duster went to." She smiled and went up to find Lizzy.

Holmes County, Ohio

Jed turned off the teakettle and poured water into the pot. After replacing the kettle on the stove, he looked over at his wife, who had circles under her eyes. "Gracie, you need to stop looking so sad," Jed said as he reached over for his wife's hand and drew her close. "I'm sure Belinda is doing fine."

"I wish I could be that sure. She looked so upset when she left. I wanted to grab her and keep her here."

"I know. I know. I felt the same way, but we prayed and this was what we believed God wanted us to do. We have to stick to it."

"After Emma has her boppli, can we go out to see everyone?"

"Of course." He stroked her back and kissed the side of her head. She pulled back to look him in the eyes.

"And if she seems like herself again, can we bring her back with us?"

"Honey, it's too soon to talk about that. She only left yesterday."

"I guess you're right, but at this moment I feel like a failure as a mudder."

"You're a wonderful mother to your children and in case I haven't mentioned it, you're a wonderful-gut wife as well. Sometimes kids get off track in their teens. She'll be fine in the end."

"I just pray she won't leave us."

Nellie came in from the barn. "What's happened, Mamm? Why are you crying?"

"I just miss your schwester, is all."

"Me, too, but I bet she's having fun. Think of all the new people she'll meet. Belinda loves nothing more than being with a bunch of friends."

"Jah, and that's what got her in trouble," Jed said with half a smile.

"I think the black cat is gonna have kittens again. She's super fat and lazier than ever."

"Well, we could use more cats around," Jed said. "I spotted some more mouse droppings in the barn yesterday."

"I wish we could keep a kitten in the house," Nellie said while she washed her hands at the sink. "Oh, I'm gonna write to Belinda later when I'm done with my chores."

"Gut idea, honey," Grace said. "I think I'll do the same."

"What will you write about? She just left?" Jed let out a laugh.

"Oh, we'll think of something. I'll send my favorite apple dumpling recipe."

"Grace, every Amish woman makes gut dumplings. She'll think you're *ab im kopp!*"

"I'm not crazy! All right. I'll just write a short note is all."

An hour later, Grace and Nellie sat down and composed a four-page letter and put it out for the mailman. Perhaps it wouldn't mean much to Belinda, but it helped a tiny bit with their own pain. Grace realized it was the very first time she and Belinda had been separated and it felt as though part of her own body was missing.

Chapter Twenty-Six
Lancaster County, Pennsylvania

Belinda felt flutters in her stomach as she prepared to meet a horde of relatives and friends for the first time. Goodness, she didn't realize how insecure she could feel. And these were mostly relatives!

She stood by the mirror in the room she shared with Lizzy and looked at the child's reflection. Lizzy was watching her brush her long golden tresses.

"You're so pretty. You look like a princess," Lizzy said in awe of her cousin.

Belinda smiled back through the mirror. "Danki, Liz. That's a nice thing to say."

"It's true. I bet any Amish guy who isn't married will fall in love with you tonight."

Belinda couldn't hold back her laughter. "You're so funny. My goodness, I'm very flattered, but it simply isn't true. No guy has ever been in love with me."

"I can't believe that. Maybe they kept it secret in their hearts," she added crossing her arms over her own heart while she sat cross-legged on her bed.

"What color dress are you wearing tonight, Lizzy?"

"My green dress. The one I showed you yesterday."

"Nice choice. I'm wearing one my mamm made for me before I left. Look on the peg by the door. It's a green one like yours, just a shade lighter."

"It's beautiful. It matches your eyes, Belinda."

She walked over and removed it from the peg, held it up to herself, and turned to look in the mirror. "So it does. We should hurry. It's almost time to go."

"Would you brush my hair? Mamm usually does it for me, but I'd like you to do it this time."

"Sure. Come on. Stand over here and I'll fix it." Memories of Rachel flooded her mind while she brushed out the snarls in Lizzy's hair. They used to always fix each other's hair before going to services on alternate Sundays. How was Rachel? Hopefully, she and Reuben were bearing their grief and looking toward the future. What a difficult experience to have a boppli pass away even before birth.

"What's wrong, Belinda? You look so sad."

"I'm sorry. I was thinking about something. Now let's see. I'll braid it before I twist it under your cap."

"You're going to love Emma's sisters. They are so nice. Aunt Ruthie is married to Uncle Jeremiah and they have a boppli named Nathanael. She's in a family way again. Then there is Aunt Katie, who used to be kinda heavy, but now she ain't. Josiah is crazy about her and he almost got killed once by a bad guy who took his money, but he's okay."

"Oh, my! That sounds scary."

"I don't have time to tell the whole story, but I will some day. It was real scary. Anyway, he's pretty nice and I think he's handsome, too. He's fixing up a house for them to live in and Aunt Katie teaches school and helps her mother—my new mammi— with *her* mamm, who was in a terrible accident and nearly died. In fact, her husband did get killed in the same accident."

"My goodness, you have had quite a time of it, Lizzy. So many bad things happening to one family."

Lizzy grinned, pleased with herself for being such a bearer of bad news. "There's more, but I can't think of it all now. Oh, my mammi had polio when she was young and her schwester got so mad, she ran away and became a famous professor in a big university."

"Really? Wow!"

"Girls, are you ready yet?" Emma called up the stairs.

"In one minute, Mamm," Lizzy yelled back.

"There, put your kapp on. Oh, Lizzy, look at me! I'm not even dressed. I'll change real quick. At least our hair looks gut. You'd better change into your dress and run down. I'll only be a minute."

"I'll try to think of some other people you should know about, Belinda, but for now that's all I can remember."

166

Belinda smiled over as she slipped on her homemade dress and adjusted the belt and apron, adding straight pins to hold everything together. "Gut. I hope I can remember all those names."

"I'll help if you forget. Just stay close by."

"Danki, Lizzy. Now run. I don't want your parents to get mad."

Belinda stood in a corner of the large living room and looked around at the crowd. Her head spun with all the names and faces she was expected to remember. Two faces stuck out. Josiah, the handsome fiancé of Katie; and Wayne, another good-looking blonde guy who was apparently the brother of Emma. She hadn't even heard about him before. He came over to talk to her once, but a girl, whose name she couldn't quite remember tagged along and she didn't look particularly happy with him when he kept smiling at Belinda. Mercy, it's not like she flirted with him. She didn't flirt with anyone, though she might have with Josiah, if he'd even looked her way—which he didn't.

Katie kept grinning the whole evening, which rather annoyed Belinda. No one can be that happy all the time. Though if you were engaged to marry a man as neat as that Josiah, maybe you could be.

Merv was so cute. He kept following her with his eyes. Belinda knew he had a crush on her, but for some reason it didn't bug her the way it did when one of the boys at church service used to follow her around. She couldn't even remember his name. It started with an "A" but she felt she was being stalked—an English expression she had learned from Carrie.

People came and went and everyone made her feel welcome. Even the old lady in the wheelchair seemed to like having her there. It made her feel so good, that at one point, she decided she would never stop being Amish. Where else could someone be treated so well by perfect strangers?

After eating a piece of spice cake with white icing, Belinda headed for the punchbowl. The fruity mixture was delicious and safe to drink. It was nearly eight o'clock and some of the guests started to leave. She reached for a refill, replaced the ladle, and attempted to step back out of the traffic. When she looked up, Wayne had arrived at her side and he smiled over at her. His cup was already half full, but he reached for the ladle and accidentally spilled some punch on her dress. His cheeks became beat-red. "I'm real sorry, Belinda. I should've waited till you sat down."

He leaned over with a couple paper napkins and started sopping up some liquid from her apron.

Embarrassed, she took a step back. "It's okay, really. It will come out in the wash. Don't worry about it, please."

"Are you sure? Maybe Emma has a secret soap you can use. You look so pretty in it, I'd hate to have it ruined."

"It's easy to wash, I'm sure. It's been such a nice evening. Everyone is so friendly."

"I'm glad you're enjoying yourself. It's hard to walk into a room filled with strangers—even if you're related to most of them in a way."

She laughed and watched while his jaw relaxed. "Jah, it sure is, but I love everyone here."

His blush returned.

"Well, I guess I don't mean 'love' exactly."

"Jah, I know what you mean."

"Wayne, there you are. Are you going to take me home in your buggy?" the girl without a name asked, her eyes darting back and forth between them, as she sidled next to the attractive young man.

"Oh, yeah, if you need a ride. You met Belinda?"

"Jah. Hi again."

"Hi."

"I spilled punch all over her dress," Wayne said, pointing down at the large stain.

"Oh, it will come right out in the wash, I'm sure and certain of that. It's just cotton."

"Jah, I'm sure it will be just fine," Belinda said, nodding.

"Okay, well, I guess we'd better go now. Looks like the party's over," Wayne remarked.

"Oh, I know a song by that name." Belinda began to sing it in her lovely soprano voice. Becky glared at Wayne while he watched enchanted at the beautiful Amish stranger who had invaded Becky's territory. After finishing a couple lines, Belinda stopped and laughed. "And so it goes."

"That's a cute song," Wayne said.

"I'd never sing such a song. I bet it was written by an Englisher."

"Oh, sorry," Belinda said, annoyed at the girl's reaction. "I didn't mean to offend you."

"Let's go, Becky. It's getting late. See you, Belinda," Wayne put his hand under Becky's elbow and guided her toward the door somewhat abruptly. Belinda felt a hand on *her* arm and turned to see Lizzy standing beside her.

"Becky's not happy with Wayne. I can see that. I think she's jealous." Lizzy scowled.

"She's got a temper, Liz. I feel sorry for Wayne."

"They aren't engaged or anything."

"Nee?" That was welcome news. Maybe her time in Lancaster County would be interesting after all. She smiled at Lizzy. "Tell me everything you know about Wayne when we get home. Okay? And also the story about the other handsome guy—Josiah."

"Sure. There's a lot to tell," Lizzy said, grinning widely.

That night before they went to sleep, Lizzy filled Belinda in on Josiah's experience with his room mates from Philadelphia. She told about how the other men ended up dealing in drugs and thought Josiah had tattled to the police about them and how the one man was in jail and the other came to get money for his release. Lizzy rattled on, exaggerating the confrontation that took place. "All the Amish men in the neighborhood went to Josiah's new house in order to scare the bad guy, who was trying to bribe Josiah. They all had guns and rakes and stuff and they would have beaten him up gut, if he tried to hurt Josiah, that's for certain," Lizzy continued.

"I can't believe it!" Belinda sat on the edge of her bed absorbed in the whole story.

"It's true, but only the bad guy got hurt when Josiah punched him."

"An Amish man punching another person? Wow! I've never seen that before."

"He didn't punch him until the bad guy said something mean about Katie. That's when he got real mad. And he got hurt too, but not so bad. He had blood all over him, though."

"And Wayne. Was he there?"

"Oh, yeah, he wouldn't miss it. He didn't hit anyone. Actually, to tell the truth, the men weren't really going to hurt the bad guy. They just wanted to scare him, is all."

"Well, you certainly live in an interesting Amish community, Lizzy. We are soooo boring next to you people."

"Oh, yeah, we ain't boring." Lizzy slid into bed and put her hands up behind her head. "I'll try to think of more stuff. There's not much to say about Wayne, except he likes to carve things and he sells them and makes gut money."

"How long has he been going out with that Becky girl?"

"Not too long. He used to like another girl, but he got tired of her. I think he likes all the girls."

"Hmm. Well I guess we'd better get some sleep.

Besides, I'm not here to cause trouble. That Becky can have her boyfriend. I couldn't care less. I just hope she appreciates him. As far as Josiah goes, he's really cute, but Katie is Emma's little sister. I don't want to stir up things by flirting with him.

Lizzy, you're lucky you're only a kinner. It gets so complicated when you grow up."

"I guess. It doesn't help to be beautiful like you."

Belinda giggled. "You're so funny. *Gut nacht*, little one."

"Gut nacht," Lizzy said as she closed her eyes.

Belinda shut her eyes also, but two handsome faces kept appearing in her thoughts. Then a third popped up. *Oh, my. I forgot all about Jeff. Ugh. I'm giving up on all men. It's way too complicated.* Ten minutes later a dull snore came from a very tired Amish girl, which if known by others, could prove quite embarrassing.

Chapter Twenty-Seven
Lancaster County, Pennsylvania

"How did you enjoy yourself last night?" Emma asked Belinda when they cleaned up together from breakfast.

"It was ever so nice. Everyone treated me real gut. Just about."

"Oh, someone didn't?"

"I guess the girl named Becky didn't like her boyfriend talking to me."

"You mean my little bruder? Wayne?" Emma grinned and stopped cleaning the counter to look over at Belinda.

"I forgot he was your bruder. There were so many people there. He's not very little, though. He must be over six feet," Belinda said in his defense.

"I guess he is, but he'll always be my little bruder, even if he grows to be eight feet tall."

"So I sang a couple lines from a song I knew—as a joke, and she looked mad."

"Well, Becky is insecure when it comes to Wayne. He's very non-committal and apparently she's had a crush on him for a long time. She and my sister, Katie, are best friends. In fact, they teach school together. Becky's more of an aide, but when Katie gets married, she'll take over the class."

"Katie's fiancé is pretty good-looking." Belinda reached for a dry dishtowel and began drying the dishes.

"Josiah. Yah, he's nice to look at. There was a time he tried to court me."

"Really?" Belinda stopped drying and looked over at her.

"Jah, and before me, he liked my schwester, Ruthie."

"Goodness. He had a thing for the Zook girls, I guess," Belinda said, grinning.

"I might have gotten interested in Josiah, but my heart belonged to Gabe, even before I realized it myself." Emma rinsed

171

out the empty coffee pot and set it aside. Then she wiped down the sink and drain board while Belinda took the last of the dishes to dry.

"Was it hard to marry a widower with kinner?"

"Not at all. I actually loved the little ones before I loved Gabe. He's quite a bit older than I am, you know."

"Does that bother you?" Belinda hung the towel over a peg and sat at the table.

Emma dried her hands and joined her. "Nee. I'm crazy about the man. He's such a great husband and father. We're so excited about our baby." She patted her tummy. "Oh, my back gave me such a hard time last night. I'm glad the midwife lives nearby. I have a feeling it won't be long."

"Do you care if it's a boy or girl?"

"Nee, though I think it'll be a boy. It's such an active boppli, and large." She smiled over at Belinda. "Have you thought about marriage yet?"

"Mmm. Only like in the distant future. I like having fun and I'm not ready to settle down. But some day I want a big family. Well, not huge, maybe just five or six kinner."

"We're hoping to end up with about that many. Gabe had two other children who died a few years ago from flu. It was very difficult on his wife and him and then when she died, he kind of pulled back from people. When we met at first he was scared to even have a relationship with another woman. I guess he was afraid of having more loss in his life."

"That's really sad. I'm so glad he found you, Aenti Emma. I can see how much he cares when he looks at you. And the children adore you."

"I hope so. I hope Lizzy will be all right after the boppli comes. I'm fearful she may be jealous. When we were first married, she kinda resented me I think. I was taking a lot of her daed's time."

"I can understand. But she seems fine now."

"Oh, jah. She does. We have a gut relationship, thank God."

"Where is she?"

"Out in the barn probably. She likes to help Gabe and Mervin sometimes. They're in the field most of the time now though. It's so much work."

"I know. My daed is outside all the time. I can't imagine him doing anything besides farming. Even though he gets worn out sometimes, he loves it."

"Katie and Ruthie are coming over this afternoon to help make rhubarb jam. Do you want to help?"

"Sure. I help my mamm make jellies and preserves. Sometimes it gets boring, but I'd rather cook than sew."

Emma laughed. "I'm not a great sewer either. I'd rather quilt than mend, though."

"I can finish painting the sills this morning, if you'd like," Belinda said.

"That's a gut idea. Then I can wash up some of the kinner's clothing. I have to wash more than once a week, that's for sure."

Katie and Ruthie showed up after lunch. Gabe stayed around the house long enough to greet them and then he decided to take off and go fishing with the children. "You don't get many June days this cool," he said when he headed out of the door with two very happy youngsters.

"Okay, don't forget, I'm counting on fish for dinner," Emma said with a grin as she closed the screen door behind them.

Nathanael was asleep in a carrier in the sitting room off the kitchen and Ruthie and Emma began setting up the canning equipment. Mervin and Lizzy had cut the rhubarb earlier so Belinda and Katie began rinsing it before preparing it for jam. The conversation was light and friendly until the birthday party was mentioned. Then Belinda noticed Katie became quiet and unsmiling.

Why would she be upset? Had Belinda done something wrong? Then she remembered Becky's reaction to the song. Of course, it wasn't the song at all, but rather the fact Wayne showed some minor interest in her.

"Becky seems like a nice girl," Belinda said, opening the conversation. If there was anything she hated, it was when people held grudges against others without trying to mend the problem first. Goodness, it wasn't like Belinda openly flirted with the man.

Katie looked up while she placed the cut stalks in a pot to simmer. "She's my best friend. We teach together."

"Jah, I know. Aenti Emma told me. She also said Becky's liked Wayne for a long time. That's ever so nice. You would be sisters-in-law someday if things work out."

Katie gave her a huge grin and Belinda could see her body relax. "Oh, jah, that's what we're both hoping."

"Pass me the tray of jars, please, so I can heat them in the water," Emma called over to Ruthie, who had been rocking her restless baby before returning to the sink. "This set of jars is ready to fill once the rhubarb is ready."

"I'm almost done melting the sugar. I hope you have enough pectin, Emma," Ruthie said, setting a tray of hot pint jars on the table.

Belinda checked the large pot with the softening rhubarb. "Not ready yet. You have a lot of rhubarb."

"Jah, we keep cutting it and more seems to pop up," Emma said. "My Gabe has a green thumb."

"He does the family vegetable garden, too?" Belinda asked.

"He doesn't want me to strain my back, so he's taken over—just for this year."

"How sweet," Belinda said, smiling over. "Most men would expect their wives to do everything even if they were pregnant."

"If it was just being a little pregnant, I would do it, but look at me!" Emma turned sideways and popped herself out in front.

"Jah, you sure are in a family way," chuckled Belinda. "It's gonna be a big boppli, that's for certain."

"You look like a teapot," added Ruthie. The girls enjoyed a good laugh and proceeded with the jam.

Holmes County, Ohio

Jed looked over at his wife and daughter while they bent over a piece of yellow fabric on the floor and laid the tissue pattern out to save as much material as possible and still have cuttings for a new frock. He set his paper aside and folded his arms.

"So who's getting a new dress this time?" he asked with amusement.

"It's for me, Daed," Nellie said, adding a straight pin to the bodice piece.

"Goodness, you have one of every color now, don't you?"

"Nee. I'd love a purple one next."

"I see. So has anyone heard from Belinda?"

"Not yet, Jed. It hasn't been that long. Maybe I'll try to call Gabe tomorrow through his friend who has the phone." Grace leaned back on her heels. "There, that should do it. You cut it, Nellie. I'm getting a crick in my leg."

Nellie nodded and reached for the long scissors and began cutting out the skirt section first.

"I'm anxious to go to market tomorrow and see how our red beet jelly sells this year," Grace said after she rose from the floor and settled on the couch next to her husband.

"It went pretty gut last year, didn't it?" he asked as he stretched his arm around her shoulder and drew her closer. They watched their daughter while she cut out the pieces for her dress.

"Jah, once people knew how gut it was. The name scares some of the English folk, though."

He laughed. "They don't know what they're missing."

Nellie stopped cutting and looked over at her parents. "Is it okay if I talk to Carrie?"

"Sure, you can talk to her about Belinda, but I don't want her to think it was her fault she had to leave."

"Why would she think that?" Nellie asked.

"You know—since we were upset about the parties and all."

"They probably wouldn't understand why you got upset anyway." Nellie went back to work, frowning as she sliced through the bright fabric.

"Her brother, Jeff, is a nice young man," Jed said while he watched. "Gut head on his shoulders. Too bad he ain't Amish."

Grace looked over at him, her brows raised. "That's a funny thing to say. You'd like him for a son-in-law? Is that what you mean?"

"I think he has a fancy for our dochder, is all, and he's a hard working man and seems like an honest sort."

"I'll be. Well he ain't Amish, so that's that," Grace said with a firm nod of her head. "Now when you're done with that, Nellie, you can start that letter for your sister. I don't want her to think she's been forgotten."

"Jah, Mamm. I miss her so much, you can't believe it."

"We all do, honey," Grace said.

175

Jed stood up and stretched. "Well, I guess I'll go outside and check on my sohn. He wanted to repair the chicken coop before it got dark. I love these long days. We get ever so much work done."

"Jah, but you practically fall in bed these nights."

"A gut night's sleep after a gut day's work? Jah, better than sleeping pills, that's for sure."

After she folded the pieces for her dress and placed them next to the sewing machine, Nellie and her mother sat down at the kitchen table and wrote a three-page letter to Belinda. It seemed to help cover the distance between them to write. Almost like talking. How nice it would be to own a phone. Their bishop was considering the cell phone for his people. Nellie prayed he would relent. It would be wonderful to hear Belinda's voice.

Chapter Twenty-Eight
Holmes County, Ohio

Market day was busier than usual. The number of vendors had increased as the weather improved. Many farmers now displayed their wares outdoors, but the Glicks stayed in their indoor location, enjoying the covering, which protected them from sun and rain.

The rains of April and the warmth of May gave crops a hearty boost. Their produce looked fresh and appealing and while Nellie laid the asparagus out in bunches, she glanced over at their friend's booth. Since school wasn't out for the summer yet, only Carrie's mother had arrived. She looked over and waved and Nellie waved back. They were such friendly people, no wonder her sister had enjoyed visiting them. If only she'd been more careful and not decided to sneak around at night, she'd probably still be at home with her. She would never do the things Belinda did. Never! It wasn't right to hurt her family the way she did. For a moment, Nellie regretted her letter, which they placed for pick-up before leaving for the market. She had gone on and on about missing her sister, and really when you think about it, Belinda brought this on herself. She was definitely boy crazy. She heard her a couple times when she and Rebecca had been talking about them. It seemed her sister was enamored of a new young man every time she listened in.

Now that Nellie had turned fifteen, she found herself thinking more about boys than before and she was excited to know that in one year she could start attending the Sings, but she vowed never to become so infatuated with a guy that she'd make foolish choices like her sister. She was more like her eldest sister, Rachel. She never upset her parents like Belinda did. She did fall in love, but only the once and he was a wonderful-gut husband for her.

Nellie had a stab of sadness run through her when she thought about the loss of Rachel and Reuben's first child. She hoped her sister would get pregnant in a couple of months, if the mid-wife felt it was safe for her to carry again so soon. That part of marriage was kind of scary to Nellie. She had heard some awful tales of births going wrong and wished she could have her boppli in a hospital with a real doctor, but that wasn't done unless the mid-wife suspected there'd be problems. Mrs. Donner was thought highly of in the community and had even done a breach birth when there wasn't time to get the mother to the hospital. Jah, she had faith in Mrs. Donner, but she hoped she wouldn't need her services for several years.

"Nellie, the lady asked you for more lettuce. Reach under the counter and restock, please." Her mother frowned at her while she scurried to do what she was asked. She set several bunches of leaf lettuce on the counter and smiled, embarrassed at her neglect of duty.

"Thank you, dear. You have a nice day," the woman said as she handed over the money. "Keep the change," she added and walked to the next stand. Nellie looked down at the twenty-dollar bill in her hand. The groceries had added up to fourteen dollars and fifty cents. Goodness, what a nice tip. She grinned over at her mother.

"You can keep the change for helping Nellie."

"I can buy more material and make another dress," she said proudly.

"Yah, you can pick up the purple material at Hattie's booth later. The one you looked at before."

"I'm so excited. I hope she didn't sell it all."

"Mercy, she had three bolts. Don't worry."

The day went well and around closing time Nellie spotted Jeff and Carrie arrive to help. Carrie came right over to the stand while Nellie and her mother began putting things away to return home.

"Hi, Nellie, Mrs. Glick. Did you hear from Belinda yet?"

"Nee. Not yet," Grace answered.

"Neither did I, but I wrote to her yesterday. We want to go see her soon. Do you think that would be all right?"

Grace's mouth dropped. "Uh, I...I...maybe. I'm not sure it's a gut idea. It might make her more homesick."

"Golly, I hadn't thought of that. It was actually Jeff's idea. I guess we should wait. I mentioned it in my letter, but we can hold

178

off. I was gonna ask if Nellie could drive there with us. My brother has a friend who lives in the area and we might be able to stay with his family overnight."

"Oh, Mamm, that would be ever so much fun," Nellie said, pleading with her eyes.

"Nellie, not now. We'll see." Grace turned back to Carrie. "It was nice of you to think of asking Nellie. We're probably going there in about a month. By then there will be a new boppli and we can tie the two events together."

"Super. Well I'd better get back and help. I see my mother giving me the eye," Carrie said and took off.

"Mamm, why can't we go sooner? I bet it would help Belinda to see her family."

"We sent her to Pennsylvania to get her away from her friends, Nellie. You know that. So why would we encourage them to visit her? Now maybe, down the road it will be okay, but certainly not yet."

"Well, I hope it won't be too long. I miss her a lot."

Grace stopped packing up long enough to hug her daughter. "Jah, me, too. I hope we did the right thing. Now here comes your daed to help us pack the wagon. We have to get home and fix a nice supper for him. He looks pretty tired."

Lancaster County, Pennsylvania

Even though everyone was kind and tried their best to make Belinda feel comfortable and at home, she missed her family, her home, and most of all, her friends. She forced herself to concentrate on whatever task she was performing in order to get her mind off her loneliness, but so far, she had found it difficult. She'd finally written to her family and also to Carrie. It really was wrong to sneak out like she did. She knew it at the time, yet it was exciting to have secrets and after all, she didn't do anything really bad.

Belinda laid in bed, listening to the steady breathing of her roommate, Lizzy. She wished she could fall asleep. Her body was tired from working around the house all day, but her mind wouldn't allow her to rest. The memory of the evening when Dan had tried his best to take advantage of her, came front and center into her mind, and she felt herself flush at the thoughts, which came with it. She hated to admit it, but she had rather enjoyed the attention—and the feelings she had. It was frightening really. Surely, without the spiked punch, she would have had far more control. So that was why her parents did not believe in drinking. They had a point. If you do things you would not do without the alcohol, then surely it was a bad idea. Without doubt, she would not drink again. If she were with her English friends, she would make that perfectly clear ahead of time. If they thought she was a prude? So be it.

Then Jeff's smile came to her mind. He was so sweet to her. If only he was Amish then maybe he'd like her as more than a friend. She was sure his feelings were that of a brother towards her. He did save her from a bad situation. How would it feel to be held in his arms? Oh, mercy, there she was, thinking about that again. Could she ever live a proper Amish life thinking thoughts about English men holding her?

Belinda moved onto her side and looked out the window. The shade was drawn slightly but she could see stars dancing in the clear black sky. Somewhere out there was the God she loved.

Father, take away any bad thoughts I have and help me be the kind of woman you want me to be. I want to be gut. You know that, but it's hard sometimes to just be a simple Amish girl. I guess

It's hard for the English girls, too, in a way. They probably do things they're sorry for later. Carrie said as much once. Please bless my family, especially Rachel, and my friends, too. And Lord, please let me go back home real soon.

Belinda felt tears roll down her cheeks onto her pillow. It was the first time she'd allowed her tears to flow and she feared waking Lizzy if she gave into her feelings. She rolled onto her back and reached for tissues. Releasing a long silent sigh, she closed her eyes and finished her prayer.

Danki for life, Lord. Even though I'm sad right now, I know you have something planned for me and will use me somehow. Give me a servant's heart and let me be a gut helper when

Emma's boppli comes. Please give my aenti and onkel a gut healthy boppli and don't let their kinner get too jealous. Amen.

Belinda smiled at the thoughts of holding a new baby and she finally drifted off to sleep.

The next two weeks went easier for Belinda. She settled into her routine and became closer to her new family. Emma was able to do less and less as she grew uncomfortably larger. The mid-wife wondered if they had miscalculated the time and said upon examination, that Emma had already begun to dilate.

Gabe checked her constantly, coming in from the field at least once every other hour. Emma assured him that he'd be the first (or second) to know when she went into labor, but Belinda noticed he looked fearful. It was no wonder after losing a wife and two children. She felt badly for him and smiled a lot when he was around, but truth be told, Belinda was as nervous as a bride on her wedding day. What if things went wrong? Who would take care of the children? How would Gabe handle it? Mercy, why did she have such thoughts?

Gabe removed the harnesses from the mules after he completed cultivating the last field for the day. All week, he'd worked extra hours to allow himself more time with Emma when her time came. Then he spotted the bishop, who was headed down the drive toward the barn. After greeting him, he offered him coffee, which the bishop turned down. The purpose of his call was to give permission for a cell phone. "I believe Emma's nearing her time and I don't see any harm in using cell-phones. I know you wouldn't get yourself one of those fancy ones that hook up with the Internet, but it might be wise to look into it, Gabe. I know you've been concerned."

"You're right, I have been. That's gut. I'll go in town today and purchase one. I suppose it's a temporary thing," he said, glancing over to see the bishop's response.

"Look, I know some bishops would be horrified, but I don't see any harm in it myself. I've prayed about it and haven't gotten any feedback from God, so I'm allowing it."

After he left, Gabe went into the house to tell Emma. If he hurried, he could be in Bird-in-Hand before the stores closed. When he entered the house, Emma and Belinda were rolling out cookie dough. After telling them what the bishop had said, he was prepared to leave when Emma let out a short cry. He turned to see her leaning over the counter, grabbing the edge to keep from falling.

"Honey, what is it?" he asked as he ran to her side and held her up.

"I think it's time. I've been getting pains all day. I just didn't want to say anything yet."

Gabe's stomach lurched and he feared he might kutz. "Belinda, Mervin is outside cleaning the chicken coop. Tell him to go get the midwife. He knows where she lives. Tell him to hurry."

Belinda nodded and left. He was sorry he had been so abrupt when he realized how frightened the young woman appeared, but he'd apologize later. Right now his concern was for Emma and his unborn child.

Chapter Twenty-Nine
Holmes County, Ohio

Carrie set the table, but since it was pizza night, there wasn't much to prepare. Paper napkins replaced the cloth ones. She filled a pitcher with root beer and added plastic glasses. They'd eat on the terrace tonight since the weather was perfect—conducive to grilling and picnics. She wished she'd planned something fun for the weekend since she had the next three days off. When she applied to waitress at the small restaurant just minutes from home, she didn't realize she'd have to work most weekends. That was the price she had to pay. She needed more clothing and though her parents would probably give the money to her, she wanted to be somewhat independent. With college starting in the fall, she'd need additions to her wardrobe.

Jeff came in with the mail. "You got a letter from Belinda. Can I read it when you're done?"

Carrie looked over at her brother and pushed her brows together. "Me thinkest my bro is enchanted by my Amish friend."

A blush went up his neck. "She's just a friend. Don't get carried away, Miss Romantic."

She laughed. "It's a losing proposition, Jeff. She'll never leave the Amish."

"I know that. Okay, I like her. Are you satisfied?"

"Just 'like'?"

"Just 'like'." He grinned over. "She's pretty cute, and sweet."

"And pure."

"Yeah. Nothing wrong with that, is there?" His eyes challenged hers.

"Not a thing. You may think I'm on the wild side, Jeff, but I'm really not. I believe in staying pure for my husband, too, you know."

"I'm glad to hear that. I confess, I thought you and Dan…"

"No. You're way off. I'm on to him—always have been. A girl's a fool to think he has any feelings besides, you know."

"Yeah, I sure do. Poor Belinda was his last target. Thank God I was there to step in."

"And she wasn't mad?"

"Of course not. She realized she was in over her head and I know she was glad I came in when I did."

"Jeff, don't let yourself get too enamored of Belinda. It wouldn't be fair to yourself, or her, for that matter. You guys are from two different worlds."

"I'm not so sure anymore. I've been talking to Joe about the Mennonite religion. A lot of it makes sense to me. They lead really good solid lives and they're strong believers."

"I don't know that much about it, but some of them still use buggies."

"Joe's parents are black car Mennonites."

"So they drive?"

"Yeah. A lot of their friends don't, but that's a personal decision."

"Huh. I guess that wouldn't be too hard then. You've always been different, Jeff. I think you could handle it. I'm too modern, I guess. I love my I-phone and clothes and stuff. I'd never be able to switch, but it doesn't mean I'm bad."

"I never said that, Carrie. I don't think you're bad. In fact, I'm pretty proud of my sister, if you want to know the truth."

"Jeffy, Jeffy, you'll always be my special brother. I love you." Carrie went over and gave her brother a huge hug. He patted her on the back.

"So since you have a job now, I guess we won't be going to Lancaster County any time soon," he said, taking a step back.

"I told you, her mother doesn't want us to go see her yet. You'll still be helping close up on market days, so you can go talk to her and find out when it will be okay to visit. I have a feeling they just want to keep her away from all of us. Personally, I think they're scared she'll leave the Amish."

He let out a long breath. "Maybe I'll pay her father a visit then. We get along real well. He's a super nice guy and smart. I learned a lot from him the day I stopped by. I'd love to have a farm like his."

"You're kidding! Do you know how hard those people work?"

"Well, yeah, but I'm not afraid of hard work. You think landscaping is a piece of cake?"

"No, but it's not like farming with mules, for Pete's sake."

"I think it would be rewarding to live off your own land and be self-sufficient."

"So convert to Amish."

He grinned. "You're tempting me."

"Kidding aside, I think you underestimate how hard it is."

"Perhaps. Anyway, I'm thinking about college in the fall. I'd take courses in the business end of landscaping. I'd like my own place someday."

"So you're not ready to throw out your Ohio State sweatshirt yet for suspenders?"

Jeff laughed and soft-punched his sister's arm. "Okay, you win. I'm still English."

"But not for long?" She questioned him with her eyes.

"We'll see. Now I'll go pick up the pizza. Call the family." He headed out to his car and pushed thoughts of Belinda from his mind. Or tried to.

Lancaster County, Pennsylvania

Gabe helped Emma up to their bedroom, pulled the top sheet and quilt off the bed and threw them over the rocker in the corner. Emma sat on the edge of the bed and panted while another contraction washed over her. Gabe sat next to her and placed an arm around her shoulders. She reached for his other hand. After the contraction passed, she tried to reassure him. "I'll be fine, honey. Please try not to worry. Women do this kind of thing all the time."

He let out a sigh. "But this is your first. Are you in terrible pain?"

"Nee. It's bearable. Do you want to be here with me when the time comes?"

"Of course, if you want me here."

"I think so. Oh, here comes another." She gripped his hand and blew out the short quick breaths her mid-wife had shown her. After a few moments, it subsided. "Gabe, get the receiving blankets from the top drawer of my dresser and lay them out." Then she asked about the children.

"Belinda will watch them, honey," he assured her as he retrieved the blankets and laid them at the foot of the bed. "Please don't worry about anything."

"I'm glad she's here, Gabe. She can be a big help once the boppli arrives."

"That's true. I'm surprised my sister had so much trouble with her. She seems so pleasant and easy to get along with."

"I know, but of course, we're not her parents."

"Jah. It makes a big difference. Should I be writing down the pains, Emma?"

"Oh, I guess. Here comes another one. They're getting stronger. I hope my mid-wife gets here soon."

"Jah, me, too. The last one was only a couple minutes ago." He held on to her hand, which she gripped with more strength than he thought she had, while he checked the clock on the dresser.

Emma's face contorted as the contraction grew in intensity and her eyes were squeezed shut. Gabe recalled watching his first wife go through labor and childbirth and knew it was only beginning. He was glad he was a man.

After a half hour passed, they realized the contractions were only about two minutes apart. Not only that, they were stronger in force each time. Emma told Gabe to run for a cleaning bucket since she felt she was about to vomit. He raced back with it just in time and held her head while she retched. Then he heard the front door open. Moments later the midwife, Mrs. Horner, appeared with her bag, along with a white-faced boy—eyes wide with fear. Gabe tried to reassure Mervin, telling him everything would be fine. "Go tend to the horse, sohn. You might want to stay outside for a while. It might get scary for you here. It'll take a while."

"Jah. See you. Gut luck, Mamm." He made a beeline for the stairs and they heard him tripping down the steps two at a time. Emma managed a slight smile since she was between pains.

"If you want to step out for a minute Gabe, I'll examine Emma and see how far along she is."

He went out in the hall and paced back and forth. He heard Emma groan and then let out a long piercing cry followed by the wail of a newborn. My goodness, that was fast, especially for her first. Relief flooded over him as he ran through the door.

"I didn't even have time to examine her. Look you have a new dochder," Mrs. Horner said, grinning. Gabe dropped on his knees by Emma's pillow. "First I must check my darling fraa," he said, his voice cracking from emotion.

"I'm okay, Gabe," she said weakly. "Can you bring our dochder to me so we can see her together?"

Mrs. Horner smiled over at the couple. "Not quite yet, Emma. I need to cut the umbilical cord first. I'm waiting for the afterbirth and I'm going to press on your abdomen to help it along. It may hurt a little."

"It can't be as bad as it was," Emma said, looking over through her tears of joy.

"Oh my!"

"What? What's wrong?" Gabe's face blanched as he rose from his position and took a quick step toward the foot of the bed.

"Nothing's wrong, but…"

Emma let out a wail. "Oh, I need to push again. What's going on? Oh, dear heaven, it hurts so bad," she continued.

"I think you are about to have another boppli," the mid-wife said, smiling while she leaned over to assist in the second birth. "Ah, it's another girl," she said as the baby slipped into her waiting hands.

Gabe let out a laugh and shook his head. "I'll be. Look at those little sweethearts. Two, just like their mudder. Thank you, God."

Emma's mouth dropped open while she absorbed this new information. There were now two babies crying with high-pitched voices.

"I could use a little help here, Gabe. Boppli one is ready to be held. Take her and wrap her in one of the receiving blankets I see at the foot of the bed while I take care of your second dochder."

Gabe picked up his red, screaming infant, arms and legs flailing, and placed her gently on the soft white flannel blanket and then covered her before lifting her back in his arms. "She's beautiful. Just like you, Emma." He brought her over and placed her in Emma's waiting arms.

"I can't believe we have twins," she said, drained from her labor. "Oh my, look at her dear little fingers." Emma touched her daughter's hand with her own finger. She even has a little hair."

"Not much, though. I don't think you'll be braiding it for awhile," he said, grinning.

"Gabe, we don't even have two girls' names picked out."

"Well, you wanted Deborah and I wanted Miriam. So now we each get our wish," Gabe said, smiling.

"You're right. I can't wait to hold my other boppli," Emma said, glancing over at the midwife, who was separating the second baby from the afterbirth. Finally, she laid her on a second blanket, swaddled her gently and handed her over to the father. Gabe was amazed at how quickly the baby settled down once wrapped in the warm blanket.

"Jah, she's a beauty, too. In fact, I can't tell them apart," he said, laughing, while he headed to the other side of the bed to place his second daughter in Emma's free arm. The first baby had settled down and it was now quiet in the room.

"My goodness," Mrs. Horner said, "I never guessed you had two in there. I never heard the second heartbeat. No wonder you were so large. I need to weigh them soon and clean them up a bit, but I'll let you enjoy this time first. I have to wash up in the bathroom, Emma. I'll return in a minute. You did gut, that's for sure."

Emma nodded and kissed the top of each of their heads. She looked up at Gabe, smiling through glassy eyes. "I can't believe it! Two!"

"Jah, quite a surprise. Wait till the kinner hear they have two siblings to play with."

"I hope Mervin won't be disappointed to have two more sisters."

Gabe laughed. "He may press us to try again," he said with a wink.

"I think we can wait a little while for more."

Belinda came to the bedroom door and knocked, though it was open. "I just heard! You had twins! My goodness, what a surprise," she said as she peeked over to the bed.

"Come on over and look. They're asleep now, but it won't be long before you hear them cry," Emma said, proudly.

"Oh, they are adorable," Belinda said softly. "Look how tiny they are." She touched the first one's cheek. "Her coloring is so gut."

"They will get cleaned up better soon. We just wanted to hold them first," Gabe said, smiling over.

"Lizzy is downstairs waiting with Mervin. Let me know when they can come up to see the new boppli," Belinda said.

"Give us a few minutes to get them weighed and washed up and then we'll call them. Gabe will come down when it's time."

"Gut idea. I'll go back now. We were just going to have a snack when we heard the first one cry. I thought it would be hours, so I brought them inside for cookies and milk."

"Jah, it happened fast," Emma said. "I must be made for this."

"I believe we are," Belinda said with a shy smile. "I can't wait."

"It's pretty exciting, that's for sure and for certain," Emma said with a nod.

God had doubled their blessing.

Chapter Thirty
Lancaster County, Pennsylvania

Lizzy sat spellbound, watching her new sisters while they slept in her mother's arms. Gabe put his arm around her and kissed the top of her head. "What do you think, Lizzy? Should we keep them?"

"Wow, they're so tiny."

Emma nodded. "They only weigh about five pounds each. Like that bag of oranges we bought last week."

"Can they see?"

"Not too clearly, yet," Emma said.

"Are they going to sleep all the time?"

Gabe laughed. "We hope so."

"Nee," Emma said, shaking her head. "They'll wake up every couple hours to eat."

"Even in the nighttime?"

"Jah, even then. They need to get bigger and they'll need lots of milk."

Lizzy smiled and tilted her head. "They look just the same. How will I know who is who?"

"That is going to be a problem at first," Emma answered. "I may have to tie a little ribbon on one, so we'll know the difference."

"Where is Mervin?" Gabe asked his daughter. "I thought he wanted to see his new sisters."

"His hands still looked dirty, so Belinda told him to scrub them again."

"Oh, gut idea. Jah, we don't want germs. The boppli are too little for much company, too," Gabe said. Turning back to Emma, he told her Mervin was going to take the open carriage and make the rounds of the family and neighbors. "You can expect a crowd tomorrow, Emma. Everyone will want to meet our new family."

"We have to watch all the kinner, though. Mrs. Horner warned me to keep them away from the boppli for awhile. Kinner carry a lot of germs."

"We'll make sure they stay a safe distance."

"Of course the adults can help hold them, as long as they don't feel sick."

"You'll need help, Emma, for quite a while. Twins can be a handful."

"I'm glad Belinda's here, even more so now that there are two to take care of."

Mervin knocked at the door and then came in to see the babies. His grin spread across his entire face. "Wow, they're cute. Man, was I ever that small, Daed?"

"Nee. You were nine pounds when you were born. But they'll grow fast, don't you worry."

"How do you feel, Mamm?"

"Pretty gut, considering. The boppli came real quick."

"I know. I couldn't believe it. I went out to work and boom!"

Gabe grinned. "I guess the gut Lord wants us to have a big family, that's for certain."

Emma smiled and laid back against the pillows. She was so glad the waiting was over. So now she had four kinner to love. There was no end to her joy. *Danki, Jesus. Danki.*

Holmes County, Ohio

"I hear a car coming up the drive, Jed," Grace remarked while she and her husband sat on the back porch after their supper. Jed leaned over to observe a car crawling almost silently toward the side of the house. "Looks like that young English fellow who's friends with our Belinda," he said, standing up. "I'll go see what the boy wants."

"We can offer him some lemonade," Grace said.

"We'll see. I'll offer him some, if it seems the right thing to do." Jed adjusted his straw hat as he walked over to the parked car.

"Hello, Mr. Glick," Jeff said after he got out and walked over to shake his hand.

Jed received it and shook it firmly. Jah, he liked the man's grasp. "So what brings you to this part of the woods?" Jed asked with a smile.

"Just wanted to see how that blue spruce was doing?"

"Think we got it in time. Come back with me and I'll show you."

"So you treated it for the needle cast?"

"Yep. I pruned it real gut and then sprayed it with the stuff you told me about. The fungal spray."

They walked behind the barn where Gideon and a friend were practicing their pitching. Jeff caught one of the fly balls and threw it over to Gideon with a grin. "Nice pitch, Gideon."

"Danki. Wanna play?"

"Maybe another time, thanks."

Jed smiled over at the two boys, reminiscing about his youth. He'd been a pretty fair pitcher himself. He should take more time to play with his son. Before you knew it, he'd be off and married.

They came up to the large spruce and stood back to examine it. "You won't know for awhile if it's going to make it, but it looks better than it did."

"Glad you told me about it before I lost it. It's a beauty. My daed planted it when I was a boy."

"It's a great tree." They stood a couple of minutes watching the boys and then headed toward the house.

"My wife made fresh lemonade. You're welcome to join us on the porch."

"Sounds good. I worked all day in the sun and I feel sort of dehydrated even though I bet I drank a couple gallons of water."

Grace greeted him and not only poured him a tall glass of lemonade with fresh mint, but added a plate of ginger snaps to the table.

Jeff helped himself to two of them as Nellie came out to join them. She gave him a huge smile, poured herself a glass of lemonade and sat on the steps.

"Have you heard from Belinda?" Jeff asked.

"Jah, we finally got a letter today. It was short. I guess they keep her pretty busy. Seems her aenti gave birth to twin girls a couple days ago."

"Oh, wow. I guess she is busy. They don't have automatic washers, do they?"

"Nee," Grace said, smiling. "They do have a wringer washer though run by a generator. It helps, but they still have to feed the clothes."

"And hang them out," Jed added. "Our Belinda will get lots of experience child rearing, I'm thinking."

Jeff laughed and shook his head. "She may never want to marry after this experience."

"Oh my, that would be a shame," Nellie said, frowning. "I wish I could go and help. I love boppli."

"I just found out your cousin, Elizabeth, is expecting, Nellie. Maybe you can help her when the time comes."

"That would be ever so nice," Nellie said, finding her smile again.

"Belinda asked if we'd seen you and Carrie," Grace said, reaching for a cookie.

Jeff's face lit up like a fourth of July sky. "Really? Well, say hello to her for me next time you write."

"Why don't you write her yourself?" Jed said, startling his wife. She never expected to hear those words from his lips. Her frown spoke of her disapproval.

"Well, yeah, I'd like to very much. Belinda and my sister write to each other," he said.

"That's gut. It probably helps her with her homesickness. Have some more lemonade, Jeff," Jed added. "Grace, pour the young man some more. He's been working in the sun all day."

Grace nodded and poured him a fresh glass. They talked about the lack of rain and the weather front that was headed their way. Then they discussed the size of the corn and the soybeans and just about everything else about the crops. Jeff also mentioned attending the Mennonite Church on Sunday with his friend.

"We know lots of Mennonites who go to that church," Grace said. "Gut people, like the Amish. Most of them anyway."

"Well Grace, not all Amish are gut. That's for sure."

"We have a few who I'm not too fond of, but on the most part, they're wonderful people."

"How do your folks feel about you going to the Mennonite service?" Jed asked.

"They're fine with it. They're pretty liberal."

Jed nodded. "What about your sister? Does she attend with you?"

"Not yet, but she mentioned she might go next week."

"It would be gut for her to learn about their ways," Grace said, nodding her approval.

"I guess now that the boppli are here, we should make plans to visit," Jed said while he poured a fresh glass of lemonade in his own glass.

"Not right away, Jed. Give the poor girl a chance to recover. The last thing she needs now is company."

"I guess you're right."

"Well, I'm headed for the shower. I'm filthy from mulching all afternoon. I hope I didn't get your wicker chair dirty." Jeff rose and brushed off a couple small leaves, which had stuck to his trousers.

"That's all right. We can hose them down if they get dirty, but they look just fine to me," Jed said. He walked Jeff to his car and patted his arm. "Jah, it might be nice for our Belinda to hear from some of her friends. It's hard on the girl to be away from everyone."

"Thank you, sir. I would like to write. There aren't many girls out there with the values your daughter has."

"I'm glad to hear she stood by those values."

"Yes, sir, she did." He didn't mention the fact that he had to rescue her. "I know she was shy about wearing some of the clothes my sister loaned her. I don't know why Carrie did that. I guess girls today don't realize how men react to clothing."

"Oh, jah, you're right about that. You see why we like our ladies in proper dresses."

"I do and I like to see girls in pretty dresses, too. They're a lot more feminine."

"They are indeed. Come back and see me soon. You need to keep an eye on that tree for me. I didn't even notice the poor thing was sick." He grinned and his blonde beard stuck forward.

After Jeff left, Jed headed over to the field where his son was practicing and they had a three-way catch. Pretty soon Grace and Nellie joined in and they played until it got too dark to catch the ball in time. A nice way to end a beautiful June day.

194

Chapter Thirty-One
Lancaster County, Pennsylvania

On day two of Deborah and Miriam's life in the outside world, family and friends began stopping by to meet the new boppli and leave off gifts and food for the family. When Emma's parents, Mary and Leroy arrived, they brought Katie and Wayne along. After spending a few minutes with the whole group, Wayne went into the kitchen and helped himself to a glass of water. Belinda was cleaning up from breakfast and rinsing dishes at the sink. She stopped and ran the cold water for Wayne. He smiled at her and she took note again of his good looks.

"I bet you're busy, Belinda, now with all this going on."

"Jah, I can't believe it. Twins! And she didn't even suspect it."

"They're pretty small. I'd be scared to hold them."

"I was timid at first, too, but they're not as delicate as you think."

"Can you tell them apart?"

"Nee, though Emma's tied a little ribbon on the ankle of Deborah, who was the first one born. Maybe once they get a little older, it will be easier to identify them."

"Gabe said they're identical."

"Oh, jah, you can sure see that," Belinda grinned over while she went back to rinse the dishes. "You have a big family, all right."

"All Amish have big families. Don't you?"

"I guess, but they're more spread out. In fact, some of my uncles live in Colorado now. It's a small community—only about two hundred. I want to go out someday. They say the mountains are beautiful."

"I'd like to travel more, too, before getting married and all."

"Jah, well, I guess you and Becky are making plans?"

"Nee. Why would you say that? I bet my schwester, Katie, told you that."

"I guess I just assumed since you two go together."

Wayne let out a long breath. "I was afraid of that happening. As soon as you go to a couple Sings with a girl, everyone starts talking. There's nothing official, believe me."

"Sounds like you don't really like her that much." Belinda's heart palpitated rapidly. She wiped her hands on a tea towel and turned toward Wayne.

"I like her all right, but I don't think I love her. Maybe I will, but I don't want to be pushed. You know what I mean?"

She nodded.

"Do you have a steady at home?"

"Nee."

"Why did you leave, Belinda?"

"I didn't want to, but my folks were unhappy with my friends, so they thought I needed a change."

"Has it helped? Are you still planning to see the same people when you go back home?"

She shrugged. "Depends."

"On?"

Belinda let out a laugh. "Goodness, lots of things. Maybe I'll meet someone here and stay on."

Wayne's grin was adorable. His bare chin dimpled and his eyes sparkled. Hmm. Looked like there might be something here.

Katie walked into the kitchen with some coffee mugs to be rinsed. She looked from her brother to Belinda and her expression was as sour as the lemons they squeezed for juice.

Belinda stepped back from Wayne, who had been inching his way closer to her while they spoke. "So, how do you like your new nieces?" she asked Katie, hoping she hadn't read too much into her expression.

"Ever so cute. Wayne, did you see them?"

"Oh, jah, I stayed a couple minutes. Boppli kinda scare me when they're that little."

"Mmm. I guess I'll wash these mugs up, Belinda, if you'll let me through to the sink."

"Oh, you can leave them on the drain. I'm on KP today."

"KP?"

"It's a military expression I heard from my English friends. It stands for kitchen patrol."

"Oh." Katie set the mugs on the drain and stood silently.

"Well, I guess I'll go check in the barn for Mervin," Wayne remarked.

"I'll go with you, Wayne," Belinda said, anxious to escape the scrutiny. Besides, she had every right to talk to Wayne since he wasn't really involved with Becky at all. It was probably something imaginary that Katie and Becky had dreamed up. As far as she was concerned, he was open season.

Wayne's face lit up again and he steered Belinda past his glaring sister, toward the back door and they headed for the horse stalls. Once they got there, Belinda patted her favorite horse on the head between the ears. "I think Katie was mad."

"Jah, probably. She should mind her own business."

Belinda nodded though she continued to give the horse her full attention. She could feel his eyes upon her and it was exciting to realize the effect she had over him.

"Think you'll stay on here for awhile?" he asked leaning against the half door to the stall, looking directly at her.

She turned. "As long as Emma needs me and my parents are still mad."

"What did you do to upset them so much?"

"I guess it was when I sneaked out at night to go to English parties."

Wayne laughed with a hearty voice. "Whoa! You're quite spunky for an Amish girl."

Belinda knew she was blushing from the heat she felt rising in her neck. "They weren't bad parties. No drugs or stuff like that."

"Booze?"

"A little, but I only drank too much, once."

He laughed again. "Tell me about it."

"I shouldn't. Oh, well, why not. Someone had spiked the punch and I didn't realize how much was in it. I was real thirsty so I kept drinking it. Then a guy, who thought he was a gift to the world, tried to get me totally drunk."

"So he could take advantage of you, I bet."

"Exactly, but thank goodness someone came in to rescue me."

Wayne shook his head. "You take your chances with some of the English. They don't think the same way we do about some things."

"So I figured out."

"You shouldn't go out with English guys. They're all the same. Amish are safer."

"I met one who's different. He's my best friend's brother and he's the one who kept his eye on me and saved me from that jerk."

"Maybe he likes you, too."

"I doubt it. He wants to have his own business and he has a car and all."

"So, you don't fancy him?"

"I like him, but that's all."

"It must seem boring here now."

"I'm too busy to think about it, Wayne. It's not my choice to be here, though everyone's been real nice to me."

"We have a gut family. I'd never leave Amish to live anywhere else. I'll take over the farm someday, but I hope it's a long way off. My parents mean the world to me."

"That's gut. And one day you'll meet the right maed to marry."

"Hope so. Maybe I know her already."

Belinda knew without looking at him who he was considering. My goodness, the men worked quickly around here. She loved flirting, but she didn't want to hurt anyone by letting them become serious about her. Not yet, anyway.

"Perhaps," she said, matter-of-factly. "Let's walk a little. I'm tired of being in the house. The only time I get out is to work in the garden or hang clothes."

They meandered over to the cornfield and walked along the edge. The sun felt good on her back and she pictured herself in shorts and a halter. What fun that would be. After walking along two edges they came to a border tree, which offered some shade from the heat.

"Let's relax before we go back," Wayne said, pointing toward the ground. "Belinda sat down and covered her legs with her skirt, hugging them with her arms. She looked up at the clouds and pointed out a storm cloud on the horizon.

He sat down beside her, but far enough to get a full view. "Tell me about yourself," Belinda said, looking over with her sweetest smile reserved for young men.

"Ain't much to tell. I finished school and I help my daed. I like farming, though, so I'll stick with that. My older brother works at a buggy shop, but he still has enough land to grow his own food and raise a few animals. He seems satisfied, but I wouldn't want to be inside so much. Everyone is different."

"Jah, true. Like my older sister. She was just fine being so gut all the time. She never gave my parents any trouble. Not like me, I'm afraid. I can't help it. I like to have fun."

"Think you'll settle down someday?"

"Probably. You can't party your whole life away. Have you been baptized yet, Wayne?"

"Nee. I'm too young. I need to be sure and certain before that. Katie's taking instruction this summer and so is Josiah. It hasn't been announced yet, but they're planning to marry in November."

"I know. Josiah seems nice."

"He gets along gut with everyone. He had a case on my other two schwesters first."

"I heard. So the Zook sisters were popular."

"I guess you could say that."

"They're all real pretty," she said, leaning back on her elbows.

"Not as pretty as you," Wayne said after he took the same position next to her and looked over.

"Danki, but it's not true."

"I can argue that."

Belinda laughed. "This area looks just like Ohio. Sometimes I forget I'm not at home."

"Are you homesick?"

"I guess so, but I'm getting over it."

"Could you ever be happy to stay here in Pennsylvania?"

"I don't know. I'd miss my family, but…"

"Even though they made you leave?"

"I know they thought they were doing the best thing for me. They care a lot, you know."

"I'm sure. Jah, it was probably hard for them to send you here."

"I get letters all the time from home."

"And from guys back there?"

"Once in a while my bruder writes a few words. Pretty much, he and my daed leave the writing to Nellie and my mamm."

"Jah, I don't like writing that much either. But if you go home, I'll write to you, if you promise to write back."

"I would. At least until I get married."

"Mmm."

"We'd better get back. Emma may need something."

"With everyone around, I'm sure she has all the help she needs."

"Well, I'm hungry anyway. I didn't eat much today."

"Okay, let's head back. Danki for walking with me."

"Anytime, Wayne."

"I'll take you up on that."

He rose first and then reached for her hand and helped her to her feet. She had a strong feeling that he wanted to kiss her, but she made sure she never got that close to him. Jah, he was good-looking enough and nice and all, but no fireworks. Not a one.

Belinda was amazed at how much attention the twins required of Emma. It seemed she was always nursing one or the other. They slept nearly the entire time in between feedings. During the day, Belinda helped by changing their diapers and keeping up with the laundry. At first Lizzy was in constant attendance, but her excitement tapered off at the routine and she spent most of her time playing with her friend from the next farm. Mervin and Gabe worked together on the acreage and with the animals, but during the hottest part of the day, Mervin took off to be with his friends while Gabe spent time with Emma and his new daughters. His devotion to his family was evident in his complete attention to their well-being. Belinda prayed one day she would have that kind of love from her husband.

Though most of their needs were met without leaving the farm, occasionally, purchases needed to be made. Belinda was given the responsibility to go into town when the list was long enough to warrant it. One Monday early in July, she took the open buggy and made her way to Bird-in-Hand. She tethered the horse and went into the general store to purchase thread and yarn. Then she went into a pharmacy to get a prescription filled for Emma, who needed an ointment for her sore breasts. While she waited for it to be filled, she took a walk around the town and then sat on a bench. An English teenager, a girl with freckles and bright red hair, sat down next to her.

"I'm beat. I walked all the way from my house, just to mail a package," the girl said while she removed a sandal and rubbed her foot. "Look, now I've got a blister."

Belinda looked down at the open weeping sore and clucked her tongue. "I bet it really hurts."

"Sure does. So do you live here?" The girl opened up a pack of gum and offered a stick to Belinda, who took one and unwrapped it.

"I'm from Ohio, but I'm staying with an aunt and uncle nearby."

They proceeded to discuss the reasons for Belinda's moving temporarily to Pennsylvania. Belinda told her about her English friends and the parties.

"People should understand you need to get out and party when you're our age," the girl, who introduced herself as Dawn Staples, remarked. It turned out they lived only about a mile apart. They spent over an hour talking and by the time Belinda decided she should head home before someone worried, they had exchanged names and Dawn had written down her phone number. "Call anytime. We have something going on every weekend. You can even come in your regular clothing. We're used to the Amish around here and I have lots of Amish friends."

"Actually, I sneaked in some jeans and a top when I packed, just in case I had a chance to go English."

"Great! Either way. So, do you ever get near a phone?"

"Oh, jah, but I can always find an excuse to stop by your place. Put the directions on the paper you gave me."

She did and Belinda saw it would be easy to follow, since they lived so close.

After they parted, Belinda went back to pick up Emma's prescription and then headed home. As she expected, they had grown concerned. Gabe commented on the need to have a cell-phone and planned to purchase one the next day.

Emma's mother, Mary, had stopped by and after Belinda washed up, they made supper together. Due to a persistent cough,

Emma's mother stayed away from the babies. One couldn't take a chance with new boppli, especially little ones like Emma's.

The paper remained in Belinda's pocket, but she was elated to have the prospects of a little excitement in her life again. Unwanted, was the realization she was going behind the backs of people she cared about once again. She'd just have to disregard the guilt. After all, she just wanted to have some fun. What harm was there in that?

Holmes County, Ohio

"Gabe wrote a nice letter, Jed," Grace said after she sat down to do some of her mending after supper.

Jed looked up from his newspaper and smiled. "Jah? How are the twins doing?"

"Gut, from what he said. They are asking us to come for a visit. What do you think? Can we get a driver for next weekend? I know Reuben would look after things for us."

"Jah, if that's what you want. Better not tell Nellie and Gideon until we make sure we're going to get there. Especially Nellie. She's been begging us to go."

"I think she misses Belinda more than we realize."

"And you, Grace? Has it been hard on you, too?" Jed's eyes met his wife's and she swallowed to keep the tears from flowing.

She nodded. "It is hard. I just hope she's behaving herself. At least Gabe seems pleased with her conduct."

"Well then, why worry about it? Maybe she'll be ready to come home once Emma can handle things alone. She has lots of family nearby, so I'm sure they will all pitch in after Belinda comes home."

"Jah, that's for sure. So will you try to reach our driver? Maybe we can stay two or three nights. I don't want to be a burden."

"I'll check with the driver tomorrow when we go to market. Jah, I miss my dochder, too. It would be gut to see her again."

"Remember not a word to the kinner till we're sure." Grace tucked the rest of her mending back in the basket by the stove and headed for bed. It had been a long day, and hot. July was not her favorite month.

Chapter Thirty-Two
Lancaster County, Pennsylvania

Gabe showed everyone in the family how to use their new cell phones. They would always keep one at home and the other would be used by any member of the family if they traveled away from the farm. Belinda had used phones a few times, but she watched while Gabe entered the few numbers he needed. It would be useful when she wanted to get in touch with her new friend, Dawn. If her aunt and uncle were cool, they'd allow her to see her friends without her having to sneak around. Perhaps she'd mention meeting Dawn first and watch their reaction. It bothered her to think she'd need to be sneaky in order to attend parties at her new friend's, so if she could be in the open about it, so much the better. One thing was for certain; she would love to party again. This time she'd avoid all alcohol. Way too dangerous.

"I'm going to talk to your daed this afternoon," Gabe said to Belinda. "We got a letter setting up the time for our conversation. He said he'd go to his friend's barn to talk. I guess we may as well tell you, we're trying to set up a date for your family to visit." He smiled over at Belinda, who gave a gasp of excitement at the prospect.

"Oh, that would be so gut to see them again. Do you have room here for all four of them?"

"Actually, my parents have offered to put them up for a few days," said Emma. "We thought they'd sleep better there since the twins are up so much at night. They also have a couple extra bedrooms."

"Would it be soon?" The thought passed through her head that they might expect her to return already. Now that she had met Dawn and had the attention of a handsome young Amish man, she wasn't sure she wanted to return quite yet. After all, her feelings could change overnight about Wayne. Goodness, what would she tell them if they asked her to return?

"We're thinking late July," Emma said. "It's too hot to work outside much and it would be easier to take time off then."

"You still need me though, right?"

Emma looked over and smiled, "Of course. I'd hate to see you leave already, but I'm not going to stand in your way. I know how anxious you are to return home to your family."

"Well, I want to make sure you have enough help before I leave. I like it here, too. It's almost like Ohio with all the pretty trees and hills."

"I'm going to leave the decision totally up to you and your parents, Belinda. I could be selfish and beg them to leave you here longer, but that wouldn't be fair. We'll just wait and see what they have in mind."

Later, while Belinda helped bathe the twins, she broached the subject of her new friend. "I met a nice English girl who lives just about a mile from here."

Emma looked up as she lifted little Miriam from the portable tub sitting in the kitchen sink. She wrapped her in a large baby towel. "How did you meet her?"

"When I went in town last week. We sat together and talked over an hour while I waited for your medicine. She's real nice, not like some English I've met. I was just wondering if you'd mind if I walked over to see her later, once the clothes are hung out to dry. I'll still be home to make dinner."

"I guess that's okay. What's her name?"

"Dawn Staples."

"I know the Staples' house. It's an old farmhouse. My cousin farms the land and pays them for it."

"Do you know the family?"

"I've seen them and waved when we've passed on our way to my cousins. I don't know anything about them, but I guess it would be all right for you to go for a couple hours. I think we should meet the girl, too. Maybe she can come back with you and have supper with us."

"I can ask her. Could I use the phone to call her first? She gave me her number."

"Jah. The phone's on the mantle in the sitting room. Belinda, you'll be real careful, won't you? You're our responsibility right now and…"

"Don't worry, Aenti Emma. I learned my lesson. I just like to be with the English sometimes and listen to their music and all."

Emma nodded. "I'll talk to your onkel first, before you call. Here take Miriam for me, please, and put her in the crib. She's fallen asleep already. I hear Deborah, so you may as well bring her down and I'll give her a bath before I feed her."

"Come to your cousin, little one," Belinda said when the handover took place. She snuggled Miriam in her arms and kissed the top of her head. She smelled so fresh and clean from Ivory soap and she yearned to one day have her own boppli to love. Nee, not quite yet. Fun first.

Holmes County, Ohio

"It's all set. I got Mr. Dickens to drive us to Pennsylvania this Saturday and Gabe's gonna make arrangements for us to stay at his in-laws. We'll stay until Tuesday." Jed watched Nellie as she clapped her hands.

"I can't wait! Is Belinda gonna be surprised?"

"I don't know if they'll tell her ahead or not. We didn't talk about that. So we have to be ready by six in the morning. It's a long drive."

Grace grinned over at her husband. "It will be so nice to see my bruder and his new family, too. Did he sound excited?"

"Jah, he did. He can't wait to show off his new boppli. He claims they look just like his *fraa*."

"What should we take for the twins?" Grace asked.

"Goodness, I have no idea. Maybe you'll find something tomorrow at market."

"I'll look around. Maybe something for Emma. They probably have all they need for the twins by now."

"Mamm, Carrie's mudder might have something for her. I know she makes her own soap for babies."

"Gut idea. I'll ask her. Now, let's get supper started.

"I have to check the new lambs," Jed remarked. "The one was sluggish earlier. I hope they both make it. Call me when supper is ready."

Wednesday, when there was a break in the late afternoon, Nellie spotted Carrie when she arrived at the marketplace. Nellie went over to their stand and they chatted a few minutes. Then Nellie told them about their planned trip to Lancaster. Carrie asked her if she would write down her phone number and give it to Belinda when they got there because she wanted to talk to her about one of their mutual friends who was getting married.

After writing it down, Nellie went back and relieved her mother, who went over and picked out some gifts. When she returned, she showed Nellie her purchases. She had bought several bars of soap and lotions for dry skin. She also had found a vitamin for nursing mothers, which was supposed to increase supply. "With two, she needs all the help she can get," she said with a smile.

Once they returned to the house, Jed helped them unload the unsold produce. Nellie checked over the clothes she wished to take on the trip and began to make a pile on her chair. She couldn't remember ever going away for three whole days. This was going to be exciting.

Chapter Thirty-Three
Holmes County, Ohio

Nellie walked back and forth along the drive. It was nearly six o'clock and the driver was due to arrive any moment. At last a green car came rolling along the road and turned down the driveway toward the house, but instead of Mr. Dickens, a woman got out of the car. She was in her mid forties. Her eyes were downcast as she walked toward the house. When she spotted Nellie, she quickened her pace. "Hello, is this the Glick's house?"

"Jah."

"Is your mother or father nearby?"

"Jah, but we're going on a trip, all the way to Pennsylvania."

"That's why I'm here, I'm afraid."

With this, Jed came out the door carrying two suitcases. He nodded and looked over at the woman.

"Mr. Glick?"

"Jah," he said, his mouth twitching slightly.

"I'm Mrs. Dickens, Tom's wife. I'm afraid Tom can't drive you today. He spent the night vomiting and I had to end up taking him to the hospital. They're doing tests as we speak, but I wanted to let you know right away. I actually called a friend to see if he could take over for Tom, but he already has a job. I'm so sorry."

"That's okay. You couldn't help sickness," Jed said. "I'm sorry to hear about your husband. Please send him my best. We can go another time, that's for sure."

She headed for her car and nodded. "Yes, when he's better, he'll come by and you can make arrangements. I have to get back to him now."

"Danki for coming to tell us. We'll say a prayer for your husband."

"Thanks so much." She took off and when she got to the road, she increased her speed.

Nellie burst into tears. "What are we going to do, Daed?"

"What can we do, Nellie? We'll just have to postpone our plans."

"I can't believe it. I'm all packed and everything."

Gideon came out the door, carrying pillows and a bag with food for the trip. When he saw his sister crying, he gaped and looked over at his father. "What's wrong with Nellie?"

"Our driver had to cancel and she's upset."

"Can't we find someone else?"

"The other driver we've used ain't available."

"Daed," Nellie stopped crying and pulled at her father's sleeve. "What about Carrie's brother, Jeff. He drives and he said he wanted to go see Belinda anyway, remember?"

"Jah, true. I don't know where he lives."

"I do and anyway we have their phone number."

"Jah? Maybe I can go next door and use their phone. I'll check with Mamm and see what she thinks." He walked quickly toward the house while Nellie and Gideon stood and waited. It was agreed upon and their father rode over to the neighbors to make the call. When he returned, he nodded to his waiting family. "He said he can be here within a half hour. He sounded excited himself."

"I think he likes Belinda," Nellie said.

"As a friend," her father said. "It can't be more."

Lancaster County, Pennsylvania

Everything was set for the arrival of Belinda's family. Mary decided she'd use the vacant dawdi haus for them. The bedroom had twin beds and room for a cot, plus the sofa in the small living room opened up into a bed. That way they'd have their privacy and be right next-door for meals. It would make it easier on Mary, too, since her cough was draining her and she had scant energy. Her family was after her to see a doctor, but she hated to spend the money. Finally she relented and Leroy made her promise to make an appointment after her guests left on Tuesday.

Oma seemed pleased to hear she'd be meeting Gabe's sister, Grace, and the rest of the extended family. Perhaps it would help occupy her mind now that her sweet soul mate was no longer there for her.

Mary missed her daed more than she had thought possible. He'd always been there for her and his love for his family had been a constant blessing.

Katie and Mary planned the meals and Katie took over the baking for her mother. She made marvelous piecrust and since they expected family to stop by to greet Belinda's parents, she baked off three blueberry and three shoofly pies, in addition to more brownies, her specialty. Josiah planned to take the weekend off from work so he could be part of the celebration. He appeared around noon and helped set up the cot, and then he and Katie stocked the small refrigerator and cupboards with snack food for the expected guests. Katie's heart fluttered when he kissed her once when no one was around. She counted the weeks now till their secret wedding date.

First she and Josiah planned to take their kneeling vows. Her grandmother still required her attention, but since she no longer taught school, Katie found time to take the required instruction. Becky would be the head teacher in the fall, and Katie was confident she could handle things, perhaps with one aide by her side.

After spending the morning doing the wash, Belinda kept a watch out the front window while she dusted the living room furniture. Her family was expected to arrive sometime in the mid afternoon. They had estimated the trip to be about three hundred and fifty miles. Since it was all highway driving, they figured on arriving around two o'clock, but it was already half past. *Please keep them safe on the road, Father.*

Lizzy was the most excited of all, and entertained the family by singing every song she knew and dancing around the house. She helped Emma dress the twins in little dresses for the big occasion while Merv and Gabe caught up with the farm work.

Supper was going to be at their house the first night, so Belinda made potato salad. Emma had jars of hard-boiled eggs in beet juice already jarred—a favorite of her father's. Her mother was bringing meat loaf and cold cuts. They planned to keep the meal simple and concentrate on socializing.

At last, Belinda heard a car on the gravel drive and she ran out to greet her family. Nellie ran over first and grabbed Belinda. They hugged for several moments and then Grace and Jed took turns embracing their daughter. Gideon even managed a brotherly hug.

Gabe and his group came out of the house to greet them also. After the driver emerged, Belinda's mouth dropped open. Mercy, it was Jeff! He laughed when he saw her expression and then came over and put his hand out for a handshake. She extended her hand while her father explained what happened.

"Couldn't Carrie come?" Belinda looked over at Jeff.

"It was last minute and she had to work tonight at the restaurant. She wanted to, but there wasn't time to cancel. Next time," Jeff said.

Would there be a next time or were her parents going to take her back home? Funny, but at this point Belinda really wanted to stay on here. Now that she had met a new friend, it made sense to remain a while longer. Besides, she was sure Emma would find it difficult to manage alone. With Emma's mother not feeling well and Oma needing special care, it would be difficult for the family to help out. Nee, she was still needed here, that was for sure and for certain.

After the twins made the rounds of the family, Belinda started a pot of coffee. As she placed cookies on platters, Jeff came into the kitchen. My, he was a lot handsomer than she had remembered and his voice was deep and gentle. What a shame he wasn't Amish. Jeff asked if she needed help and she nodded. "Jah, you can pour cream in the pitcher there next to the cups and saucers on the tray. Cream's in the small bottle in the fridge." He did as he was told and then waited for more instructions.

"I think we have everything. Oh, Jeff, it's so gut to see you again. How have you been?"

"Well, as I mentioned in my last letter, I've been working nearly twelve hours a day landscaping, but it's slower now. I'm glad, because we've had a heat spell and it's hard working in that hot sun hour after hour."

"Jah, I bet. At least you have an air-conditioned house to go home to. We never get a break here—until it cools off in the evening. I wish we could change some rules, but it won't happen."

"You look wonderful, Belinda. Pennsylvania must agree with you."

"Oh, it's nice here, that's for sure. Everyone is gut to me, but I miss home."

"Do you think your folks will want you to go back with them on Tuesday?"

"I don't know. We haven't discussed it since they just got here, but I think Emma still needs me to help. Her family is unable to be here that much. Her sister, Ruthie comes by a lot, but she's got a boppli and is in the family way again, so she can't be here all the time."

"You're so nice to want to help Emma like that, Belinda. Do you like caring for the twins?"

"Jah, they're adorable. I only change them for her and hold them if they cry too much. Plus I try to keep up with the laundry and make meals."

"Have you met any people your age? Besides family?"

"I met a girl when I was shopping in town and it turned out she lives only a mile from here, so I went over to her place a few days ago and we hung out. Gabe has a phone now so I can call her when we want to get together. Truth is, I don't get much time to myself yet. There's always so much to do. But tell me about you and Carrie. What else is new?"

"Carrie likes waiting tables and she makes pretty good money. Did I mention in my last letter that I've been accepted in the fall at community college? I want to learn more about the business end of things—bookkeeping and stuff. If I have my own business someday, it will come in handy."

"You did tell me you might go to college. That's gut. You'd be a smart businessman, I know that."

He grinned. "You do?"

"Oh, jah. You've got gut brains."

He laughed as he lifted the tray and they headed back toward the large back porch where people had congregated. Emma sat in a wide rocker with one of her babies. Grace held the other twin and told stories of her children when they were infants. Jeff set the tray on a round table in the center of the porch and went back to help bring out the coffee pot.

It was wonderful to hear her family's voices again and her heart ached. Maybe she could leave with them. What a difficult decision if it was left up to her. She looked over at Jeff, who fit right in with the families. She wondered if he just might decide to become an Amish man. Oh, mercy. How ridiculous. He had his life planned out and it certainly didn't include an Amish wife.

While she was pondering her decision, they heard a buggy pull onto the gravel. It was the rest of the Zook family. Mary and Leroy got out and then Wayne. A few minutes later, a second buggy pulled in and Josiah emerged with Katie. Mary explained that her mother had not felt strong enough to make the trip over, so she'd insisted everyone come without her. She planned to spend the time reading her Bible.

Everyone made the hug rounds and Belinda enjoyed hearing the laughter and "happy noise," as Lizzy called it. This was the part of being Amish that most captivated her. This she could never leave.

Chapter Thirty-Four
Lancaster County, Pennsylvania

After supper cleanup, Josiah and Katie invited Belinda and Jeff to go for a walk with them. The foursome sauntered around the cornfields, enjoying the cool breezes, which were coming in from the west. After walking over to the horse corral, the couples stood to watch the new foal born to one of their mares—a lovely chestnut Saddlebred. She came over to the fence and received accolades from the group while she swung her flaxen tail. The foal trotted along beside its mother.

Josiah put his arm around Katie, who looked adoringly into his handsome eyes. It might be nice to have a man enthralled the way Josiah is, Belinda thought, as she moved away from the fence. "Come, Jeff, I'll show you the barn and leave the two lovebirds to themselves for awhile." Josiah showed his appreciation with a full-faced grin while Belinda and Jeff moved on. They heard Katie let out a giggle.

"It's a great farm," Jeff said when they approached the large bank barn. He commented on the large windmill off to the side.

"Jah, Gabe told me he added it when he moved in. He said it was a big job to replace the open well with an underground one. I think he said he bricked it. Anyway it supplies the water for the troughs as well as drinking water.

"I'd like to be self-sufficient like you Amish are," Jeff said, placing his hands on his waist while he looked up at the windmill, which spun feverishly in the wind.

"It's okay. Sometimes I wish we could be more modern, but most of the time, I'm happy."

"I'm glad your father called me so I could get to see you again."

"Me, too. I've missed you and Carrie a lot," Belinda said, while she walked over and sat on a bale of hay by the doorway. Jeff came over and sat beside her. He had a nice smell about him, sort of pepperminty. Plus, he always looked so neat.

"Maybe I can take you to Sight and Sound while I'm here. What do you think?"

"I'd love it, but you're here only a couple of days and I'd feel bad not to spend time with my family after they drove all this way."

"I doubt they have any tickets left, anyway. Maybe next time we can plan ahead and I'll come by myself...I mean Carrie and I can come."

"Jah, she's gonna be mad if you come without her again," Belinda said, looking over and smiling into his startling blue eyes. They were the color of a summer sky and her heart danced at his nearness to her. Goodness, what an attraction! What were his feelings for her? She hoped they were more than friendship.

They talked about his job and the twins and everything they could think of while the sky became darker and night drifted in. "I guess we should head back," Belinda said. "I bet my parents are wondering where we were all this time."

Looking down at his watch, Jeff's brows rose. "I didn't realize how long we'd been out here. Hope I didn't get you into trouble." He rose and took her hand to help her rise. She loved the strength she felt in his arm when he helped her up. They walked back to the farmhouse, where the rest of the family was moving from the porch to the inside.

No one seemed concerned about their disappearance, so they sat on the steps before going in. The mosquitoes were beginning to bite and Belinda swatted one on her arm with her other hand. "Nasty insects."

Jeff agreed and pointed out the zillions of fireflies drifting skyward from the fields. "When I was a kid I liked to catch a few and put them in a glass jar. Did you ever do that?"

"Oh jah. Many times, but we had to let them loose before we were allowed back in the house."

He laughed and nodded. "We did, too. Sometimes they didn't all make it. So where am I supposed to sleep tonight?"

"Goodness, I have no idea." Belinda stood and picked up a couple empty glasses from the table to carry them inside. Jeff rose also and collected several used paper napkins. When they arrived in the house, Belinda's parents were talking with her aunt and uncle, and Lizzy was showing Nellie all the quilt blocks she'd sewn in preparation for her own quilt.

Belinda and Jeff walked over to the others and stood listening while they discussed the arrangements. Emma turned to Jeff. "Oh, there you are. You're going to sleep in Merv's room, if you don't mind. He has twin beds in there."

"That's fine," Jeff said. "I can sleep anywhere—even the barn if you want."

"Nee, we have enough room. I guess the rest of the family is set-up with you and Daed, right?" Emma asked her mother, Mary.

"Jah, we've fixed up the dawdi-haus for you," she said, turning to include Grace, Jed, and Nellie.

After a few minutes, Merv hooked up their large buggy and drove some of the guests back to the Zook farm while Nellie squeezed into Mary and Leroy's buggy next to their son, Wayne. Katie rode with Josiah back to the farmhouse.

A few minutes after everyone left, Gabe and Emma headed upstairs each carrying one of the twins with Lizzy trailing behind "Outen the lights when you head for bed, Belinda," Gabe reminded her. Unless Merv hasn't gotten back home yet. You get to bed real soon, okay?"

"Jah, I will. Gut nocht, Onkel Gabe, Aenti Emma. Hope you get a gut night's rest."

Emma smiled back. "Jah, that makes two of us."

Belinda was acutely aware of being alone with Jeff. Her heart fluttered as she went to the sofa to sit down. The light from the near-full moon competed with the dwindling light from the kerosene lamps. Jeff came over and sat next to her, though he stayed toward the opposite corner of the sofa. For several moments there was silence. Then Jeff cleared his throat and asked her again about her life in Pennsylvania.

"I miss everyone at home, but it's pretty nice here. I wish I could see Carrie, though. Is she dating anyone special? I asked her in my last letter, but I haven't heard back."

"She's working more hours now, so you may not hear from her often. She goes out with guys when she has a chance, but no, she doesn't have anyone steady yet. She seems all right with it. Dan's away for the summer. He got a job as a lifeguard at the Jersey shore."

"Oh, I'm sure that pleases him—to be sitting like Adonis, being admired by all the girls in bikinis," Belinda said, grinning.

Jeff laughed, nodding. "I'm sure he's enjoying himself."

"I get scared thinking what might have happened if you hadn't come in and saved me that night. Danki, again, Jeff. You were sweet to keep an eye on me—your baby sister's friend."

"That wasn't the only reason. I'm really fond of you, Belinda."

"Oh, like in 'fond of chocolate'?" she asked with a wink.

"Maybe a tad more than that, though I like my chocolate," he said.

"Do you want to play chess?" Belinda asked, preferring to be on a safer course. She didn't want to pursue his line of conversation. Knowing their future could never include marriage, she preferred to keep him as a friend. At least, that's what she told herself.

"If the light's good enough, I'll take you on."

"I hope you're not too gut. I'm still learning. Onkel Gabe taught me."

They moved over to a card table near the window and set the lamp on the sill for light. The game was already set up so they sat and slowly moved their pieces about the board. Within ten minutes, Jeff had removed her two bishops and the queen. It didn't look too hopeful, but Belinda plugged along for another few minutes before being checkmated.

She sat back in her chair and folded her arms. "You're too gut for me, Jeff. I need more lessons before taking you on again."

As he smiled back at her, she heard Mervin coming down the drive. After he came in and said good night, he went upstairs to bed.

"Maybe we should turn in, too," Belinda said, hesitantly.

"Belinda, before you go up, I guess I just want to say… well, I hope you'll come back to Ohio Tuesday. I really miss you."

"We didn't see much of each other before," Belinda said, smiling coyly at him.

"I guess that's true, but I can't stop thinking about you."

Belinda hesitated before responding. "Jeff, you know our lives are never going to join. We're too different."

"I'm not sure we are. I'm thinking about taking up the Mennonite way of life, Belinda."

"Mercy, you wouldn't do that because of me," she said, her eyes questioning.

"Not really. No, I've been disillusioned with the way our society has been headed for a couple years now. It seems to deteriorate more all the time. People's values are not what they should be or were. I can't do anything to stop the moral decay, but I can change the way I live and find a community of like-minded people."

"And you think that would be with the Mennonites?"

He nodded. "My friend, Tom, has been talking with me for months now and as you know, I've been attending his church. I haven't approached my family yet, but I plan to soon."

"How do you think they'll take it?"

"I don't expect much reaction. They're pretty cool."

"My daed likes you, you know that," Belinda said.

"I like him, too. I like your whole family—what I know of them, anyway."

"I think Nellie likes you."

He grinned. "She's a wee too young for me, I'm afraid. Well anyway, at least you know one thing. I want you back home so we can get to know each other better."

Belinda reached over and touched his hand with hers. "I can't let myself care, Jeff, because I don't think I could ever leave the Amish. I know I've acted differently in the past—like I don't care and all—but truthfully, once I get this restlessness out of my system, I plan to take my vows and then I'm committed to live as an Amish woman for life."

He nodded. "Would you consider the Mennonite religion? It doesn't seem that different from Amish, except a bit more lenient."

She withdrew her hand. "I've never considered it before. I'd have to think more before answering you."

"So you haven't totally eliminated it as a possibility?"

"To be honest, until just now, I've never even thought about changing my religion."

He grinned over and moved toward her. His leg accidentally brushed against hers. She felt a thrill pass through her when she looked over at his handsome face.

"You look so lovely in this light," he said softly. His head came closer and she wondered if he planned to kiss her. Then they heard steps on the staircase as Mervin came down two at a time. He looked over while Jeff drew back.

"Sorry, hope I didn't interrupt anything. Just forgot to lock the door."

"Nothing to interrupt," Jeff said, rising. His cheeks were ruby red and his look of disappointment was not lost on Belinda.

After locking the front door, Mervin nodded and headed back upstairs. "My room's on the left, Jeff. Don't make a mistake."

"Now what did he mean by that?" Belinda said, un-amused by his insinuation.

Jeff let out a chuckle. "Think I know, but he needn't worry. I'm not like Dan."

Belinda stood up and walked toward the stairs. "Thank goodness for that. I wouldn't be sitting here in the dark if I thought you were."

"See you in the morning, Belinda. Hope you sleep okay."

"I hear the twins crying, but I don't do anything at night. Gabe's there to help if necessary."

They stopped at the top of the stairs before parting. Jeff took both her hands in his, leaned over and kissed her lightly on her cheek. Then he turned and she watched while he entered Mervin's room. What were her feelings for this gorgeous English man?

Chapter Thirty-Five
Lancaster County, Pennsylvania

Belinda's night was spent tossing about—not only her body, but her mind as well. Her dream of becoming part of a new group of teens here in Ohio was a strong draw, but then her attraction to Jeff pulled her in another direction. She liked Wayne, but though she found him physically attractive, her feelings for Jeff were deeper. Was she ready to think about getting serious with anyone? And Mennonite? Could she consider becoming one? She thought about having electricity and maybe even an air conditioner and heat you can turn on with a dial. They were definite advantages over the Amish way of life. Or were they?

What would her parents say if she were to consider leaving the Amish for the Mennonite community? Would they still shun her? She didn't believe that would be the case, since she knew of an Amish man who married a Mennonite and he still saw his family. He seemed real happy when she him with his wife and kinner, though they were never included in community activities. Was Jeff merely attracted to her because he thought she was pretty? And different? Goodness, he'd be college educated and she only went through eighth grade. Perhaps, she'd feel inadequate. Though she almost beat him in chess. Well, maybe not almost…but she wasn't horrible.

After their normal early breakfast, Gabe and Mervin prepared to go to take care of the animals and they invited Jeff to tag along. He followed them out after taking his dishes to the sink where Belinda was filling a dishpan with soapy water. "See you later, Belinda," he said and she smiled over.

"Jah. Don't let them make you do too much," she teased.

"Hey, I never milked a cow before. Why not try?"

"It's harder than you think," she said as she inserted the glasses in the hot suds."

After he left, she finished cleaning the kitchen. The plan was to head over to the Zook's place around noon. She was glad there wasn't a service today. It allowed more time for her to spend with the family.

Jeff spent the morning with Gabe and Mervin while Belinda helped Emma bathe the twins. She loved helping, though the little girls weren't particularly thrilled when she tried to shampoo their scant blonde hair. Emma laughed when Deborah screwed her face up and screamed while Belinda rinsed her scalp with a cloth.

"Goodness, she has a temper. She must have gotten that from her father's side," Emma said with a grin.

"I'm scared to see what my kinner will be like," Belinda said. "I'd better not marry a guy with a temper. His, plus mine, would send my kinner up a wall!"

"I think Jeff is interested in you," Emma said when she took the wailing baby into her towel-wrapped arms.

Belinda reached for Miriam, who was lying peacefully in her carrier. "He might be. He hinted at it last night, but I'm afraid. I don't want to like him too much. After all, he isn't Amish."

"Your daed mentioned Jeff was considering the Mennonite church, but he hoped he'd have more opportunity to educate him on the Amish faith. Please be careful not to get serious."

"We don't know each other that well, Emma. Don't make too much out of it. He's more like a brother."

"Oh, jah, I'm sure," she said, with a wink.

Around eleven, with chores completed, Gabe harnessed their buggy for his new family and they headed over to the Zook's place while Lizzy and Mervin sat in the back of Jeff's car behind Belinda, who sat in the frontseat. The kids sat motionless with their seat belts fastened, staring out the windows as the landscape scooted past them.

"Your car is really nice," Belinda said as she turned on the radio. Jeff turned the volume down on the Christian music station he had it set on.

"Wait, let's hear the music," Lizzy said. "I like that song."

Jeff turned it back up and started humming along. Belinda smiled over at him. He had an interesting profile with his chiseled features. She pictured him with a beard. Still handsome. He looked over. "Like it?"

"The music?"

"What else?" he asked, his brows arching.

"Oh, jah, the music. Very nice. I've heard it before somewhere."

"I like jazzier stuff," Merv said, folding his arms over his chest. "Can you change it?"

"I can, but your sister is enjoying it, Merv. Let's wait," Jeff said.

"Okay."

Belinda turned toward Merv. "Since when do you listen to jazz music?" she asked.

"I heard it once at my friend's house. It was real cool. Ever hear a saxophone?"

"I'm not sure," Belinda answered. "I mostly have heard guitars and pianos."

"Aenti Ruth plays a violin," Merv offered. "She played it for me once and she's real gut."

"Oh, Emma was telling me. She learned when she was living in Philadelphia, right?"

"Jah. She had a boyfriend who was English," he added, matter-of-factly.

"Oh, I hadn't heard that one," Belinda said, her eyes widening. "I'll have to ask Aenti Emma or Lizzy about that."

Lizzy's ears perked up. "I thought I told you that one," she said, a look of disappointment spreading across her face.

"Nee. That's one you forgot, Lizzy," Belinda said with a smile.

"She liked Onkel Jeremiah better, though. That's why she came back home," Merv continued, matter-of-factly.

"Oh, jah, Jeremiah is ever so nice."

"I heard Aenti Mary say her sister, Esther, the lady who lives in Philadelphia, wants to come in a couple weeks to see her mudder, but she doesn't want her to come."

"My goodness, you are quite the gossip," Belinda said, reproaching the young man.

"Nee, but I keep my ears open. Aenti Mary didn't know I was in the next room when she was telling Mamm about it."

"I'd like to meet Esther. Do you think she's glad she left the Amish?"

"I don't know. Who knows? She's got a lot of money plus and she married a rich guy, so they travel a lot."

Jeff had kept silent during the discussion, but then he added his own comment. "It's not money that makes a person happy. In fact, it's not the lack of money, either. It's the inner peace you can have when you know Christ and keep Him in your mind and heart."

"I don't know if Aenti Esther believes in God," Merv said. "I don't know her much, but she's nice to me." He looked out the window. "I think we're gonna beat my parents big time."

"Well, yeah, I guess so," Belinda said. "Cars are a wee bit faster than horse and buggies."

"I wish we had a car," he said wistfully.

"Me, too," Lizzy added. "Though I like horses a lot."

"Liz, you can like horses and still have a car."

"Oh, jah. I guess you're right. Do you like horses, Jeff?"

"I do. I took riding lessons for three years. I hope some day to own my own."

"Then you'll need a lot of land," Lizzy said as she patted the soft fabric of her seat.

"That's what I hope to do, Liz. Buy a nice farm someday and live off the land."

"But what about your landscaping business?" Belinda asked when they made the turn to the Zook's farm.

"I can do both, maybe. The business should give me the money I need to purchase the farm. Then in time, maybe I can give up the business and just farm my own land."

"Goodness, you have a lot of fancy plans," Belinda said, amused at all his future planning.

"I have a few I haven't told you," he said, glancing over briefly.

"So maybe you should tell me," she added, teasingly.

"Someday. So here we are," he said as he pulled in. "Glad it's so easy to find. Gabe drew out directions last night. Only two turns."

"Jah, we all live close to each other. Emma has two brothers who live next to the Zook's."

"I can't learn any more names," Jeff said with a grin. "I have a hard time keeping everyone straight as it is."

"Jah, sometimes I get mixed up with all my cousins and second cousins. It's fun, though."

After parking behind the barn, everyone got out and the kids ran ahead. "I hope we'll find a couple minutes to be alone," Jeff said while they walked slowly toward the farmhouse.

"It's not going to be easy, Jeff, but I'll try to get outside with you later. It's so much cooler today, thank the Lord."

"It's a perfect day, though we may get thunderstorms later this afternoon." He took out his I-phone and checked the weather app.

Belinda peeked over. "Amazing. All that information in that tiny thing. Onkel Gabe's phone doesn't do much."

"Sometimes we depend too much on technology. I like my phone, but it can be addictive."

"I know. I've even seen people driving with phones at their ears."

"Worse than that, is when they text and drive. It should be against the law."

"They have laws for everything else. Jah, why not that one, too?" She looked across the driveway at a young man in front of them, who turned and waved. "There's Wayne. I wonder if his girlfriend, Becky, will show up."

"I saw him watching you yesterday. I think he may have a crush on you. But then what guy wouldn't?"

Belinda bit her lip. "That's silly. Lots of guys don't even notice me."

"No way, girl. You have no idea how lovely you are."

"Stop talking sweet talk, Jeff. You warned me about guys who do that." She tipped her head and gave him a half smile.

"Oh, yeah, I did, didn't I? My mistake. I should have said, 'don't listen to them—just me,'" he added, grinning back.

Wayne stood and waited for them to catch up with him. After they greeted each other, they went inside, but not before Belinda noticed Wayne had a sour expression, probably because she came in with another guy. This was fun, though maybe she shouldn't be leading anyone on. But isn't this just part of growing up?

A few minutes later, Emma, Gabe and the twins appeared. There was so much excitement in the house now, Belinda could barely hear. She noticed Katie helping her grandmother over to the porch while people began to congregate outside. Mary and Ruth held back in order to start lunch. Belinda was about to go back in to offer her services when her mother, Grace, came over to her.

"Belinda, Daed and I want to talk to you in private. Should we go in the living room?"

"Sure. I think just about everyone is outside now or working in the kitchen."

"Gut. I'll get your daed and we'll meet you inside. It won't take long."

Belinda went in and sat down on an upholstered side chair and waited. She could hear the voices of her family out back as her parents came in to join her. If she could guess by their demeanors, it would be good news.

Her parents sat down across from her and her father placed his hands on his knees and smiled over. "We had a nice talk with your aenti and onkel and they have been very pleased with your behavior. Emma says you've been a big help with the boppli and made life much easier for her. So we're proud of you, dochder."

"You're not supposed to be proud," Belinda said, grinning.

"Oh, jah. That's true," her father said, smiling back.

"So," Grace began, "we think it's time for you to return home with us. Emma said she's strong enough now to take over and as long as you promise to never sneak out of the house again, we can start all over."

"Mmm. Are you sure she won't need me a little longer?" The faces of her new friends, and the possibilities that loomed, popped into her mind, coloring her own thoughts.

"Nee. She has plenty of family around in case she needs help. We all miss you, Belinda, and we feel it's time for you to come home."

"As long as it's okay with everyone, I guess I may as well go back with you," she said.

"And your promise?" her father asked, giving her his full attention.

"Does it mean I can't see my English friends ever again?"

"We ain't saying that, Belinda," her father said, his lips turned down. "But no sneaking around and no parties. If you want to get together with Carrie, or a couple of her other girlfriends, that would be okay. We'll expect you to tell us, though, where you're going and get permission first. Is that understood?"

"Jah, I guess so. I still need to see people and have fun once in a while, you know. It's not like I'd do anything awful."

"Jah, we know that," Grace said. "I think you've learned a lesson though. Don't you agree?"

"I do. I'm sorry I hurt so many people by being bull-headed."

Jed nodded. "It's probably your age. Hopefully, you'll put others ahead of your own wishes now."

"So, we'll make plans to have you go back with us. It will be a little tight in the car, but we can manage for five or six hours, nee?"

"Ach. My legs will be cramped, that's for sure," Belinda said, now pleased with the decision. This way she'd get to know Jeff better, too and just maybe…

Chapter Thirty-Six
Lancaster County, Pennsylvania

The day was tiring, but enjoyable. Belinda found time to spend alone with Jeff. Actually, not quite alone. Nellie made a point of following them around and Belinda wondered if her parents hadn't given her sister instructions to do just that. When they walked down the road to a stream, Nellie took off her shoes and waded across to pick wildflowers in a nearby field. While she was busy, Belinda and Jeff sat on the edge of the stream and chatted. He was so easy to talk with. She'd never experienced such a pleasant relationship with a man before. Usually, she felt it necessary to do all the talking and with Jeff, it was an exchange of words and ideas. He seemed genuinely interested in what she had to say and she found him intelligent and with good humor. She laughed at some of his unusual observations and in turn, he listened intently when she described her life as a young Amish woman. She was careful not to sit too close to him. Too many feelings were aroused when she felt his hand on her arm or he touched her cheek. Much too intimate.

When she told him she would be returning to Ohio with them on Tuesday, he seemed ecstatic. "I'm so glad. Carrie will be excited, too."

"I'll be able to still see her, but I won't be attending any of the parties. I agreed not to."

"And you won't try to sneak out?" he asked with a grin.

"Nee. I'll behave like a perfect little Amish girl."

"It shouldn't be too hard. After all, the parties turned out to be a bit dangerous for you."

"Ach. I was so naïve. Never again. No more alcohol for me, that's for sure."

"And no more Dan?"

"That goes without saying. I don't even want to see him again."

"Do you think your parents trust me enough to see you privately once in a while?"

"Jeff, we shouldn't see each other that often. I'm afraid we'll start caring too much about each other."

"It may be too late for me, Belinda. I think about you all the time."

"Oh, Jeff, don't. You know it would never work for us, don't you?"

"I don't know what I think. Belinda, do you have any feelings for me?"

"You know I do. I consider you one of my best friends."

"I wasn't thinking about friendship so much. Do you have any feelings beyond that?"

"I...I don't know what I feel for you, exactly. I know I think about you a lot, too, but when I do, I get kind of a pit in my stomach. Like it's wrong somehow to allow my thoughts to dwell on a man who isn't Amish."

"I doubt I could accept the Amish way of life, but what I know of the Mennonites, I think I could handle their traditions."

"They're pretty restricted, too, you know. You'd have to give it a great deal of thought."

"As I told you, I already have. I've gone to the meetinghouse at least a dozen times with Tom. Have you ever been to one of their services?"

"Nee."

"Would you consider going with me once?"

"I'm not sure I should. Let me think about it."

He nodded. His mouth had turned down when they discussed their relationship, but he smiled again when Nellie made her way back across the stony bottomed stream, trying to balance with a handful of Queen Anne's Lace and wild tiger lilies. He stood and reached for her other hand since she nearly fell on the slippery rocks.

"Whew, that was close," she said as she dropped her skirt and began putting her stockings back on. Jeff looked the other way to allow for her modesty.

"The flowers are beautiful, Nellie. We'll have to get back home to put them in water before they wilt," Belinda said.

"I'm gonna give them to the old lady."

"Oma?"

"Jah. She's nice. She told me stories about when she was a little girl like me."

"That's Aenti Emma's mammi."

"I know. She told me. She talked about her daughter, Esther, the one who left the Amish. She looked so sad when she talked about her. I guess they still have problems getting along. I hope you never leave the Amish, Belinda." Nellie looked first at her sister and then pointedly over at Jeff, who stared down at the ground.

"Goodness, don't worry about things like that, Nellie. Come on, let's get home now. We should give the others a hand with the next meal."

"It seems that all we do is eat. Eat and clean up."

"Jah, you're right," Belinda said when she and Jeff led the way through the wooded area to the road. Nellie walked along behind them.

"I can't think of anything better than that," Jeff called back, chuckling.

Belinda nearly collapsed into her bed that night. Between cooking and cleaning up, the confusion and noise, plus her walk, the mattress felt like a cloud. Before falling asleep, she envisioned her life back home. Would it be satisfying? Had she really changed her mind about wanting free time to do whatever she wanted? Even though she liked the idea of seeing more of Jeff and Carrie, she wondered if she could really just settle down and behave the way her parents expected her to. Perhaps, the decision to return, made more by her parents than her, was a good idea. She truly hoped she could be the kind of daughter they expected now that she'd been away from home and family. Why the strong hesitation? Was it because she had no choice anymore and that saddened her? She tossed for several more minutes until sleep overwhelmed her. Unconsciousness was welcome.

Monday morning she slept in until seven. When she came down for breakfast, Gabe and Jeff were already working in the fields. Emma cleaned up the dishes while the twins slept in their carriers. Merv and Lizzy put their dishes in the sink and went outside to help with the animals. It was divinely quiet.

"I'm glad you slept in, Belinda. You looked exhausted last night. I really appreciate all the hard work you've done for us. Your parents are pleased with you also."

"Danki," Belinda said, slightly embarrassed by the undeserved praise. "I guess my parents talked to you about my leaving with them."

"Jah. We'll miss you, but things seem to be straightened out now with your family and we can't expect you to stay here forever."

"I hope you'll visit us soon. I'll miss the children. All of them. Lizzy is a sweetheart."

"Jah, that she is. It may be hard for a while to do any traveling, but hopefully in the future... You're all coming back for Katie's wedding, though, I'm sure."

"I hope so. It would be ever so much fun." Belinda poured cereal into a bowl and added milk before sitting at the table.

"Jeff would be welcome, too. Of course, you'd probably need him to drive anyway."

"He's not our normal driver, Aenti. I don't know if you realized that."

"Oh, that's right. He's just a family friend, right?" Emma laid her cleaning sponge aside and sat next to Belinda.

"More or less. I mean, I met him first. His sister's a real gut friend of mine. Then he and Daed hit it off since they both like farming and gardening and all."

"I see. As long as you're just friends, though I know now he feels more than that towards you, Belinda, judging by the way he follows your every move with his eyes."

"Does he? I didn't know." *If Aenti Emma noticed, who else might have?*

"Just a warning. You don't want to hurt your family any more than necessary."

Belinda nodded and looked down into her bowl while she stirred slowly with her spoon. "I never meant to hurt anyone. I just want to have some fun in my life before I commit to marriage."

"I think I understand. Ruthie was that way, too. I never seemed to have the wanderlust like she did."

"Is it true that Josiah liked you and Aenti Ruthie before he fell for Katie?"

"Goodness, things get around, don't they?" Emma's face turned pink. "He was never in love with Ruth or me and we certainly weren't in love with him. I think God had it planned that he'd end up with Katie. They get along gut."

"What about Wayne? He doesn't seem to go along with everyone else's idea of being paired off with that girl, Becky. He thinks he's being pushed."

"I've wondered myself why Katie keeps trying to play matchmaker. Certainly Becky can have just about any young man she favors. She's a sweet girl and a gut Amish woman."

"No one wants to be pushed into something. My Amish friend back home tries to fix me up with her brother and if there's anything I can't stand…"

"Jah, it doesn't usually work out. Oh, I see Deborah is waking up to be fed."

"I'll change her, if you'd like."

"Nee. You finish your breakfast. I have to get used to doing things alone. We're expected over at my parents' place for the noon meal."

"Should I do the diapers before we go?"

"That would be great, Belinda. Goodness, I forget how much there is to do around here now."

Jeff and Belinda took the two children in their car again while the rest of the group headed over to the Zook farm. When they pulled up Belinda noticed Ruth and Jeremiah's buggy was already tethered to the hitching post. Then they saw Wayne run out of the house toward the barn. He barely looked their way.

"Goodness, I wonder if something is wrong," Belinda said as she opened the car door. The children had already gotten out of the car and were heading toward the house. Grace met them at the door with a strained look on her face.

"It's Oma, Mary's mamm. She just fell out of bed and she's in terrible bad pain. Wayne's gonna get help."

Jeff offered to take her to the hospital in his car.

"Nee, we're afraid to move her. There's a doctor nearby who makes house calls if it's an emergency. Poor dear. She's all upset."

When they got inside, Belinda heard the woman crying softly from the next room. Katie came out of the bedroom, her eyes filled. "I can't believe it. She was doing so gut. And now…"

Belinda looked over at her mother who was standing next to Mary. "What can I do to help?"

"There's nothing anyone can do till the doctor comes. We're just trying to make her comfortable."

Mary went swiftly into the kitchen and came back with ice cubes wrapped in a towel. "Maybe this will help with the pain. Poor Mamm."

"Mamm, let me do it. You're all flushed," Ruthie said reaching for the ice. "You just told me how awful you were feeling."

"Jah, but…"

"Nee, not buts. Go sit down and take care of yourself. Your cough sounds terrible and you don't want to make your mamm any worse by giving her your sickness."

"It's just a cold."

"Nee, it was 'just a cold' three weeks ago. Now you need to be seen. Maybe when the doctor comes he can check you out, also."

"My concern is my mudder, not myself, Ruthie. I can see a doctor in a couple days if I'm not better." Mary watched from the doorway while Ruth sat cross-legged on the floor next to Oma and rested the cold pack against the woman's hip. "Here, Oma, this should help a little."

"Danki, Ruthie. It hurts real bad, honey. Do you think it's broke?"

Ruthie shook her head. "I hope not. Just try not to move."

"It hurts more if I do, so I'll just lie here. Can you get my other pillow off the bed? This floor is awful hard."

"I'll get it," Belinda said, coming in through the doorway. She removed it from the bed and knelt down to lift the old woman's head high enough to insert the pillow.

"Danki. That's a little better." Her eyes glistened from her tears.

Emma and Gabe arrived with the twins and entered the house, surprised to be greeted with such bad news. Emma came right over, knelt beside her grandmother, and stroked her tear-stained cheek. "Goodness, Oma, what a shame you fell." She looked over at her sister, Ruthie. "Is an ambulance coming for her?"

"We didn't call one, but Wayne went to get Dr. Mason. He's so close that unless he was out, they should be along soon."

Ruthie nodded. A few minutes passed and finally Belinda heard a car making its way along the drive. It was the doctor. Leroy immediately let him in and led him to Oma. Emma and Ruth stayed in the room with him while everyone else left to allow the doctor more space.

When they got back into the kitchen, Belinda noticed Mary had her head in her arms. Leroy stepped over to her. "Mary, you look terrible. Let me feel your head." She dropped her arms and he laid his hand across her brow. "My goodness, woman, you're as hot as a poker. Shouldn't you be in bed yourself?"

"Leroy, how can I do that? Look at what's going on."

"Honey, you could have pneumonia, the way you've been coughing lately."

Grace moved over to Mary and laid her hand on her shoulder. "Mary, go lie down. We'll take care of things here. We don't want you to get any sicker. Goodness, if we'd known, we would have waited before coming. This has been way too much for you. And now…"

"I feel badly, Grace. I wanted everything to be so nice for you and look at me. Jah, I'll take you up on it and lie down for a while after I hear about Mamm. I hope she hasn't broken anything, but at her age…"

"Jah, I know."

Several minutes passed. The family congregated in the kitchen and waited. Silence prevailed. Josiah had arrived and he stood with Katie in the hallway. Finally, the doctor came out of the room, leaving the girls with Oma.

"I've called an ambulance. I'm pretty sure she's broken her hip. All indications point to a fracture. The sooner she gets surgery, the better, if it is broken. I've sedated her for the pain."

"How will you know if it's fractured?" Leroy asked.

"We'll take x-rays. If they aren't conclusive, we'll do an MRI, but usually it will show up on x-ray. I've called over to Lancaster Hospital and they'll be waiting for her."

"Doctor," Leroy said after clearing his throat. "I hate to bother you Mary, is sick, too. Could you take a look at her since you're here anyway?"

Dr. Mason looked at his watch. "I have appointments in an hour, but until the ambulance gets here, I'm not leaving anyway, so to answer your question—yes, of course, Leroy."

Belinda looked over at her parents as Leroy led the doctor upstairs to his bedroom. Grace came over and put her arm around Belinda's shoulders. "Honey, your daed and I were talking and we think you might have to stay a while longer to help out. Between Mary's illness and now Oma needing care, this poor family will have a difficult time. Katie can't do everything and a few days after surgery, they'll probably send the woman home. That's the way it's done now. Quick! Quick! Quick! I know they won't want her in a nursing home."

"But I'm no nurse. I can't stand it when people get sick and kutz and all."

"She probably won't vomit, but she'll need help turning in bed and learning to walk again. At least you could be here to help out with meals and everything. Then in a couple weeks we can send a driver for you. What do you say? Do you mind terribly?"

Belinda was surprised at her disappointment. Here she'd been wavering, not wanting to miss an opportunity to be with cool English kids her age, and yet now that Jeff seemed interested in her, she had looked forward to seeing more of him. And of course her friend, Carrie. Now she was in a position where she'd look unkind to refuse to stay on to help. And after all they'd done for her. It left her little choice. "If they want me to stay, I will, but you'd better ask first. I might just be in the way."

"I'll talk to Mary after the doctor leaves. Your Daed agreed it wouldn't be right for us to stay any longer. We'll just be in the way, but you could be a big help."

"Mmm. I guess so." Belinda let out a sigh. "I hope it doesn't mean I'd never be able to leave the house. I'd go crazy."

Grace nodded. "Jah, you probably would." Her mouth curved upward in a slight smile.

After several minutes went by, they heard the ambulance arrive and at the same time the doctor came down the stairs. Wayne opened the door for the two EMT's, who came in carrying their equipment. The doctor followed them into the bedroom and closed the door.

Leroy leaned against a counter, his eyes downcast. Ruthie walked over to him. "Daed, what's wrong with Mamm?"

"He thinks it's bronchitis, but he wants her in his office tomorrow and he'll do testing. It seems that when it rains, it pours around here, nee?"

"I've been after her to go to the doctor for weeks. She's as stubborn as you were, Daed. You know I'll try to help out."

"I know you're not feeling so gut with the new one coming and Nathanael needs you. He's just a boppli himself. We'll manage okay."

Grace and Belinda stood listening to their conversation. They stepped closer and offered Belinda's services to the family for a while longer. "We know things are going to be difficult for awhile. Especially when Oma returns to the house. Katie can't do it all."

"Mary will be well soon, I'm sure," Leroy stated, but his eyes looked fearful. "Well, maybe if you could help us for a couple weeks till Mary gets back on her feet, we'd be very grateful."

"Jah, I'd be happy to help out," Belinda said, though it didn't sound very convincing, even to her own ears.

Katie and Josiah had walked in behind them and just heard the last part of the conversation. Belinda turned to face them. "I guess I'll move my things over here so I can help you out, Katie. Everyone thinks it will be better if there are two of us taking care of your mudder and grossmammi."

"I can manage fine," Katie said, somewhat too quickly.

"Katie, you just told me how you didn't know how you'd manage," Josiah said. "Belinda is willing to help out. Don't turn her away." He looked over at Belinda and smiled. "That's real nice of you Belinda. I know Katie could use your help."

"Jah, well. Whatever you think, Katie."

"I guess for a couple weeks, it would help out. Emma's too busy to help us here and Ruthie has her boppli to worry about. We don't want him exposed to Mamm's sickness, either. Okay, you can stay in the dawdi haus if you want after your parents leave."

"Okay."

"I'll go help you bring things over," Josiah said.

Wayne took a step forward. "I can help her."

"Well, why don't I drive her in my car," Jeff said, his words short and bordering on harsh. "It's a lot faster than using a buggy." The two men stared at each other and then each nodded.

The bedroom door opened and the EMT's carried Oma out on a litter. They walked carefully as they moved her toward the front door. She appeared more comfortable as the medication worked in her system.

Ruthie and Jeremiah decided to go in the ambulance with her, so Emma took their baby, Nathanael, in her arms. He squirmed to get down and crawl, but she held him tightly and spoke softly in his ear to quiet him down.

In the meantime, the twins wailed for their next meal.

Gabe looked bewildered at the scene taking place. "I'm glad you're gonna be here a while longer," he said to Belinda. She smiled and reached over for Nathanael, to allow Gabe and Emma a chance to attend to their crying infants.

"I can drive people over to the hospital, if you want," Jeff said.

"Nee, that's okay, Jeff," Ruthie said. "We have a driver who will come by to pick us up when we call him. I'll take the cell phone with me."

"I should stay with Emma and help there until Oma comes home again," Belinda suggested.

Katie picked right up on the plan. "Jah, with Mamm sick it doesn't make sense to come here yet. It will be different when Oma is discharged, but for now, I can manage alone. Besides, Wayne's a big help."

"Jah, and your old man isn't helpless, either," Leroy said.

"So, don't worry about bringing my things over, Jeff. When the time comes to move over, I'll have all the help I'll need. Truth is, I have very little anyway."

Belinda walked out with Jeff and watched the ambulance take off for the hospital. "I guess the day didn't go quite the way we thought it would," he said, putting his hand under her elbow. "So now you'll stay on for awhile. When you're ready to come back to Ohio, just give me a call. I can always take off a day or two."

"Danki, Jeff. I'm sorry I have to stay on."

"I understand. You have to promise to write often, though."

"If you write back. Carrie is so slow. I've written twice as often as she has."

"I promise. If you have access to the phone, you have my number, don't you?"

"I do. I memorized it," she confessed.

He glanced over at her while a smile spread across his face. "How about that. So you have no excuse not to call once in a while."

"I promise to call you at least once a week."

"Good. Don't change your mind. I can call you, but I know it's the family phone."

She shook her head. "True. I will call. You have my word. Let's go back in so I can help Katie with lunch. What a day."

"I guess you can't call it boring, anyway."

"Nee. Anything but." They went inside and the family worked together to get sandwiches and drinks on the table, but it was no longer festive. Life can change in a heartbeat.

Chapter Thirty-Seven
Lancaster County, Pennsylvania

Oma had to undergo surgery the following morning. Her femoral neck, which they explained was located in the upper part of the femur, was fractured. They planned to remove the head and neck of the femur and install a prosthesis. They called it a partial hip replacement. While they felt the surgery would be successful, they also warned that hip injuries in the elderly could be dangerous, especially if the patient was inactive afterward. When the family explained she'd come home rather than go to a re-hab center, the doctor told them he'd give them instructions when he discharged her.

That morning, Ruth and Katie went to the hospital, while Belinda took care of Nathanael. Her family waited around long enough to get a full report about Oma's surgery. It delayed their departure by several hours, but they still expected to get to Ohio by late afternoon. As she held Nathanael, Belinda waved goodbye to her family. Jeff drove slowly out of the drive. His normal cheerful demeanor was missing. Belinda was disappointed they hadn't spent more time alone together, but it couldn't be helped.

After they left, the day dragged on. Belinda did a wash and hung it out to dry. Nathanael crawled on the grass and chewed a wooden clothespin, drooling so much she needed to change his cotton shirt twice. Perhaps there would be time to call her English friend. It would help if she had something to look forward to.

Around one o'clock they got an update. Oma was still in recovery, but doing well. Several neighbors stopped by to get a report and left articles of food for the family. News travels quickly.

After things calmed down mid-afternoon and all three children were napping, she and Emma sat on the porch drinking lemonade. Belinda swirled the ice in her tall glass with an ice teaspoon, watching the pale lemony liquid as if she saw it for the very first time. "I was wondering...that is, if you think you can manage till Aenti Ruth returns for Nathanael...if maybe..." She stopped and looked over.

Emma's expression was quizzical. "Jah? You were wondering what?" she asked.

"If maybe I could go see my friend for an hour or so."

"Of course. Goodness, you certainly have earned some time off. You've been such a big help, but between Lizzy and Merv, we can handle things for a while. Gabe checked about your friend's family. Apparently they're gut neighbors to some of our Amish friends."

"Danki. I'd need to use Gabe's phone to call her, just to make sure she's home."

"He left it on the counter over there. Feel free to use it. You know we trust you, Belinda."

"I'm glad. I wouldn't do anything to shame you. I just need friends, is all."

"I know and I'm sure it's been difficult for you."

Dawn was excited to hear from Belinda and asked her to come right over. When Belinda arrived, she came out to greet her along with two other girls, both in Amish clothing. Dawn was wearing a halter and shorts, but her friends looked just like Belinda did. Hot and boring. Dawn introduced the girls as Annie May, a short, skinny girl with thousands of freckles, and Fran, who was quite tall with black hair and dark eyes. She had a lovely deep tan and her teeth gleamed in contrast.

The girls went into the air-conditioned home and sat and talked while Dawn's mother spooned out strawberry ice cream for them. Then she left the girls alone and they proceeded to discuss clothes and boys. "Do you know Wayne?" Belinda asked her friends.

"I've met him. He's dreamy," Annie May stated. "I heard he has a girlfriend already."

"Jah. Becky something. I know her, but he's not committed to her."

"How do you know?"

"I've talked to him." Belinda liked to feel she was 'in the know' and continued talking about the other young people in her family. "Do you know his sister, Katie?" she asked.

"Jah, by sight," Fran answered. "She seems nice."

"She's almost engaged," Belinda said, knowing it was to remain a secret.

"Really? Everyone has a guy except me," Fran said, scowling.

Dawn laughed and shook her head. "Not like you haven't had a chance. Eric would love to go out with you."

"I know, but he's a lousy dancer."

"You all know how to dance?" Belinda's eyes lit up.

"Oh, jah, we dance a lot."

"Show me your steps and I'll teach you what I know."

They raced up to Dawn's bedroom and turned on music. For the next hour the girls danced and giggled and danced some more. By the time Belinda broke away to return home, they had bonded into a foursome. Now this is fun!

After a successful surgery and a week of occupational therapy, Oma was allowed to return to her home. The afternoon before her return, Belinda and Gabe moved her clothing over to the dawdi-haus. After Gabe left, Mary came downstairs for the first time. Belinda was shocked to see how pale and gaunt she appeared. Her coughing had decreased significantly and since she was on antibiotics she was considered safe to be around, though she planned to leave her mother's care to others until she was totally rehabilitated.

Leroy grinned without ceasing. He had his wife back and he watched her every move, anticipating her needs and fulfilling them straight away. Katie poured a bowl of fresh asparagus soup and encouraged her mother to eat it. They sat around the table together while she tasted it.

"It's nice, Katie. You're a gut cook. Josiah should be pleased."

"Danki." Katie's face lit up at the compliment. "He's coming over in a little while. I hope it's okay."

"Of course. You know it is. I'm going back to bed though when I finish this. I feel so weak."

Leroy's smile turned down. "You want to go back already?"

"Nee. Not quite yet. I'm going to finish the soup. Can you call Esther and tell her Mamm's coming home tomorrow, Leroy? I'm too weak to call. I'm relieved the bishop has allowed cell phones now. It helps a lot when something like this happens."

"Jah, it does. I'll call her. She wants to come help out you know. She told me Martin is taking off a week to come with her. She can't stay too long though, because college classes start the following week."

"I guess we can't refuse her."

"Why would you do that?"

"Well, look at me. Do you think I need more company?"

"Mary, she's not company. She's your sister."

"She feels more like company. It was her choice to leave the family and now all of a sudden, she wants to be treated like a bosom sister."

"I thought you'd forgiven her, Mary. Let bygones be bygones."

"It's easier to talk about it than do it. I try."

"Well, maybe you need to pray about it more. God forgives us as we forgive others."

"I don't need you to give me a sermon, Leroy." Her eyes flashed over at her husband. Belinda wished she wasn't present to hear this exchange, but she was secretly glad Esther was coming. Maybe she'd shed light on the whole bit about leaving the Amish life style.

"Honey, I don't mean to preach, but—"

"I'm tired, Leroy. Help me back upstairs." She pushed the bowl away though it was still half-full.

"Jah. Okay. Discussion closed for now." He helped her to her feet and supported her while she gained enough strength to ascend the stairs. Belinda watched as they stepped in unison. *He's a gut man. So patient.*

Philadelphia, Pennsylvania

Esther poured a second cup of coffee for Martin and settled back into the sofa, plumping up a decorator pillow to conform to her back. The sun streamed through the large glass windows touching her eight-foot tropical plants, encouraging their upward growth.

Martin, who was sitting on the other end of the sofa, put his newspaper to the side and smiled over. "So she got through the surgery well. That must be a relief."

"Definitely. You never know at her age. The family was told it could take a year before she could return to normal, whatever normal is after her terrible car accident. That poor lady has really been through it this past year."

He nodded and reached for her hand. "I think Amish women must be strong from all the work they do."

"My mother certainly is. I'm concerned though because of her state of mind. With Dad's passing…"

"I know. I've considered that, too. Did you talk to Mary about our coming?"

"Earlier I had mentioned it, but I didn't think she sounded very pleased with the idea."

"She's been sick, honey. Probably that affected her reaction. We can stay in a hotel."

"I think that's a good idea, though I don't want to offend anyone."

"We should play it by ear then. I can make tentative reservations, just so we'll have a room available."

Esther sipped from her cup, staring straight ahead.

"What's troubling you, Esther? Is there still friction?"

She nodded while she pushed her cup and saucer aside. "I thought things would be better by now. Mary just doesn't seem capable of forgiving me for the past."

"That is really *her* problem, honey. She knows she should forgive."

"Yes, we all know that. It's a lot harder to do it."

"Have you totally forgiven your mother for the polio thing?"

"You mean for not getting the polio vaccine in time to save Mary?"

He nodded.

"I think so. When I see Mary limping, it comes back to me, though. I hate to admit it. I probably would still be Amish if it weren't for her decision to follow the bishop's ruling instead of her own conscience."

"Then you wouldn't have met me."

She smiled over at her husband. "You're right. Amazing how our lives twist and turn. Every decision we make determines the next choice we're confronted with."

"That's why we have to go to God when we're at a crossroad."

"I prayed a lot before I went to Philadelphia, Martin. It was the most difficult decision of my life."

"He moved over and put his arm around her. "It was right for you, Esther. You know it was. Look at the way your teaching has impacted your students. I don't think a week goes by that someone doesn't comment on your positive influence."

"I hope it's made a difference. Now I just need to keep my emotions in hand and try to reach my sister. My first concern though is Mother."

"She'll be fine."

"If Dad was still alive, I wouldn't be so concerned, but then again, she has all her family around her. Almost all." Esther leaned in against her husband. "I don't know how I managed without you all these years. You're so perfect for me, Martin."

"And you for me." He turned her face toward his and kissed her gently. "I guess I'll pack up when we're done. I won't need a suit or tie, I guess."

"Take one, Martin. Just in case."

He nodded, his expression somber. There would be only one occasion for him to wear a suit in Lancaster. God knows, He prayed it would not prove necessary.

The phone startled Esther. She answered it and Leroy's voice came through the phone. "Esther, I'm sorry to call you last minute like this, but it's about Mary."

"Oh, no. What's wrong?"

He seemed to hesitate before answering. "Well, you know she's still feeling poorly from her illness. Would you mind waiting a few days or so before coming out, just to give her a chance to recuperate?"

"If that's what she wants. We were hoping to help out, Leroy. I wouldn't expect Mary to prepare any meals for us or anything."

"Jah, I realize that." There was silence for a moment. Then he resumed the conversation. "She's upset from everything that's going on and I just thought it would be better to wait, is all."

"Certainly. I'll try to understand. I know my sister well enough to know she'd prefer not having anyone around until she's well again. We'll call in a couple days and see how everyone is doing. I hope my mother won't be disappointed if we don't show up."

"Nee, I talked to her. She understands. By then, maybe she'll be doing better, too. I think it's just more sensible to wait. Please don't take it the wrong way."

"No, I won't. Thank you for calling and give Mary and Oma our love."

She hung up and stared at Martin. "She doesn't want us."

He nodded. "So I gathered. Mary is sick, Esther. You know he's not making it up."

"I know. I want so much to help, but not only isn't it needed, it isn't wanted either. Will it always be this way?" Her eyes filled. Martin sat closer to her and stroked her hair.

"You can only do so much, Esther. The rest is up to Mary—and God. Now let's unpack and watch some television. We'll plan to have dinner out tomorrow night. I know just the place."

"Thank you, darling. I love you." He kissed her tenderly as they embraced.

Chapter Thirty-Eight
Lancaster County, Pennsylvania

Several days later, Oma was released from the hospital. After setting up appointments for an occupational therapist to stop by twice a week, the nurse handed Leroy several instruction sheets, in addition to medications and prescriptions. An ambulance transported her to their home, where Belinda and Katie helped her into bed. Exhausted from the trip, she had little to say to the waiting family. Her eyelids were red and swollen from her constant tears, and she looked old and rather pathetic to Belinda. Poor lady. Her suffering was taking its toll.

Gabe had brought Lizzy over in the morning to help cheer his mother-in-law when she returned. Belinda brought in a small bouquet of flowers Lizzy had picked earlier and placed them next to Oma's bed.

"Danki. Aren't they pretty?"

Lizzy stood by the threshold and grinned at the compliment. "I picked them just for you," she added.

"I do appreciate it, honey. They'll cheer me up real gut."

Mary had come downstairs long enough to greet her mamm and she tucked a quilt around her mother's slight frame. "Now you rest. We'll keep the neighbors out of your room until you're up to seeing people."

"Jah. For now, I just want to sleep a little bit. When's Essie coming?"

"Esther will be here tomorrow. She wanted to let you rest your first day home."

"I suppose that's a gut idea. I'm glad you're feeling better, Mary. I've been worried about you."

"You shouldn't worry, Mamm. The antibiotics are working. It just takes time. I'm just ever so weak."

"Well you get back upstairs and rest. I'll be just fine. Katie and Belinda will take gut care of me."

Mary began to cough and quickly left the room. She continued with her spell of coughing. Belinda went over, led her to the kitchen, and helped her sit on a chair.

Leroy walked over to her side. "See? I told you not to come down today. You need more rest. The doctor told you to just walk around upstairs till you're stronger. They know best."

"Jah, but I'm getting weaker. I need to move around more."

"You can do that upstairs, Mary. I don't want you getting worse."

Belinda reassured her that her mother would receive all the care she needed. "That's why I stayed on, Aenti Mary, just so I can help you out."

Mary smiled over as her coughing ceased. "That was real nice of you. I know you must be anxious to get back home, Belinda. It shouldn't be long now. I am getting better."

"It's fine. I like it here anyway. Your house is even closer to my new friends than Onkel Gabe's house."

"Oh, how nice you have friends nearby. I just hope you have a chance to see them."

Leroy helped Mary back to her room and Lizzy went outside to play with the new lambs.

While Oma napped, Katie worked on bread dough while Belinda made tapioca pudding, which was one of Oma's favorite desserts. They worked silently until the dough was laid to rise on the back of the coal stove. Katie placed a clean linen towel over it and began the coffee. She placed the yellow enamel percolator over the front burner and removed her apron.

"Before we start the laundry, we can have coffee together on the porch. It's much cooler there," she said to Belinda.

"Jah, that would be nice. It's probably the only chance we'll get to relax today. Do we need to bathe Oma?"

"She was bathed at the hospital this morning. It can wait until tomorrow. They want her to get up several times a day, though. You can read the instructions." She took a stack of papers from her apron pocket and placed them on the kitchen table.

"Goodness, that's a lot to read."

"It's important."

"Jah, I'm sure." Belinda glanced over at Katie's cold lips. Was she still upset because Josiah and Wayne had paid attention to her, wanting to help move her things? Surely, she didn't think Belinda was competition. Though she admitted Josiah was real good looking, he was taken, that was for sure, and Belinda had no feelings whatsoever for the attractive young Amish man. Now Wayne? Maybe there was an attraction there, but the one thing that had changed was her feelings for Jeff. She found herself thinking about him constantly.

She still hoped there would be time in the evenings to be with her new friends. That was the only thing that helped with her loneliness. When she was with them, she didn't even think of Jeff. Was it appropriate to waste so much time concentrating on a young man who was not even a marriage prospect? Even if he became a Mennonite, she was still Amish. Oh, life could be so complicated.

"Want more kaffi?" Katie asked, breaking Belinda's pattern of thought.

"A little more."

Katie poured fresh hot coffee in both cups. "You'll probably be able to go back to Ohio as soon as Mamm is better," she noted while stirring cream into her coffee.

Belinda surrounded her cup with both hands and stared at the dark liquid. "Katie, I want to make something clear. I have no designs on Josiah. He was just being friendly the other day."

Katie's brows rose. "Goodness, I'm not worried about Josiah. He's as faithful as a puppy. Nee, my concern all along has been the way you flirt with my bruder, Wayne. I don't want my friend, Becky, hurt. He seemed interested in her until you came along. Why don't you just try to discourage him?"

"I haven't done anything to encourage him. I'm nice to him because he's nice to me. There's really nothing between us."

"Well, maybe you should make that clear to him so he can go back to seeing Becky. She's pretty upset."

"Don't be mad at me, Katie. It's not my fault he doesn't like her anymore."

"Then stop flirting with him." Her eyes darted across at Belinda's, challenging her.

Belinda felt offended. Had she been a wedge between him and Becky? Perhaps she had overdone the smiles and sweet words a bit. Did she really care for Wayne as more than a friend? When it came right down to it, he was just another challenge. She loved the attention young men paid her, but if it meant destroying relationships with her own people, was it worth it? In her heart she knew it was a sign of vanity. It certainly wasn't the way a good Amish girl behaved. It was time to back off.

"I guess I have been partly responsible," she stated. "I'll just be more careful in the future. I don't want to lead anyone on and I certainly don't want to be responsible for hurting your friend. I'm sorry, Katie. Really."

Katie looked surprised at the admission from Belinda. She reached over and patted her hand. "Danki. Maybe in time, he'll notice Becky again. He's never really had a girlfriend and I'm not sure he's ready for one. He's pretty immature when I think about it."

"Guys take longer to grow up, that's for certain," Belinda commented, grinning at Katie. "So let's get those clothes going. It's a perfect day to hang them out."

Katie took their empty cups to the sink and checked on Oma, who was fast asleep, before heading for the wringer washer in the basement. Belinda and she sang while they worked.

Holmes County, Ohio

Jeff had trouble concentrating on the book he was reading. Exhausted from planting two dozen six-foot cedars, he had a right to be tired. It was good to finally relax by the family pool. So far it had been a cool August, but tonight the humidity made the cool water inviting. He avoided towel drying after his laps, instead, he sat and dripped dry. Running his fingers through his wet hair, he tried to read again. Normally, his landscaping books held his interest, but he couldn't get over his disappointment at Belinda having to remain longer in Pennsylvania.

She was even lovelier than he remembered her. The simplistic dress and her pure beauty unmarred by artificial cosmetics only added to her attraction.

That restlessness could be a problem, though. He wouldn't be there this time if she found herself in trouble. Would she keep away from temptation? Such a spirited young woman, yet so unaccustomed to the world about her. She had mentioned meeting an English girl and making plans to get together with her and her friends. It was troubling. He'd feel much happier if she were back in Ohio, with her family—and him. Perhaps he'd pay her a visit again soon. In the meantime he could at least keep in touch with her parents. Her father seemed more relaxed around him than her mother. Of course, that's to be expected. After all, her father loved farming and he, too, wanted to live off the land. Their mutual bond for nature had drawn them together from the start.

He'd made a decision while preparing the holes for the evergreens that morning. It was time to explain his decision to follow the Mennonite religion to his parents. Though he didn't expect a problem, it was still a major move on his part. Though there was considerable latitude in the rules he'd need to follow, it would still be a major change in his life. The clothes were the simple part. Would it embarrass his family? It shouldn't, he thought, almost stating his answer aloud.

Too bad they had gone to a dinner and movie tonight. When they asked him to come along, he'd refused due to his need to relax and think without interruption. After considerable prayer, he made his final decision. Now that it was made, he was anxious to get it over with.

Earlier, he had called Tom, who was elated at his decision to become Mennonite and they arranged to discuss it with the pastor. It would require instruction and adult baptism, which was one of the reasons for his desire to join the church. He liked the idea of making the public sign of baptism to show his acceptance of Christ as his savior. His decision to follow Christ with his heart and mind was made earlier in his life when he first realized the atoning sacrifice of the cross. His rebirth had come through many sources, though it was the conviction of the Holy Spirit that he was a sinner and needed the blood of repentance, that provided him with the final impetus to step out in faith. He had read a lot of books by great Christian theologians, talked with knowledgeable people, and searched his Bible for answers. While these things all contributed to his re-birth, it was only when he opened his heart and gave himself over to Christ with sincere humility that his life took on new meaning. It hadn't been instantaneous as with others he'd heard about, but it was deep and meaningful and life changing.

Without a thought, he reached for his cell phone and dialed Gabe's phone. When Belinda's voice came across, he smiled, picturing her in her setting. "Belinda, it's me, Jeff. I hope I didn't disturb you."

"Nee. I'm glad you called, Jeff. I'm sorry I didn't call you sooner. It's been so busy here, but I was just wondering how you were. How was the trip home?"

"Good. We made it back around seven. How's Oma doing?"

"As you know, she made it through the surgery real gut and she's home now. Katie and I just got her down for the night. My back is sore from lifting. She looks so frail, but she's like deadweight until she gets in a sitting position."

"You have to be careful. We don't want you out of commission, too."

They were silent for a moment. Then she asked questions about his job and he told her all about the work he was involved in. "I've made a final decision, Belinda. I'm going to join the Mennonite church."

"Oh, wow. That's a big decision. What did your parents say?"

"I haven't told them yet, but I plan to in the next day or so. I think they'll be fine with it. Carrie wants to attend with me Sunday and I hope you'll join me sometime when you're back home. Have you thought anymore about it?"

"Not really, though I don't think my parents would mind, if it was only once or twice. I'm glad you're following your heart, Jeff."

"I'm following more than my heart, Belinda. I'm following Christ now."

"Yah, that's more important, that's for certain. I'm proud of you for making that decision."

"Goodness, did I hear an Amish girl say she was proud?"

Her giggle came across the wireless phone and melted his heart. Oh, how he wished he could touch her lips with his.

"I hear Oma calling, Jeff. I need to go. Katie's upstairs and won't hear her."

"Of course, Nurse Belinda. I'll call you in a few days, if not sooner. Take care of yourself."

"You, too."

He heard the phone click off at her end and pictured her rushing to the side of the elderly woman. Would she one day be his? Was it too much to ask for?

Lord, you know my heart. Please make it happen. I realize how much Belinda means to me now. You've known all along I would love her like this, even before I knew. I pray she will one day be my beloved wife. If it be your will, Lord, please make it happen.

Jeff laid the phone aside, along with the book, and returned to the pool. He dove in the deep end. The complete silence and peace he received as he immersed his total body in the cool water refreshed him. Her laugh resonated in his mind and he surfaced with a smile of contentment. He needed to be patient and just wait for Belinda.

Chapter Thirty-Nine
Lancaster County, Pennsylvania

The next few days were difficult. Oma did not seem to be improving. She wanted to sleep most of the time, but the family had been warned to keep her relatively active. At least she needed to make an attempt to use her walker and even the bathroom. It was a struggle to get her to comply and Katie shared her frustration with Belinda. The two girls worked side-by-side and any friction they felt before, disappeared.

Josiah came by each evening. His part-time job helped financially as he spent time completing their future home, though it looked more and more as if they'd be staying on in the dawdi haus once they were married. Neither of them complained, but Katie expressed disappointment once and appeared to show less interest in their future home.

Mary was finally able to come downstairs every day and she spent more time fussing about the house, doing minor chores. Her disposition improved as she became stronger.

Esther was coming today with Martin. Mary had not given them any flack over their decision to stay at a hotel outside of Lancaster. She was privately relieved. Even if they were family, it would mean extra meals and wash and general confusion. No, it was better this way while their mother was practically confined to her bed. Maybe next time things would be different.

Mary sat with her mother and read to her after they returned her to her bed. "Katie and Belinda, why don't you do something fun for a change. Go for a walk or something. You two have been so confined and Oma won't need attention for a while. I'll be here if she needs anything and Wayne can check once in a while."

Katie smiled. "Actually, I'm going to take a nap. I had a poor night's sleep and I'm really tired. How about you, Belinda?"

"I think I'll call my friend and see if she wants me to stop by."
After Katie went upstairs, Belinda called Dawn.

"My friends are here with me. The girls you met and so are a couple of the guys we know. Hurry over, Belinda. We can dance. My mother isn't home."

Belinda used an old bike that used to belong to Katie and she made her way over to Dawn's. Sure enough, it was party time. The music could be heard from the street and Belinda's heart palpitated quickly at the thought of dancing—and with guys.

After introducing everyone, one of the boys, who was Amish, asked her to dance. He had a bad case of Acne and his teeth were slightly crooked, but she didn't care. He was a great dancer and he led her through several new steps of swing dancing and then line dancing, which she had never tried. Fortunately the living room was huge and could accommodate their group of ten lively teenagers. Belinda was in her glory. This was worth all the hard work she did, just to be free for a couple of hours to be with kids who weren't afraid to live a little. And how could anyone object? After all, half of them were Amish!

When she took a moment to check her watch, she realized she'd been there nearly three hours. She was struck by a wave of guilt. What if she was needed at home? What if Oma had fallen again?

"Oh dear, I have to leave," she told the group when they stopped to split a pizza.

"Already?" asked her dancing partner, Ezekiel.

"Jah. I have to take care of someone at home. She just had surgery. But I'll come back later if I have a chance," she added.

"Gut. I enjoyed dancing with you." He gave her a huge grin and she realized he was probably reading too much into her willingness to dance with him. Goodness, here she was again— leading guys on without even realizing it. Katie was right. She was a born flirt. Oh, dear, what now?

She pedaled home quickly, relieved it was getting cool at last. When she arrived, Mary had returned to her room for a rest and Katie was preparing supper. She expected a sour remark from Katie, but instead she asked her if she had a good time.

"Jah, it was fun. We danced a lot."

"Oh." Katie put an end to the discussion with a look. Belinda reached for the potatoes and began peeling them.

"Put in extra. Aenti Esther called and they're on their way over."

"I can't wait to meet her. I heard she was real rich."

"Jah. But she never had boppli."

"Maybe she didn't care," Belinda said in her defense.

"Don't believe it. Every woman wants to have a child."

"That's quite a statement, Katie. Not everyone feels the same way you do."

"What about you? Don't you want boppli someday?"

"Jah, of course I do, but that doesn't mean everyone feels the same way."

"I guess. How's your back?"

"It didn't hurt at all today. I think the dancing helped."

Katie smiled over while she brushed egg white on the top of the bread loaves before inserting them in the hot oven. "I guess I should take up dancing then. Mine's killing me. I'm glad you're here to help, Belinda. Danki."

"I'm glad to be able to help. I just heard a car. I bet it's Esther." She wiped her hands and Katie went to wash the flour off her own. Sure enough, an attractive woman in a stylish sleeveless white dress headed up the front path with her husband at her side. They made a handsome couple and for a moment Belinda understood why some people left the Amish. What a beautiful dress. She was quite glamorous, even at her age. Belinda never felt so plain.

After saying hello to everyone, Esther went in to see her mother, who was propped up on several pillows. Katie had made sure her kapp covered her white strands of hair. Her cheeks were sunken from losing weight and her arms looked thinner to Esther, but her smile was the same. The same tender smile she remembered seeing when she was a young girl—sweet and sincere. Yes, her mother was glad to see her, even if her sister was not. Mary had not yet come downstairs, though her bedroom faced the drive, and Esther was quite sure she'd heard the car arrive.

"You look good, Mamm, for all you've been through." Esther took her mother's hand and leaned over to kiss her cheek. The scent of lavender, her mother's favorite, met her senses. It brought back a flood of childhood memories and it was all she could do not to weep. What marvelous times she'd had growing up, surrounded by family and friends. Sweet days of work followed by picnics and Sings and reunions. How blessed to be raised in such a home.

"Oh, Essie, I knew you'd come."

Martin joined them after a few minutes and talked with them about the surgery and her progress.

Oma smiled affectionately at him when he spoke. "You take gut care of my dochder, don't you?" she asked, though it was more of a statement than a question.

"I do my best," he said with a smile. "She keeps me in line."

Esther smiled over at him. "Most of the time."

Oma nodded. "I'm glad you have each other. My happiest days were those I spent with my dear husband, raising our family. Jah, we had a special bond. We were best friends."

"I know what you mean, Mamm. Martin is my best friend."

"That's the way it should be. Only one person should be more important, and that's Jesus."

"Yes. We realize that." Esther nodded.

"So you believe?"

"Yes, we both do."

Her mother closed her eyes briefly, nodding approval. "Then I'm content with my family. We will all be together again someday. For that, I'm blessed."

Esther looked over at Martin, who smiled. "We are all blessed, Oma."

"I'm glad I got to meet my dochder's husband before I left this earth," Oma said, quietly.

"You'll see more of us, Mamm. We're staying almost a whole week."

"Oh, I'm ever so glad. How could you take that much time off?"

"We're both on vacation right now."

"I see. Not much of a vacation to come visit an old lady in bed."

"There's no where else I'd rather be right now."

Oma smiled as she looked into her daughter's eyes. "I forgive you for leaving, Essie. Don't forget that. Don't feel bad when I pass on. You're a gut dochder."

"Oh, Mamm." Esther couldn't talk. She just sat and held her mother's hand until the elderly woman finally fell back to sleep. Then she and Martin slipped out of the room.

Mary was waiting in the kitchen for them. Leroy had arrived from the barn along with Wayne. They greeted each other with hugs and handshakes.

Esther was shocked at Mary's appearance. Her illness had taken so much out of her sister. She wanted to mend their differences before leaving again. She'd have nearly a whole week. Surely that would be enough time.

Chapter Forty
Lancaster County, Pennsylvania

Oma joined the family at the table for supper, though only briefly. Sitting proved painful. Katie and Belinda did the majority of the work, but Wayne made himself useful by carting out the garbage and he even scrubbed the pot from the mashed potatoes while the girls wiped down counters and put the leftovers away. Belinda noticed his eyes glance her way several times, but she'd decided to put an end to any illusions he had about a future with her, so she kept their conversation simple and impersonal. He seemed to take the clue, since he disappeared once he placed the pot on the drain board.

Mary and Esther sat in Oma's bedroom with their mother while the men went on the porch to talk about men things such as sports, farming, and even a little politics, though the Amish men deferred to Martin on that subject.

Belinda broached the subject of returning to her friend's house, claiming she left something there, though she couldn't be precise when Katie asked her what she'd left. Katie shrugged and suggested Belinda get permission first from Leroy and ask to use the buggy, since it would be growing dark earlier now that it was August.

Leroy nodded and gave his permission so Wayne prepared the buggy. While he waited for Belinda to climb in, he warned her to be careful. His scowl told her he was not only concerned for her safety, but also her behavior with her friends. "Of course, Wayne. I'm always careful. It's not really any concern of yours, anyway."

His jaw clenched and he stepped away from the buggy, arms on his hips. When she looked back, as she turned the curve in the drive, she saw him kick a milk can over. Goodness, what a way for an Amish man to behave!

The party was still going strong and Dawn's mother was nowhere to be seen. Belinda noticed empty beer cans scattered about the disheveled room, along with a half empty whiskey bottle sitting on a desk. There was also a strange sweet scent, which she figured was emanating from the lit candles scattered about the first floor rooms.

Ezekiel came right over when she arrived and handed her a can of beer, which she refused. "Nee, no alcohol for me. Do they have coke?"

"Sure. They have everything. Her parents just separated and her mom works late, so we party almost every night. I hope you can come back again, Belinda. I really like you."

Things were moving much too quickly. She was there to have fun, but not to tie up with a guy. She spotted Annie May who removed her kapp, allowing her hair to fall free. A young man she didn't recognize pretended to braid it and they laughed together at his feeble attempt. Dawn waved to her and then left the room with a tall, good-looking redhead who had his arm around her waist. Two couples danced together on the bare floor. The rug was still rolled up in a corner of the room, but as dusk approached, no lights were lit. Only the glow from the candles remained. Several people were smoking and Belinda began to cough. The sweet scent reached her nostrils and she realized it was most likely marijuana. She hadn't counted on this. Perhaps it was time to go home.

Then an Amish guy walked over to her with a beer can in his hand. He nodded and introduced himself as Aaron. His good looks held her attention. His eyes were the clearest blue she'd ever witnessed. He handed her the can and since she was thirsty, she decided to take just one sip. Surely a swallow or two wouldn't hurt her. After all, she didn't want to seem like a prude. And he was Amish, like she was. Certainly he wouldn't take advantage of her. They talked about their lives and she explained she was only in Pennsylvania temporarily to help out.

"So you'll have to leave us? I've just met you, Belinda. You're a doll." He handed over the beer can again and she took another sip and tried to hand it back. "Nee, you finish it. I'll get another." There was a table behind them with a fresh supply and he reached for a can, pulled the tab and drank nearly the whole thing at one time.

Belinda's thirst got the better of her and she finished the beer from the can. She could feel the effects already. Oh, goodness. She dropped the empty can in the trashcan by the sofa.

Aaron's eyes appeared glassy and he swayed awkwardly. Without thinking, she reached up and grabbed his arm to steady him. He grinned and placed his other arm around her, pulling her close to him. Her heart beat wildly as she tried to turn her head to avoid his lips. He smelled of beer and his unwanted kiss was rough. What was she doing? She had made a promise to herself not to get in this position.

"I...I think I'll get some air," she said, backing away from his embrace.

"Honey, where are you going? Stay here with me."

"Nee. I'll come back later." She pushed her way past several people, all in different stages of inebriation, and found the front door. When she exited, she looked around for her buggy, but it was nowhere in sight. Then she heard the door open and close behind her and there was Aaron.

"You wanna go somewhere?" he asked, grinning at her while heading her way. Mercy, he was just an Amish guy, not someone to fear. She stood still as he approached. "I'll drive you home later," he added.

"You drive?"

"I'll just borrow Dawn's car. Sure, I drive. I can teach you how if you want."

"Nee. That's okay. I was just wondering where my buggy was."

"Probably in the back. Dawn's younger brother likes to take care of our horses when we come. I'm sure your horse is okay. Come on back in, Belinda. I won't hurt you."

"I know that!" how annoying that he thought she was afraid of him—or anyone else!

"So let's be friends. We can dance, if you want."

"I think you've had too much to drink to dance."

He laughed and reached for her hand, which she gave him—just to prove she wasn't afraid of partying with people. She could control herself, no matter what the others were doing. They walked back in and true to his word, he led her to the dance area and held her, swaying to a slow piece. She closed her eyes and hummed to

258

the music. His hand moved slightly on her back as he brought her closer. She pushed back, moving away from him. It was time to leave. Why was she still here, anyway? She didn't need to prove anything—certainly not to a guy she didn't even like!

Suddenly, both the front and back doors burst open and uniformed police stood guard at each exit. "Okay, someone turn on the lights in here and then don't anyone move."

Several girls shrieked and people raced around stubbing out their cigarettes and dumping alcohol down the sink.

The police then had everyone sit on the floor or the furniture and a third policeman entered with a clipboard. He proceeded to ask for identification, names and addresses, and ages. Belinda's heart felt like it would leap from her body. Oh, what was she going to tell her family? Why had she come? What a nightmare!

Eventually, there were three arrests and multiple warnings. When the policeman saw she was Amish, he scowled at her and shook his head. "You should know better, young lady. Shame on you. I'll pay your family a visit tomorrow."

"Please don't tell them. I'm only staying there for a while. I won't come back here, really."

He looked over his clipboard with a frown so deep, she felt ashamed of her behavior. Aaron looked over at her and shrugged, with a half smile.

The police waited while those just given warnings, exited. When Belinda went out front, her buggy was waiting for her, tethered to a tree. There were three other buggies attached to the same tree. She cried as she made her way back home. What a shameful thing to do. Why didn't she leave immediately when she saw the beer? Down deep, she had guessed the sweet smell was more than incense from the candles, yet she had looked the other way. All in the name of 'having fun.' What a disgrace she was. No wonder her parents had made her leave. It was a wonder anyone would take her in. She made the English girls look like saints, for heaven's sake.

"Oh, Jeff, why did I go there? You would have protected me." The tears flowed, unabated, while she prayed for God's forgiveness. How shameful for an Amish girl like herself to behave the way she did.

When she arrived home, she was thankful to see Wayne still working in the barn. He took the buggy without looking directly at her. Relieved that he hadn't looked at her swollen eyes, she walked toward the house. Hopefully, everyone else would be too busy to notice her. She'd head right for bed and maybe the policeman would not follow through on his threat.

Belinda saw Katie when she entered the kitchen through the back door. Katie was busy chopping nuts and barely noticed Belinda as she went through the kitchen. She said good night and headed straight for the connecting door to the dawdi haus, making her way to her bed. She collapsed fully dressed on the mattress and resumed weeping. She'd never felt so ashamed and so alone. If only she could talk to Jeff. He'd help her through this, but she couldn't face the family and the cell phone was in the living room, where they had gathered. *Oh, Jeff, I wish you were here.* She pictured his smile and could almost hear his voice. She had an ache to see him, to hear his laugh, to touch his strong hand…Then the realization came to her.

She was in love with Jeff!

She knew with certainty what she felt towards him was the real thing. She had been attracted to other guys—Aaron, Wayne, and even Dan, but there was never anything more than physical attraction with these other men. With Jeff, it was so much more. He was her friend—her confidante—her protector. Oh, how she wanted to talk to him and hear his voice, reassuring her.

It took hours for her to calm down enough to sleep, and when she awoke she realized it was almost nine o'clock the next morning. Why didn't someone knock on her door? On top of everything else, she wasn't even in time to help with breakfast. What would everyone think of her?

Esther and Mary were sitting at the kitchen table when she arrived. They looked up and smiled. "You must have been really tired to sleep in this late," Mary said.

"I guess so, but I'm sorry I wasn't up to cook breakfast," Belinda said as she reached for a glass of juice.

"It was fine. Esther was here to help today."

"How do you like Pennsylvania, Belinda?" Esther asked.

"It's ever so pretty. Much like home."

"Yes, so I understand. I've never been to Ohio."

"But you've been to Europe, haven't you?"

"Several times. We're traveling to California next month for a long week-end, but we'll fly out, so we miss seeing a lot of middle America."

"I'd love to travel someday, but I guess if I remain Amish…"

"You can still travel, can't you?" Esther looked over, her brows drawn.

"Not so much. Once the boppli come along."

"Oh, true." Esther drank from her mug and looked down at the red plaid tablecloth.

Oma called in from the bedroom. "Girls, I need to use the bathroom."

"I'll get her," Belinda said as she set aside her juice.

"Nee, we'll do it. You eat your breakfast, Belinda," Mary said, rising from her chair, with Esther following suit. They disappeared into the bedroom and Belinda let out a sigh. Even with so many hours of sleep, she felt worn out. Her thoughts went back to the party. Hopefully, the policeman was just trying to scare her. Surely, he wouldn't waste time coming over here.

Katie came in from hanging clothes and she joined Belinda with a cup of coffee. "You must have been real tired to sleep so late. Did they have dancing?"

"Jah. I learned some new steps. If you ever want to learn any—"

"Nee, that's okay. I wouldn't have anywhere to try them out, so why bother? Anyway, did you have fun?"

"I guess so. I don't think I'll go again though. I didn't feel comfortable."

"I thought a lot of the kids were like us Amish."

"Jah, but kinda wild."

Katie giggled. "Mercy, wilder than you?"

"Katie!" Belinda joined her laughter.

A loud rap came on the front door and Katie rose to answer it. She looked out the front window before opening the door. "Oh, my, it's a policeman! What could he want?"

Belinda's stomach fell to the ground. What a day this would be.

Chapter Forty-One
Holmes County, Ohio

Jeff sealed the letter to Belinda and dropped it off in his mailbox for pick-up before heading to her parents' home. He had promised her father to help with the retaining wall he was building beside the barn. Reuben and Gideon planned to be there also, and since it was Jeff's only day off, they decided to get together early, hopefully to complete the job in one day. The rains had washed away a good deal of the soil and the only remedy was a wall to hold up the remaining earth before it affected the foundation of the barn.

After three hours of hard labor, the men took a break and sat under the trees drinking from a pitcher of sweet iced tea Grace brought over. She set a plate of molasses cookies on the ground next to them and returned to her wet clothes waiting to be hung. She and Nellie worked together hanging them on the clotheslines strung between two old apple trees. The warm breeze would facilitate the drying, allowing another load to be hung by afternoon.

"So have you heard from Belinda?" Jed asked Jeff casually.

"I got a letter yesterday. It was short. She's working pretty hard. She said her back was bothering her a little and she was glad that Mrs. Zook's other daughter was going to come and help. She sounded a little homesick."

"Jah, I hated leaving her again. She seems a lot better, don't you think?"

"Sir, I never thought there was a problem with Belinda. She's a very decent girl. You should be very proud of her."

"Pleased, not proud. We Amish, you know, love being humble," he said with a wink.

The men laughed. After another half hour they resumed their job and worked in concert as if they'd worked together their whole lives. It felt good to do something just to help and not for the money. Jeff had found more to be grateful for. His new friends meant a great deal to him, as well as a certain beautiful young woman.

Lancaster County, Pennsylvania

"Can I help you?" Katie asked the policeman as he stepped inside. He showed her his badge and spoke in low tones. "I'd like to speak to the guardians of Belinda Glick, please. I understand she lives here with you."

"I…I'll have to get them. You can sit down."

Belinda listened from the kitchen and felt her heart nearly bounce out of her chest. When Katie returned, she looked at Belinda with a puckered brow as she headed toward Oma's room.

Mary sorted out an underwear drawer while Esther read aloud to their mother. They all looked up as Katie beckoned her mother to follow her into the hall. After she explained about the policeman, Mary went into the living room and Katie nearly ran over to the barn to bring her father back. They walked hurriedly back together and marched past Belinda into the front room without even a glance her way.

Belinda dropped down onto a chair and put her head in her hands. *Mercy, I need mercy.* Her hands trembled as she heard the policeman give an account of the night before. When he mentioned drugs, she heard Mary gasp. *I didn't take any. Please, don't let them think I did, Lord.*

After several more minutes, she heard him say it was merely a warning since she hadn't been caught actually smoking or drinking, but he thought they needed to know. Then she heard the door close behind him. Their voices became muffled and she was unable to make out their words, but she knew things were not good. Not good at all. Then she heard them call her name and she walked reluctantly into the room to accept her due punishment.

Leroy stood with his thumbs behind his suspenders. Mary remained seated on the sofa, her head down. "Katie, you can go now," Leroy said.

Katie looked over at Belinda as she walked past her and there was a mixture of anger and disappointment in her expression.

"So what do you have to say for yourself?" Leroy asked Belinda.

"I just wanted to have fun. I didn't know they were going to have pot and stuff there. Honest."

"We trusted you, Belinda. You're our responsibility and we've been pleased with your attitude and helpfulness, and then this." He raised his arms in apparent frustration.

She burst into tears. "I'm so sorry. I didn't know. I would never have gone over if I'd suspected they were using drugs. Never!"

"I believe her, Leroy," Mary said haltingly. "She's not a bad person."

"Nee, I ain't saying she is! But now what do we do? Do we send her home? I'll have to call Jed and tell him, you know that."

Mary lifted her hands off her lap in a helpless gesture. "I guess so."

"Can I call and talk to my mamm, first?" Belinda asked through her tears.

Mary looked from Belinda to her husband. "Jah? What do you think, Leroy?"

"I guess, but I'm going to stand right here, Belinda. No lies."

"Nee. I promise. I just think it would be better for Mamm to tell my daed, is all."

"Mary, where's the phone?"

"On the mantel behind you."

"Here. You call. We're listening." He handed Belinda the phone and her hand shook as she used the speed dial. It was several minutes before her father answered. Oh, no, it was supposed to be her mother. She hesitated before answering.

"Daed, it's Belinda."

"Wait, honey. There's too much noise here. Hold on." She heard him call out to others to stop work while he talked on the phone. She thought she heard Jeff's voice, but obviously it was her imagination. "Okay, I'm back on. Why are you calling at this hour? Is there anything wrong?"

Through her tears and snuffles, she was able to give an account of the party and the officer's visit, without sounding like she was a totally sinful daughter. She emphasized her lack of knowledge beforehand. Her father remained silent throughout her dissertation. When she was done, she held the phone closely to her ear and waited. And waited.

At long last, he made only one remark. "We'll come get you tomorrow. Pack your things."

Oh, dear Heaven, what a ride that would be! Six hours of the silent treatment. Mercy, she'd rather be punished to a week in solitude on bread and water. You could even skip the bread!

He hung up and she stood there holding the dead receiver. Oh, if one could only relive certain days. How different it would be.

"Daed's picking me up tomorrow." Her words were wedged between sobs.

"I'm sorry that it ends this way. We still care about you, you know that," Leroy said, patting her on her shoulder. It only made matters worse. She leaned against him and sobbed more.

Mary came over to her and laid her hand on her arm. "Now, now. It doesn't help any to get all choked up like this. It ain't the end of the world."

"In my world, it is," Belinda said, looking over through swollen lids. "I'm such a bad dochder. I deserve to be punished."

"We'll see. I'm sure your parents will forgive you."

"Why couldn't I be like Rachel? She never did anything wrong. Nellie, too. She's just all gut. Maybe I was adopted."

Leroy held back a laugh. "We've all had our moments to regret, Belinda. Believe me. No one is perfect, but we have a God who forgives."

"But He's not my earthly father."

"All the more reason to forgive each other," he added. "You'll see, everything will turn out okay. We're going to need your help eating up that ice cream Katie made this morning."

"Oh, no. See? I even slept in late and didn't even lend a hand. I'm a total failure."

Mary shook her head and clucked. "Now don't be so hard on yourself. Come on. Help me dish out the ice cream and we'll try to salvage the rest of the day and have a gut time. Jah?"

Belinda tried to smile through her tears as Mary went for a washcloth. Now if only her parents will see things the same way.

Chapter Forty-two
Holmes County, Ohio

Jed set his cell phone back on a large stone and looked over at the others watching him. "It was Belinda." His mouth was set in a straight line and he looked down at the ground. "We're gonna have to get a driver and bring her home tomorrow."

Jeff felt his legs weaken as he stared at Belinda's father. What could have happened for this decision to be made so quickly?

Gideon's mouth dropped open. "Why? What did she do?"

"We'll discuss it later, sohn. Let's get this wall finished. I'm getting tired." The men began to pick up where they'd left off and once they finished a section, Jed suggested a break. "We can finish up another time. I need to go inside and call our driver." He began to head toward the house, but Jeff caught up with him, and walked beside him.

"Sir, let me get Belinda. I can take the day off. All I have to do is call. My boss just finished a big job and talked about giving us some time off before the next one started. Please. Let me do this. Belinda may be upset and it might help to have me, as her friend, to talk to."

"She's gonna be upset all right. You might not want to get her when you hear what happened. He relayed her account of the party and then told him about the policeman turning up at the door.

Jeff winced when he heard about the drugs. "I'm sure she didn't take any."

"I hope you're right. I don't know what gets into that girl sometimes. She's caused this family a lot of heartache, that's for sure." His eyebrows drew together and he swallowed several times in succession before continuing. "If you still feel like driving all the way to Pennsylvania and back for the girl, well, so be it. I'd appreciate it, but I'd want to pay you."

"Sir, I'll be happy to go, but I don't want payment. You know that."

"I insist. At the cost of gasoline—"

"I have money saved up. My car's good on gas. I'll call my boss now and make sure it's okay with him." He reached in his pocket and made the call confirming what he had told Jed. His boss was agreeable to giving him several days off if needed.

"Maybe I should have Nellie go with you."

Jeff's heart sank. They'd have no time alone. "I'll get to bed early and try to get started before daybreak. Can Nellie be ready by five?"

"Nee. I forgot she's helping her mother all day with pickling. You'd better go by yourself. It's gonna take me time to figure out what to do with Belinda, or I'd go, too. Chances are, she's gonna spend the whole trip crying, anyway. She sounded real bad."

Poor Belinda. Surely, she was just as upset as her father was. Jeff had been afraid her naiveté would catch up with her. She needed protection from the outside world. His protection. When he arrived home, he threw some clothing and necessities in a travel bag and told his parents where he was going. At first Carrie wanted to go along, but when she saw his expression, she backed off. "I guess I wouldn't be back in time for work anyway. Just give her my love, Jeff."

He smiled over and nodded. "She'll need it, I'm afraid. It sounded like she'd be permanently grounded."

Carrie shook her head. "I know Belinda, and she'd never do anything that bad. People often exaggerate. I'll pray for you to have a good trip, bro," she said as she went in the kitchen to make salad for dinner.

Lancaster County, Pennsylvania

Mary finished explaining the situation to Esther and Martin as they sat on the porch together, while Oma took a nap. Leroy rocked slowly, puffing on his pipe.

"She was such a wonderful-gut help while she was here. I hope her family won't judge her too harshly," Mary said, looking over at her sister.

267

"Sometimes we do judge unkindly without knowing all the facts."

"Like I've done with you, Esther?" Mary's brows arched.

"I wasn't thinking about that, but perhaps it applies. You were so young when I left, you couldn't have known all the factors that went into my decision to leave."

"Nee. I realize now. At the time, I just saw Mamm's suffering."

"And not your own? You didn't think about the polio and how it affected you?"

Mary cleared her throat. "I figured it was God's will."

"But he also willed scientists to develop a vaccine to save people from contracting the disease. It was Mamm's decision to follow the bishop's will."

"She knew later it was a mistake. She's told me herself. I don't hold ill feelings. Poor mamm has suffered enough."

Leroy took the pipe from his mouth and laid it on a plate. "It seems a lot of people in this family have suffered because of that decision, Mary. It's time you and Esther stopped using it as a wedge between you."

"Is that what it's become?" Mary asked, her eyes grave.

"Maybe."

The group was silent for several moments. Then Martin broke in. "Mary, your sister has lived with this decision her whole adult life. She didn't make her choice lightly."

"I know. Esther, I've forgiven you a hundred times over, but my stubborn Amish blood still seems to hang on to a grudge. I don't want it between us anymore. Will you forgive me for my pig-headedness? I want us to be close. Goodness me, family is so important. We can't go on like this."

Esther reached across the patio love seat and took Mary's hand in hers. "Dear schwester, there's nothing to forgive. Yes, we must stop looking backward and enjoy the years we have to bond again."

"Show me you've forgiven me my mulishness by checking out of the hotel tomorrow and staying here with us. Especially now that Belinda is leaving, we have the whole dawdi haus open. There's even food in the fridge."

Esther laughed. "My bags will be packed first thing in the morning. Oma will be pleased to see us working side-by-side again."

"Jah, her Essie and her 'little Mary Contrary' will be friends again."

A bridge had been crossed.

Holmes County, Ohio

Jeff was on the road by five AM after a mere six hours of sleep. He had bottles of water in an ice container and a bag of chips for emergencies. He put Christian music on the radio and sped out of the drive. The trip seemed to take longer than before as his anxiety level increased. Belinda wasn't expecting him to be the driver. Would she be upset to see him instead of their regular driver? What exactly would her reaction be to his coming to her side, yet again? She was an independent woman—at least she thought of herself as independent—and yet she kept finding herself in situations that required more discernment. Would she continue to make poor choices? Did he really want a woman who could prove untrustworthy? Was that truly Belinda though? Wasn't the real woman actually a sweet Amish girl who just didn't realize the dangers in the other world? After all, she lived almost sequestered amongst people who knew and loved her. How would she know that apart from her world there were those who saw only their own needs and desires? Dangers lurked, sometimes unexpectedly, and there would be events that would present themselves under the guise of innocent moments. How much had Belinda experienced by attending a party where she barely knew the guests? *Dear Belinda, let me care for you. If you only knew how much I loved you.*

He stopped only twice to use the facilities at the rest stops and grab a cup of coffee. At last he crossed the county line. Lancaster County. What beautiful land. He could live there if he had to. He could settle anywhere, as long as it was with Belinda, the girl of his dreams.

He pulled up beside the house. No one was around, so he went around the house and found everyone sitting on the porch eating lunch. He'd made it there by noon even with the road construction, which had slowed him down.

Belinda's mouth dropped. He wished he had thought to take her picture, but that was the last thing on his mind. She looked so fragile, her blond hair tucked sedately under her freshly starched kapp and her modest green dress accenting her cool jade-colored eyes. What a vision.

"Jeff, how nice of you to come for Belinda," Grace was saying. He barely heard her as he watched Belinda rise from her chair with a bashful smile working its way across her lovely oval face.

"Oh, right. It was easier for me to come than to try to line up another driver."

"Would you like some lunch? In fact, do you want to stay the night and leave tomorrow?"

"Not unless Belinda's too tired to leave today." He looked over and she shook her head.

"Nee, I think I should get home right away, but please eat something first, Jeff. There're fresh apple dumplings left, after you eat some sausage and noodles."

"How can I refuse? May I freshen up first? I need to wash my hands."

"Of course. You know where the bathroom is."

After eating, Wayne brought over her few belongings from the dawdi haus and laid them beside the table. He looked over and frowned. Jeff picked up on it and tried to smile. "Thanks, Wayne. I guess we'd better get started."

Everyone came around and gave hugs to Belinda, who began to cry again. Her emotions were so close to the surface now that it took very little to bring her to tears. Mary wiped her eyes, also, and Oma, who was starting to droop, took her hand and kissed it. Then she turned to Jeff. "Take care of my little nursemaid. She's a sweetheart."

Jeff smiled over. "I'll try, if she'll let me."

Everyone but Oma walked over to the car and waited while they set her luggage in the trunk. As the car pulled away, Belinda turned to look out the back window. Everyone was waving and she waved back. Then she wiped her eyes on a hankie, which she kept wadded up in her hand.

For several hours, she and Jeff would be by themselves. What did he think of her at this juncture? Did he have any respect left for this foolish young Amish girl? She was about to find out.

Chapter Forty-Three
Somewhere between Counties

Belinda stared out the passenger side window and watched the landscape fly past. Jeff turned on the Christian music station and they listened silently to the latest popular songs. Belinda was too embarrassed to engage Jeff in conversation at this point. What on earth did he think of her? No one could put up with her behavior. Was she beyond redemption?

"Hey." His soft masculine voice interrupted her thoughts and she turned to face him.

"Hi." She made an effort to smile.

"What's going on, pretty girl?"

"Mmm. I wish I knew." She turned her head and looked straight ahead as the traffic thickened. People going about their business—working, shopping, just out for a drive. Each in his or her own world, while *her* world was crashing in. How would this all end? Maybe her parents would give up hope and send her to a foster home somewhere far away, so they could erase her from their minds.

"What happened, Belinda? Tell me about it." He reached over with his right hand and held it open, waiting for her to place her own in his. Hesitantly, she rested her hand in his palm and he gently squeezed it.

"It's the same old thing. I never learn, Jeff. I thought it would be fun to go to my new friend's house. After all, she had Amish friends as well as English. So when she said they were going to have dancing, I went back after supper. I'd been there earlier and nothing so terrible was going on. We merely taught each other some dance steps."

"Were there guys there?"

She tried to read his voice to know what he was thinking behind his words, but he had spoken them simply in normal tones. "A few. No one special."

He nodded. "So why did the police come?"

"I don't know who reported it. Maybe a neighbor. It was kinda loud. Anyway, they came in, both the front and back doors at the same time—like a raid or something."

"Were you scared?"

"Jeff, I was terrified! I thought I was going to jail."

He held back a smile. "Usually not on a first offense."

"Well, anyway, they asked a bunch of questions. They found pot and maybe other stuff, I don't know. Then they arrested a couple of the older guys. The rest of us just got a warning, but the policeman who talked to me at the party, came yesterday to talk to the Zooks. It was so embarrassing. I could have died."

"But you didn't smoke any pot, did you?"

"Nee, but I did drink a little beer."

"Oh, Belinda, no. After the last time?"

Tears began to form in her eyes. She was so tired of crying. She bit her lip and struggled to keep them at bay. "Only part of one beer. Well, I guess a whole one."

"I hope it didn't lower your resistance to guys' advances."

She remained silent and he turned to glance at her, and then returned his gaze to the road ahead. He let out a long breath. "Tell me what happened."

"This one Amish guy started dancing with me."

"And?"

"Well, he got too close."

"And?"

"For heaven's sake, Jeff. This feels like the third degree!"

They were silent again and it was uncomfortable for Belinda. She knew she'd end up telling him what happened. She always did. That's the way it was with Jeff. He knew everything about her. More than she did.

"Okay. He kissed me."

Jeff banged his left hand on the steering wheel, staring straight ahead.

"I didn't want him to and I didn't like it. Not one tiny bit!"

"Mmm."

"Jeff?"

"What?" His tone was definitely one of annoyance and disappointment. Another person she'd hurt. It was just too much. She burst into full-blown tears and he turned and gaped at her. "Listen, we can't talk like this when I'm driving. I'm pulling over at the next exit and taking a break."

They drove without speaking until he pulled into a parking spot by a Sheetz station. Only her sobs could be heard. After turning off the ignition, he pulled the lever to move his seat back and turned his body toward hers. "So you let this stranger kiss you, drank beer, and knew people were doing drugs, but you did nothing about it."

"It sounds terrible when you say it like that."

"Belinda, it was terrible! When are you going to learn? I can't always be there to bail you out."

She put her head in her hands and wept, her body shaking like leaves on a breezy day. Jeff's heart reached out to her and he moved closer and put his hand on her shoulder. "Belinda?"

"What?" she said through her tears, without looking up.

"I love you." His voice cracked as he spoke the words that had been on his heart so long.

Her sobs began to subside and she took her wadded hanky out and dabbed at her eyes. Then she peeked over her hands. "What did you say?"

"I love you."

"As in, 'I love you like a friend?'"

"No, as in 'I love you with all my heart and I want to marry you.'"

Belinda began to laugh through her tears. The sound from her mouth was a mixture of sadness and joy. "Oh, my goodness, do you know how much I love you? Do you have any idea?"

Jeff shook his head, his grin reaching from one cheek to the other. "Why don't you tell me?"

"I do! I do love you! I just realized it myself since that horrible party. I wanted so much to be with you, to have you near me and then I realized you weren't just a friend or like a brother, but you were someone I wanted to cherish, to live with the rest of my life!"

"Oh, my darling. I can't believe you're saying this. I've dreamed of hearing those words."

"I'm so slow, Jeff. Heavens, I've probably loved you for months now, but wouldn't admit it to myself."

"Belinda, I bet I'm the happiest guy alive right now. But it's not going to be easy. You know we're still living in somewhat different worlds."

"I don't care. I'll go English! Yah, I'll yank over for you."

"Hold on, my love. It's not that simple. First of all, I've decided to become a Mennonite. You know I've been thinking about it, even before we met."

"I know you have. It's not that different from Amish, and I haven't been baptized, so I don't think my parents would shun me. Goodness, we could certainly meet half way and be Mennonites, couldn't we?"

"I hope it will work out that way. All I know is I want to make you my bride and whatever it takes…"

Belinda leaned over as he moved closer to her side of the car. The bucket seats complicated it, but Jeff took her chin in his hands and kissed her gently with his lips. Her heart leaped. Oh my, this feeling was so much better. So right! Jah, Jeff was the man for her, for sure and for certain. "I don't want this moment to ever end," she said, smiling tenderly at him.

"This moment will end, but our love doesn't have to," he said as he leaned over to kiss her again. This time she returned his kiss. Then she moved back and let out a long sigh.

"I guess we should get back on the road."

"I guess so," he said. "We have a lot to talk about now, but God's made it plain to us. We have something special, Belinda."

"Oh, jah. That's for sure and for certain." She settled back in her seat as he started up the engine. God had indeed brought them together.

Whatever the future held for them, they would get through it, because not only did they have each other, they had the Lord, and He was first and foremost in their lives.

If God be for us, who can be against us? Romans 8:31 KJV

31864269R00167

Made in the USA
Lexington, KY
01 May 2014